Nyifie Brothers Publishing

Copyright © 2024 by Sterling & Stone
This edition published by Johnny B. Truant and Nyfie Brothers Publishing.
All rights reserved.

No part of this book may be reproduced in any form or by any electronic or mechanical means, including information storage and retrieval systems, without written permission from the author, except for the use of brief quotations in a book review.

Thank you for supporting my work.

THE VAMPIRE MAURICE

THE VAMPIRE MAURICE (A FAT VAMPIRE SIDE SERIES) - BOOK 1

JOHNNY B. TRUANT

INTERVIEW WITH THE VAMPIRE

DR. ANNABEL RICE was tapping her pen on her pad, thinking about football players.

She'd been considering football players, in fact, since the moment the vampire had shown up for his appointment. Then, as the vampire reclined on the couch like a psychiatric cliche and said nothing at all, Annabel's attention had moved from football players to football in general, then to the evening's agenda, then to her horrible husband, who'd set the agenda to punish her and who she couldn't quite divorce despite many attempts to do so. Every time she raised the issue, he distracted her by cleaning a bathroom. It was a tactic that shouldn't have worked, but Annabel hated cleaning — especially bathrooms — and thus found reasons to let the issue slide ... for now, at least. She was also not a fan of paperwork or research or phone calls, all three of which seemed necessary for divorce. So thus far she'd let the marriage drag on like something undead, doing her very best to avoid him just as she'd tried to avoid tonight's football game. She'd told him he'd have more fun with his friends, without her along to girl it up. But because he hated her, he'd told her she really should go. When she'd refused, he'd cleaned a bathroom. Her house, owing to her professional success and prudent investments, was large and had many bathrooms. Damn the house and the way it sided with her husband's manipulations.

"How should I begin?" the vampire asked her.

Annabel stopped tapping her pen. The appointment was open-ended. The vampire — a first-time patient — was her last of the day. He'd told her on the phone that he had plenty of money to spend, if she had more than the usual hour to give. Once her football evening was booked, she'd been able to sincerely reply that she didn't care how long he stayed. It might mean she'd have a great excuse not to go home on time. Oh how tragic that would be.

"However you'd like."

"But where? When? The story is so long."

"Why don't you begin with why you believe you're a—?"

The vampire cut her off, raising a hand. The hand ended in black-painted fingernails. The vampire himself was dressed all in black and had a shock of long black hair that wouldn't stay out of his eyes. When he'd arrived, he'd had a sword on his belt. She'd made him leave it behind the reception desk. Doing otherwise felt like something her insurance company might have a problem with. If she had to guess, he was perhaps eighteen or nineteen years old and looked precisely like the reason she and her horrible husband had never had kids. It was perhaps a professionally irresponsible opinion (particularly for a shrink), but Annabel often thought privately that kids were such douchebags these days. Upon meeting him, she'd confirmed that his extended appointment was still okay only because he'd given her a black AmEx card to pay for it. Probably his father's.

"Stop," he said. "We can't begin that way."

"What way?"

"With you believing I'm delusional."

"That's interesting," Annabel said. "Tell me more."

"Are you shrinking me?"

"Do you *feel* that I'm 'shrinking' you?"

"Seriously," the vampire said.

Annabel crossed her legs. "Tell me about your mother."

The vampire sat up. He was scrawny, short, all legs and arms. The kind of kid that others beat up, if that was still in fashion.

"Perhaps I should turn on the light," he said, in a way that seemed meaningful but that meant nothing to Annabel.

"Whatever you'd like."

The light instantly snapped on. There was no delay. The vampire was no longer sitting on the couch in front of her. Instead, he was all the way across the room in less than a blink, holding the light switch between thumb and forefinger.

"Do you see?" he asked.

"Better than when the lights were dim," Annabel said, shrugging. "On or off, I'm happy. Whatever you prefer."

This answer seemed to surprise the vampire. His voice became almost disappointed.

"Aren't you wondering how I got to the light switch so fast?"

"You're very good at light switches," Annabel confirmed, since he seemed to be digging for a complement.

"I'm not asking for validation here."

"Are you sure?"

She made a note on her pad: *Delusions of the supernatural.*

The vampire answered his own question, since she hadn't: "I moved too quickly for you to see."

"Did you?"

"You seriously didn't notice?"

"I was focused on your words."

Now he seemed flummoxed. "Maybe I should do it again."

She made another note on the pad: *Insecure.*

"Look over here for a second," he said.

Annabel, whose mind was drifting back to her horrible husband, said, "Mmm-hmm" without looking up.

"I really am a vampire," he said.

"Tell me about that."

"You don't believe me."

"It's not a matter of belief. It's my job not to judge what my patients tell me, Mr. Toussant."

He seemed unsure what to say, so he said, "Call me Maurice."

Annabel, similarly unsure, said, "What kind of a name is 'Maurice' for a vampire?"

"What kind of a name is 'Anne' for a person who *talks* to vampires?" he snapped.

"It's actually Annabel."

He wordlessly returned to the couch, but something had changed on his face. He seemed less teen-like, older than his years. Despite his ridiculous garb, he struck her as a person wearing a costume. Not really a tortured, world-hating kid after all.

He reached out. Took her hand. For some reason she did not object. The pen hit the floor.

She found herself staring into his eyes. They seemed bottomless.

"How are *you* feeling?" he asked her.

"That's ..." She blinked, suddenly dizzy. "That's ... not really relevant."

"I think you're feeling good. Relaxed. I think your preconceptions, given this feeling, are drifting away. And I think you're suddenly open to ideas you haven't been open to before."

"I feel open," Annabel's mouth said without permission, "to ideas I haven't been open to before."

"You will remain yourself, and you will retain your professional ability as a psychiatrist," the vampire — who, for some reason, she now believed might actually *be* a vampire — told her. "But now that we've had this little chat, you will find yourself fully believing what I tell you. Your only skepticism will be as to my motivations and emotional defenses. You will, in other words, act exactly like the good doctor you are ... were she to find herself with an honest-to-God vampire for a patient."

Something clicked. The dizziness she'd been close to feeling vanished. Annabel found herself entirely coherent and cogent — but also very interested in this honest-to-God vampire who'd come to her for therapy. *Why aren't there more vampire patients out there?* she wondered. *Why do people not believe vampires exist?* It was so obvious that they must, now that she thought about it.

The vampire — Maurice — let go of her hand.

"*Now*," he said, his voice different, "where should I begin?"

Annabel wanted to blink, but her mind was sharp now. She said, "Start with what brought you to me."

The vampire on her couch turned his gaze to the ceiling. He considered, then began.

"I've only ever turned three humans into vampires ..." he said.

2

———

EVERYTHING

I'VE ONLY EVER TURNED three humans into vampires. *Three.* That's far below normal — one of the ways I've never seen eye to eye with my kind. Some vampires, before Council took over and made us what we are today, would turn three or four on a single night. There are eight billion humans on the planet and only 70,000 of us. So the way they saw it, Why *shouldn't* they turn as many as they could? Vampirekind has a lot of catching up to do.

And the Council calls *my* creations "wanton."

My first was Celeste. She was on the brink of death when I found her, and that meant I had two choices: turn her and save her, or let her die. I had to decide right then, right there. When you turn someone, you create a bond that lasts forever. Even across great distance — even if maker and made want nothing to do with each other — the bond lasts in what we call "blood ties." It is (or should be) a great responsibility that I've never taken lightly. But with Celeste, there was no time to think. It would be a funeral or a shotgun wedding, tying us together for the rest of time.

So I turned her. Luckily, the shotgun wedding worked out.

We had a real wedding a few years later, and will be celebrating our 1000th anniversary soon. I'm not sure what gift to get her. The etiquette lists top out at platinum, for a piddly 70 years. It's kind of bullshit.

The third vampire I made was Reginald, who I also turned to save from dying. He's what got me thinking. He's what made me wonder if, perhaps, there's a pattern to those I turn.

Reginald is only about a week old, in vampire terms. He's atypical to say the least, and that puts him at risk. Not just from the Council, and not just because the Vampire Nation's problem child Maurice just added a wanton creation charge to his laundry list of crimes. The problem is bigger — no pun intended — than that. See, you don't change after you become a vampire. You're stuck, forever, with the body you had on your undead birthday. And Reginald's body? Well ... it's not really up to vampire standards as they exist today. Modern vampires are strong, fast, and beautiful, just like Hitler would have wanted. Reginald is none of those things. *Brilliant*, yes. But does the Council see what's more than skin deep?

Not bloody likely.

If I had any delusions that the Council would look the other way on Reginald, they vanished when I got my summons. I even invented a little game to occupy my mind while they were dressing me down over what I'd done. For every time Logan or one of his people said "fat vampire," I'd take a drink as soon as I got home. Vampires can drink but don't usually bother — we metabolize liquor so fast, it barely affects us. But still I ended up shitfaced the next night, worrying into my wine.

When I turned Reginald, I knew I was doing wrong by the letter of the law. I knew I'd get slapped; I even knew he'd probably end up on trial for his life and fail. But still I told myself, "It's the only humane choice." I'd gotten him into the situation that almost killed him. He was at the bowling alley because of me; he'd come out back because I told him to; he met Moira because she and the others had come to serve me with their idiotic summons. If I'd turned Reginald down when he'd pitched our little "bro date," he'd have lived a normal life. So how could I, in good conscience, let him die?

But now I'm starting to wonder if that's really why I did it. Maybe it's all one big rationalization.

The more I think about it, Celeste and Reginald have a lot in common. Celeste, Reginald ... and *me*. We're all misfits. Then and now, we were all chewed up and spit out by our peers. None of us ever fit in when we'd been human, and none of us fit in as vampires. I've never had much use for my kind, and few of them like me. I've always preferred to live away from it all: the decadence, the arrogance, the cold-blooded killing.

So did I turn Reginald to save him, or because he reminds me of myself? Did I turn him for his own good, or mine? Was my goal to save a life, or gain a companion? Was I selfless? Or was I self*ish*?

In the midst of it, my mind returned to Daisy — the second vampire I turned. *Daisy*, who I hadn't thought of for what felt like a very long time.

My feelings about Celeste are obscured by our life together, and my time with Reginald is still too new to assess for truth. But Daisy? She feels like the tiebreaker. If I can find a clear purpose in my time with Daisy, I might just find my answers.

And so I asked myself: What *about* Daisy?

Why did I turn *her*?

What did she mean to me, other than everything?

3

FAMILY

IT WAS May of 1929 in Chicago and Mort, coming around the corner in the little apartment we all shared, grunted at me: "Your aunt is in the can."

Then he rammed me in the shoulder hard enough to knock me against the plaster. This happened often enough, at this particular bend in the hallway, that the wall behind had been beaten down to the lathe. It wasn't just me that Mort knocked into the wall when passing. Elsie and Evelyn, the twins, got some of it, too. But for me it was the worst. I was supposed to be the foreign cousin, and that meant I needed to constantly be reminded of my place. I still had a pretty thick accent. They all had accents, too, but theirs had just a bit of either Irish or Brogue. I hadn't cared enough to figure it out. I liked the Flynns better than the vampires I'd known, but not by much. They were shelter, and they were camouflage. Not much more.

I didn't bother to correct Mort. I'd told him a hundred times that Celeste wasn't my aunt, just as I'd told the rest of the family. But something in their brains had broken when Celeste tried to add her glamour to mine, and after that none of them had been quite right. Unlike me, Celeste is shit at glamouring.

I've told her not to do it, but she always thinks I'm just affectionately joshing her. I'm not. She's going to kill someone.

And anyway, it was fine. My original glamour on the Flynn family still held, for the most part. I told them all when we came to Chicago that we were their French cousins. I convinced them that they'd come overseas to visit us last year. I also told them that Celeste and I were man and wife ... but at that point Celeste had interrupted my glamour and tried to explain our apparent age difference, which I'd planned to make their brains ignore. Her diversion served only to draw attention to it, and afterward they could never quite shake the perception no matter how much I tried to wash it away. They seemed to decide that I was 15 — not 19, which was actually as far as I got as a human and the age I see in the mirror — and that Celeste was in her 30s, which had been true when I'd turned her. And with that, they'd decided I was having sex with my aunt. My compromise was to glamour them into believing that in France, that kind of thing was normal.

The bathroom door opened. Celeste watched as I brushed plaster dust off my back.

"Mort run you into the wall?"

"Yeah."

"Maybe you should shove him back."

Not a good idea. My lightest shove would probably knock Mort into the next building. It was easier to lay low and be a victim. My revenge, if he pushed me too far, would be to glamour him into erectile dysfunction.

I kissed Celeste. Then I grabbed her ass.

"*Incest,*" she warned me.

"Only as far as they think."

She whispered in my ear. Her own accent was thicker back then. In the near-century since, she's lost most of it and gained a midwest lilt. It's unfortunate. France is sexier than Ohio, sorry.

"Eww!" said a small voice down the hall. It was one of the twins, hair short and ready for bed in pajamas that were too elaborate. She'd gotten into her mother's face powder and looked like a ghost. Her head turned and she called to her sister: *"Elsie!* They're doing it again!"

Celeste rolled her eyes. *"Mon dieu."*

"Ooh. Say more."

She shoved me away, moving toward our room. We had the master, with three layers of blackout shades nailed over the sun-washed windows. The tenement apartment only had two bedrooms, and I'd be damned if my wife and I were going to stay with the kids. So I'd glamoured Henry and Irene into having the splendid idea to sleep on their children's floor while the guests took their bed. I wanted a place to lay low and blend in, but there's no way I was going to do it without privacy.

I watched Celeste depart, then stared Evelyn down. She and her sister thought I was 15, too. The whole family did, despite my contradictions. I'd decided not to rock the boat. We'd glamoured them so many times in the first weeks — and Celeste's hatchet job had weakened them like rotted lumber — that I was afraid to do much more. Besides, I've never liked glamouring. It's so ... *vampire.* It's intrusive, and you emerge feeling like a monster. The Flynns had already been kind of stupid when we'd shown up and taken over, but I had no desire to turn their minds to mush. We wouldn't be here forever, so I was content to roll with it.

Evelyn stuck out her tongue. Then she put her thumbs in her ears, fingers up. I stuck out my tongue to retaliate. My fangs had descended in arousal when Celeste had whispered in my ear, though, and I didn't realize until my tongue struck them. Evelyn's eyes widened and she ran.

Oh well. Nobody believes a 9-year-old.

I washed up, then dressed in slacks and a simple button-up shirt. Irene, who'd appointed herself my surrogate mother, kept trying to get me to wear knickers. I insisted on more dignity. I was like 60 times older than her.

I moved into the small kitchen with the peeling wallpaper and sat next to Henry at the table. He was wearing his charcoal suit and reading the sports section, his hat on top of the rest of the evening paper beside him. Irene was at the sink, washing dinner dishes. She had wavy curls in her short brown hair and was wearing a yellow crepe frock that looked a bit more expensive than it actually was. I always admired that about Irene: She could stretch a dollar like nobody's business, without it looking stretched. Most of the children's clothes were her own creations, as was the dress. We contributed to their bank account on the sly, but Celeste would never let me give them much. In France, we'd been wealthy. Here, with so much of our old lives left behind, we were only well-off. The Flynns were dirt poor, but we couldn't raise their standard much without drawing attention, and attention was the last thing I wanted. Drawing eyes — especially local vampire eyes — would be bad for us, for the Flynns ... for everyone.

Without looking up from his paper, Henry asked me if that was any kind of outfit for work. His voice was a dial tone, if we'd had such things. I'd have called Henry the calmest person I'd ever met if a better adjective (sorry, Henry) wasn't "boring." He had little round glasses, a balding head, and was interested in precisely nothing. I don't think he had hobbies, and he dressed too well for his immigrant's job at the shipping company — for which he dressed exactly as he was now, for an evening meeting with his buddies. But since Henry didn't heft boxes, his pride told him to wear a suit to work with customers. It raised eyebrows, but it did earn him respect.

Eventually Henry looked up at me. On the surface, it should have seemed strange that the boy who lived with them had a nighttime job in the storeroom of the local grocery, but that was just one more thing my glamour had convinced him not to think too much about.

"I'm not going to work on the loading dock tonight," I told him. "It tires me out too much for the next day, so I made a change."

That got me a look, and a raised eyebrow. My mention of "the next day" had him thinking that was the important part of my sentence, when in fact they might have noticed I never, ever cared what happened during daylight. I slept in, like a good teenager.

"We've talked about school, son."

Yes, we had. Or rather, Henry had, while I listened. I never asked, but something in Henry's psyche seemed stuck on the idea that all young men under his roof should be able to go to school, and that it was his duty to explain regretfully why they couldn't afford to — why working was necessary to pay the rent instead. There were too many contraindications to list (I'd lived more life than he knew; my human age was beyond school years anyway; I hadn't gone to school as a kid and wasn't about to start now; I'd incinerate in the sun on the walk there), so it had been easier to listen. Henry seemed to think I cared. I did not.

"I don't mean school, Cousin Henry," I told him. "I'm still working at the store. But Mr. Reys gave me a promotion."

Well ... Okay, I'd glamoured Reys into giving me that promotion. And it wasn't precisely a *store* that Timothy ran, but who was counting?

Henry set down his paper. He looked me full in the face.

"You don't say," he told me.

"Yes, sir."

I got another long glance. Then he ruffled my hair. "Well, good for you." He looked me over. "Office?"

"Register."

Because obviously, people bought groceries in the middle of the night. *Go, glamour.*

"Dressed pretty well for the register, don't you think?"

"I learned from you," I told Henry. "'Dress for the job you want, not the one you have.'"

He gave me a tiny smile.

"Honey," Irene said, "I think your friends will be waiting on you."

Henry looked at his watch, then gulped his dinner coffee and stood, planting his hat on his head. "Holy smokes! I guess you're right. I won't be late, Buttercup."

He gave her a kiss, gave me a glance that seemed almost proud, and was gone.

"You too, young man," Irene said.

I stood. Irene seemed to size me up, as if about to say I was too skinny. At every meal, she badgered me to eat, but I always had an excuse. I took my meals on the street, in the shadows.

But this time she said nothing. She kissed my forehead and let me go.

I found Celeste, kissed her goodbye, and was out the door and a dozen feet down the hallway when the door behind me banged open. I turned to see Mort running after me, still in the knickers I refused to wear.

"Maurice!"

I stopped.

"Good thing I caught you," he said. "You forgot something."

"What's that?" I asked.

He punched me in the stomach. I pretended it hurt and dropped the lunch pail I'd been carrying.

"Fucking frog," he said.

4

WORK

FOR THE 15-YEAR-OLD boy the Flynns thought I was, a job in a store would have been impressive — especially for an immigrant kid, not working hard labor, able to dress to impress his substitute father.

For the 19-year-old I actually looked like, working behind a store counter still would have been a damn fine job. I might have earned twelve bucks a week or so — and even my part of that, after tithing out the family whose roof I shared, would have meant living high.

But for a vampire who'd passed his 1900th birthday, I'll admit I needed a bit more excitement than a day's wages, if I had to live in the slums and bide my time. Celeste and I had left France to get away from the decadent and dramatic vampire life, but mostly we'd just wanted to *get away*. In New York, where we'd spent three years between France and Chicago, we'd run into few vampires — mostly because I'd tried very hard not to. In Chicago so far, we'd run into none. Chicago, in 1929, was home to a different kind of monster: the kind that lived in sunlight and took their blood with tommy guns. Before the St.

Valentine's Day Massacre, I'd been told people in the windy city saw Al Capone as a modern-day Robin Hood. That had changed, obviously. But, what ... was I supposed to be afraid?

So: What interested me, to help pass my time?

Business.

And *excitement.*

The store I worked at? It wasn't actually a store. There were groceries on the shelves out front where the building faced the street, and plenty of people came in during the day to shop there. But I didn't work days; I'd never worked at the store itself. No. I worked in the speakeasy — called The Bomber — that Timothy ran out of the back.

By the time I arrived each evening, the glass doors out front had been locked. I had to go around the back, to the narrow alley where there was a loading dock only used by the partitioned-off speakeasy, never by the market. We took grocery deliveries through the front door, hooch through the rear. The small man-door beside the loading dock had a slit through which our bouncer, Mason, would ask new arrivals for the week's password — just like in the movies.

I liked to mess with Mason.

Mason was at least 6'4" and had cut the slit himself, to suit his own eye level. As a result, he ended up looking at the foreheads of people of average height. Being short, if I stood flat against the door he couldn't see me at all.

I knocked. Stood. The little peephole slid open above me, then slid closed again.

So I knocked again and got the same result.

The third time I knocked, Mason demanded, "Who the fuck is there?" Only then did I say, "It's Maurice." I always acted like it was a perfectly sensible mistake, not like I'd been hiding just to twist his mind. I did it a few times every week and he never knew I was taking the piss out of him. Mason wasn't very smart, either.

The door opened. He looked down at me and said, "Oh, hey. Sorry, Maurice."

I told him it was no problem, then moved behind the bar with a hidden grin. I put on my bartender's apron and began moving the bottles and glasses to where I liked them. There was a second bartender, Mick, who sometimes took over for me midshift, sometimes on my nights off. Mick had a terrible system. It's almost like he didn't take pride in our work.

The Bomber had an impressive liquor selection, I thought, for a little place that mostly served the local cops who were supposed to arrest Timothy and shut the place down. The cops took bribes and got their drinks for free, so on paper the operation should have been struggling. It wasn't, though. I hadn't seen the books, but the paying customers — of which there were many — must have made up for it. We'd gotten lucky in terms of location. The speakeasy was right on the border between my working class neighborhood and one that was decidedly middle class, edging on upper. We got working stiffs, but we also got ladies in furs and men wearing spats. My interest in business was taking notes: The fact that Timothy spent extra to get so much variety in his booze was the *reason* we got such a diverse clientele. Some places didn't serve much more than glorified moonshine. We were the opposite of that.

I looked across my domain. All those sparkling bottles with their foreign labels, all those shining silver siphons. The clean glasses, the smell of fermentation spiked with the crisp kiss of distilled spirits. I'd enjoyed alcohol when I was human all those years ago — enough to fall down drunk a time or two, for sure — and still enjoy it today. It seldom affects me, but I like the taste. Especially wine, especially when the mood is right.

As I prepared and our little ragtime ensemble set up in the

corner, I caught Timothy's eye. He gave me a nod. He hadn't wanted me for this job. In his human eyes I'm just a kid — and a skinny kid, at that. Barmen are supposed to be big and broad, at least old enough to entertain and offer stories to counter the ones told by drinkers. When I first showed up, he laughed me away. The speakeasy was well-known in our area, and when he made it known that he needed a new tender, he got plenty of applicants eager to be part of the scene and drink for free. But when I got my shot — in a kind of try-out Timothy designed — I proved myself to be faster and more efficient than all of them. That streak continued during trials night, during which one finalist per hour worked the bar. That's where I killed it. I've never flat-out glamoured our customers, but there's a spectrum to everything ... and during my hour, everyone left happier, tipped better, and lost more of their worries to drink.

Besides, I pushed things the rest of the way in my favor by demonstrating my strength. I can carry the big barrels out of trucks and into the bay all by myself. It feels like showing off, but I at least limit it to one barrel at a time. If I didn't mind their questions and fear, I'll bet I could take three at once. And juggle them.

"Maurice," Timothy said, after peeking into the back. "You all set up?"

I nodded. The bar was ready for the rush.

"Then come out to the bay, will you?" he said. "Truck's here."

Ah. My special talents were needed.

"Sure thing," I told him.

5

HOOCH

THE DELIVERIES WERE MADE by two dirty grunts and a big guy who always wore a suit and a fedora. A big fat guy who looked like he might have a lot of muscle hiding beneath. They called him Little Sammy, probably for irony. As far as nicknames went, Sammy was lucky. I heard through the grapevine that a guy he worked with was called Paulie Nutsack.

I came to the edge of the dock and waited for the truck to jockey into position. It was a big, ugly thing covered in canvas, and something wrong with its engine caused it to belch blue smoke and roar like an animal. The cops should have wondered at the truck, but they knew enough to leave it alone. Same for the locals who lived in the building opposite. When Sammy's truck arrived, you looked away. Everyone knew who ran this town.

The truck parked sideways, blocking the alley. As its engine cut, I heard another. I looked up to see a black Ford pull in behind it.

"Dammit," I muttered. The truck was easy. When the car came with it, there was always a hassle.

Beside me, the Bomber's barback-slash-waitress looked up.

Her name was Daisy. She was my best human friend at the time, despite barely being friendly at all. She wasn't rude. She *was* weird, though. I never got her exact age, but she seemed about eighteen or nineteen — the age I'd be, if I were human. But there was never anything between us — not from my side for sure, and not from her side in a way that was, for some reason, obvious. It just never seemed an option, and nobody would have thought it. It was as if she'd been born my sister, somehow, two millennia late.

I hadn't seen her. Daisy was quiet. She tended to vanish into backgrounds like shabby paneling.

"Sorry, Daisy," I said.

But Daisy didn't mind profanity. She repeated, like a child: *"Dammit."*

Daisy had longer hair than Irene, longer than most of the current-day fashions. It actually ran past her shoulders, and she never put it up. In speakeasy circles, it made people stare. At the time, women's hair was based on fifty variations of the exact same thing. You could cut it in a pageboy bob, an orchid bob, an Egyptian bob, a Charleston bob, a Dutchboy bob, a Coconut bob, an Eton bob, a water bob, and, amusingly, the ever-*chic* vampire bob. Daisy was having none of it. She had brown hair with the undulating waves of a waterfall — a style that would have been beautiful in many eras, but was long for the time. She always let it hang. It wasn't a statement. It wasn't defiance. It was just ... *Daisy.*

Daisy was a terrible waitress. It wasn't her fault. She wasn't caustic or clumsy or forgetful or inefficient. She was just so odd that she unsettled our clientele. It was hard to say why, but still I understood right away. There was something slightly off about the way she looked at people (a second too long), the mannerisms she used (technically fine, but conveying tension or unease that her mouth never spoke of), and the tone of her voice. She should have been perfect bait for the male half of our crowd, because in any decade Daisy would have been stunning. But she wasn't perfect in practice. She made a quarter of the tips as any other server and got twice the complaints — except that when Timothy asked what she'd done wrong, the complainer usually couldn't articulate. *She's just wacky, I guess,* was the most common response. Timothy kept her anyway. I loved him for it.

"You good, Daisy?" I asked.

"It's cold out."

She didn't say more. She didn't actually answer my question.

We watched the grunts raise the truck's rear. Inside were boxes of bottles and three wooden barrels of beer. The crowds weren't in yet. The noises of the workers and the rattle of the bottles in the truck were the only sounds, beyond the putter of engines in the street beyond. I looked down at something in the corner of my eye and saw that Daisy had drawn a tattoo on her arm with a pen: Oswald the Rabbit.

"Oswald," I said.

"Oh." Looking down. "Yes. Of course."

"You draw that?"

"I wonder if these men have families," she said.

I assumed she was talking about the gangster and his henchmen. Little Sammy was at the truck's open cab, writing something on a slip of paper, and Daisy was staring at him unabashed.

"Sure. Why wouldn't they?"

"I don't know. I just wonder sometimes."

"What about *your* family?" I asked. "You hear anything?"

Because just a few weeks ago, Daisy's father had disappeared. Everyone knew it was because he'd racked up way too many gambling debts and someone had called in the loan. Her mother was in denial. It left her even more aimless than she'd been even before.

She looked away. I probably shouldn't have asked, but Daisy always seemed so fragile and I felt a strange need to protect her, or at least show concern. She really didn't belong at the speakeasy, with a speakeasy's crowd. But her family needed money, particularly now, and when Timothy had asked if she'd like to graduate from the store to the bar, she'd leapt at the chance. Well. As far as quiet Daisy leapt at anything, I mean.

Two men had emerged from the black car behind the truck. One was dressed in an immaculate, expensive-looking wool suit with pleats in the trousers. He wore a fedora cock-eyed on his head — the same look as Sammy, though Sammy wore it worse. The other, smaller man from the Ford looked like a pageboy. He carried a notepad as if waiting on instructions from the first. The tall one was named Santori. The boss.

Santori stood at his car, waiting to be noticed. The rule was, *Santori* didn't move. *Others* moved to him.

He caught Timothy's eye, then raised two casual fingers to beckon him over.

"Puffed Wheat," said Daisy.

I looked over. She nodded toward the pair, indicating the short man next to Santori. The lackey holding the notepad, looking like a pageboy.

"They call him 'Puffed Wheat,'" she explained.

Poor bastard. We didn't see Santori often, but I'd seen the kid before. He was probably in his mid twenties and came off as a sad sack. The mob seemed to use him as a utility player: most often Santori's bitch, but also available to be the bitch of any wiseguy who needed a hand. But the poor bastard had a hairlip and a cleft palate, and couldn't say S sounds cleanly.

He was thertainly and thubstathally thupportive of the

mob's thpirits dithtribution business ... but that didn't stop them from buthting his ballth and thitting all over him every chance they got.

What the hell; every group of alphas needs a punching bag.

"Puffed Wheat" was a perfect name for him, I decided. I wanted to go closer and see the face of the man who'd earned such a disrespectful moniker, but everyone knew: You didn't get near Santori or his people unless summoned. And that bothered me, too, because there was something off about both of them. Something I didn't like, but couldn't put my finger on. Other than their involvement in organized crime, of course.

By now Santori had Timothy pressed up against an alley dumpster, berating him about something (late payment, maybe) when Sammy shouted my name. He said it like I was the world's biggest asshole, and should know it by now.

"Yes, sir?" I said.

"Get on it!" He motioned to the truck, which I guess I was supposed to unload. I'd figured that was Sammy's men's job, but apparently I was wrong.

So I went to the truck. Sammy's pair of henchmen must have been union. They stepped aside to let me do the work.

"Maurice," said one of Sammy's henchmen, nodding beneath a newsboy cap.

"Lefty," I replied.

"I'm Righty." He pointed at the other grunt. "He's Lefty."

"How am I supposed to tell you apart?"

"I'm left-handed," Righty told me.

Then he went around to the truck's side, leaned against it, and lit a cigarette.

I unloaded the boxes and crates first, working by myself. Daisy stood on the elevated dock in her plain crepe dress as I passed her over and over again, her hands clasped in front, her manner its usual nervous state. She wasn't actually nervous, I'd decided a few weeks back. Just one more Daisy-brand peculiarity that set our customers on edge.

When it came time to unload the barrels, I had to climb all the way to the truck — right up next to the cab, where the sounds were strange. I stopped before picking up the first one. There was a smell. Something unusual. Something I hadn't smelled before in the back of Sammy's truck, and that a primal part of me wanted very hard to place.

But of course, that part had placed the smell already.

Blood.

I looked around the truck's interior. We all knew who we were dealing with; that was the excitement that made the job worth my time. Yes, the Organization ran the booze. Yes, these men were in some sort of downline that peaked at Al Capone himself. Day to day, that reality never bothered me. It was only a problem when the income and rent cycles overlapped wrong and Timothy came up late on his payments. Times like now.

I could hear Santori still threatening Timothy, but my mind was already distracted by the truck's strong odor.

And I realized: Someone had died in here. Or had been killed elsewhere, and transported in here, right beneath our casks of beer.

"You taking a leak in there?" came a voice. Then a big fat face, predictably chomping a cigar.

"No sir, Mr. Sammy."

"Then move it. I've got a schedule to keep."

Farther out, I saw Santori move into view. He had Timothy's collar in his fist. He'd dragged him over to peek into the truck. Santori's eyes matched mine, and I wanted to shiver. Something about the man made me edgy. Something about the way he looked at me, like he knew me.

"Your fucking kid stupid or something?" I heard Santori ask Timothy.

"Yes sir," I told Sammy, answering his question rather than Santori's. The blood smell had me foggy, and I wasn't sure if normal human ears would have picked up what Santori had said. Anyway, you weren't supposed to talk to Mr. Santori unless spoken to. Mob bullets wouldn't kill me, but taking a beating — should they decide I'd earned one — still hurt.

I hefted the first wooden barrel and turned, now eager to please, even if just for Timothy's sake. But still, it was hard to move. The smell of blood was so *strong*. The box of the truck had amplified it, like scent in full surround. Outside, the only light was the one above Timothy's back door, and in the gloom, I may as well have been swimming in the swoon of red Heaven. It made my fangs want to lower. It made my vampire heart — which does still beat — double its pace.

It was the first time since reaching Chicago that I found myself in a vampire's fugue, surrounded by humans I wanted desperately to rush through, slitting throats, making them bleed.

"Just finishing up," I told Sammy.

The first time I'd wanted to do it, yes. But definitely not the last.

UNICORNS AND MURDER

WHEN I GOT BACK to the Flynns' apartment, it was around 4am. Celeste didn't have a job (she wasn't bored into one like I was) and came and went nights, alternately exploring and hunting. I found her in the bathroom with blood all over her face, trying to clean her blouse in the sink.

"You missed a spot," I said, dabbing at the corner of my mouth with an invisible napkin.

"Ha ha."

"What, did you find someone with too much fight in them?"

It had to be that or another bad glamouring job, though I didn't want to say it. It wouldn't be the first time. Celeste's physical presence was even less intimidating than mine, and she played it up with clothes twenty years older than the age she'd been when I'd turned her. She liked to ride the streetcars at odd hours with a tiny bag perched on her lap, waiting for someone to offer to help her disembark. Then she'd glamour her prey and feed. But because her glamouring skills were so terrible, sometimes the orders she gave them involving blood were misinterpreted. Sometimes her targets cut themselves in a trance using the nearest sharp object, sometimes they threw themselves violently into her fangs, sometimes they tried in vain to draw *her* blood, and once a young man had gone calmly with her to a Red Cross office, where he'd banged into the locked doors. It could get messy.

"Mugger," she explained. "He tried to grab my purse."

"And you stopped him with your teeth."

"He surprised me. He got it clean."

"You chased him?"

"I really like that bag, Maurice!"

I didn't ask if she'd killed him. It could have gone either way. In the 20s, forensics weren't really a thing and the killings that grabbed headlines were big and flashy. We could get away with anything if we weren't seen — or, honestly, even if we were. My wife never killed anyone who didn't deserve it, but I didn't want to ask if trying to snatch her favorite purse was a murderable offense. Probably. I was more concerned about raising alarms. Celeste was wicked fast when she turned her legs on, and if anyone had seen her run this guy down, people would start to whisper. Rumors would spread, about creatures that came out at night. There had to be other vampires in Chicago like there'd been in New York, but I didn't want their attention any more than I wanted a visit from some cop I'd have to glamour.

She saw me thinking and read my mind. Not literally, but also kind of literally. I'm her maker, after all.

"Nobody saw me, Maurice."

"Are you sure?"

She was in a mood. Nothing got blood out of clothing. Now we'd have to access a bit more of our stashed money to buy more, and in Celeste's mind all of what we'd left France with was earmarked for the next stage of our housing. We had a centuries-old mansion in France that in later years I had painstakingly shipped overseas brick by brick and reconstructed here (don't ask; live long enough as a vampire and you get rich and very bored), but for the time being she'd have been happy just to get out of the tenement.

"*I know, I know,*" she said, not answering my question and turning again to my thoughts. "We can't leave this stupid human ghetto yet. I *swear*, Maurice. I've never met a vampire who's so afraid of his own kind!"

"Will you keep your mind out of my blood?" I said.

"Maybe I could, if you didn't feel things so *loud,*" Celeste told me. She'd changed into a nightdress to scrub her blouse, somehow missing all the blood still crusted around her mouth. Now she propped her hands on her hips, and I felt a lecture coming.

I moved to pre-empt it.

"I'm not *afraid* of my own kind," I said. But who was I kidding? My desire to lay low *was* loud. It had been loud enough to ship ourselves overseas in the hold of a cargo ship, then loud enough to move us from New York where we'd started to make a home. No wonder she kept catching it from me, like a whiff of bad odor.

"Nobody here knows about our problems back home," she said. "Nobody cares. Everything I heard in New York said that the Deacon in the States is too obsessed with his government to look outside his own circle. They're so much more *together* here. It's not all castles and orgies. Nobody hides under bridges, leaping out like horrors from the pitchfork days. Our people here are part of society. *Legitimate.*"

And with that, I could feel what Celeste was thinking, because this time she was the loud one. But I didn't want to have this fight again. The itch I had could be scratched by involvement in the fringes of human society. I was fascinated with the arbitrary nature of human laws, with the dissonance in good folks that Prohibition had caused. I took my energy out on the speakeasy scene, on tales told of the gangsters and the way they ruled this city beneath its skin. They took what they wanted, like vampires did. But they did it as frail things with limited lives — a practice that struck me as equal parts daring and tragic. One bullet could end a human life, and yet they all carried guns. But for Celeste, things were different. The monotony of a job bored her even more than boredom did, and without a job there were few ways for a supposedly poor immigrant to rub elbows with ... well ... with *anyone* other than her husband after the sun went down. When I left, she could only wander, feed, talk to nobody she didn't plan to make into a meal. We were at an impasse. Without me, she'd found nothing in America ... and every time she told me she'd heard about vampire friends she might join, I pulled in the other direction.

"Have you heard something?" I asked. "Locally, I mean?"

It was the wrong thing to say. She read my subtext, rolled her eyes, looked away.

"No, Maurice. I haven't *heard anything*. If I had, do you think I'd spend every night chasing down criminals, walking the streets, eavesdropping on human conversations from half a mile away just to have something to occupy my mind? I know you have this ... this *prejudice* against—"

"Don't make it sound like I'm a bigot," I said.

"Oh, no. You're not a bigot. You're just self-hating. That's why I can't have friends: because *you* don't like what you are. Well, guess what, Maurice? It's not going to change. We are what we are. And you know what? We're not bad people. Yet you seem to think that every other single vampire is some sort of—"

This time, someone else interrupted us. Mort, standing behind me in the hallway, out of bed to use the bathroom or get a glass of water. We'd been too loud, and the place wasn't large.

"Did you say 'vampire'?"

Celeste rolled her eyes. "Go back to bed, Mort."

"No way. You said *vampire*. Do you know something? Does this have to do with that thing down by the shipping docks?"

"What thing by the shipping docks?"

"All those people who got killed. You didn't hear?"

I looked at Celeste. Her face gave no sign.

"Bunch of Teamsters. Just ... *dead* yesterday morning. The sunrise shift found them, and they were totally shredded."

"*Gangsters*," Celeste said. I couldn't tell if her tone conveyed accusation about my line of work and those I brushed elbows with at the speakeasy. I refused to hear her thoughts, listening only to her words. I kept my head out of blood ties whenever I could, despite being very good at it. I preferred to hear only what a person elected to tell me, without any unfair subtext.

"*Shredded*," Mort went on. "Like Mother's roast comes off the bone. They wouldn't let the paper print the pictures, but my friend Bobby? His dad took them, and he showed me, and ..." Mort looked at us with wide eyes, then swallowed. It was strange to see him without his usual bravado, but here he was in the dead of the night: a kid scared shit out of his mind. "The guys on the next dock said they ... *saw things. Heard* things."

"What kind of things?"

"Creatures. Like right out of the comic books. Creatures with big fangs. Like ..."

I didn't want to hear him say it again. Those were different times. Quieter, darker, without all the noise and connectivity we have today. People still believed in things they shouldn't — oh, yes.

I held up a hand. When I looked back at him, I did so with glamour.

"Mort. You're just sleepwalking. You're dreaming. You didn't hear anything from us. In fact, you didn't even see us tonight at all."

Mort's gaze softened. His brain went feeble. He nodded.

"And you had a wonderful day filled with everything you love," Celeste added, because she liked to spread joy whenever she could.

"I rode a unicorn," Mort said.

Then he left. I waited for the door to close before turning to my wife.

"Seriously? Now he believes in unicorns."

"*I* didn't say anything about unicorns," Celeste replied. But she'd also turned away from me and back to the sink, all the anger she'd had moments ago now gone. She was embarrassed. She knew it was always a bad idea to give such vague instructions to humans under glamour, especially to stupid people like Mort. Without specifics, Mort's mind would invent all sorts of "everything you love" to fill his memories of yesterday, and none of it would be consistent. He'd probably wake and tell his father about how he'd spent the day at Comisky Park and met Ted Lyons. Oh, and Babe Ruth had been in town too for some reason, and all three of them had gone out for burgers.

The hallway was too quiet. We'd blacked out the window in the bathroom, too, so no light came from the street or the buildings across the way.

"Had you heard about that?" I asked. "About the docks?"

"It was probably gangsters, like I said."

"But it was at the docks," I said. "*At night.*"

"What, you believe Mort about 'creatures in the dark'? You think they're shipping vampires in? Not everyone is as paranoid as you, Maurice."

"I think that sounds exactly like the work of vampires," I answered. "I'll bet if I were to go glamour the police, they'd tell me those Teamsters didn't have nearly enough blood left in them."

"Because you like glamouring so much?"

Celeste wasn't done being annoyed after all. She gave me a stare.

"Don't you dare snoop around, Maurice. I don't care about 'laying low' the way you do, but I *do* care about how it'll look if word gets around that the first impression you made in town was anti-vampire." She wrung out the blouse, sighing at the still-present bloodstain. "Besides. You know how Mort is. He believes every dumb thing he hears. Vampires don't act like that even back home. A mass slaughter, when there's so much easy blood to find? Deacon Logan wouldn't tolerate it. The US Council would have sent the Guard already if it was our kind, and *that* would be hard to miss."

But as her words departed and Celeste went back to fussing over the ruined blouse, I caught one final wave of her thoughts. In that wave I realized that she had, indeed, seen something. Nothing to do with the docks slaughter, but *something*. Something that would have bothered me — which was surely why she was keeping it secret — but which gave her hope. Something that had made her night before I'd returned, quiet and indistinct as I sensed it was.

Whatever Celeste had seen, it had made her believe.

There were vampires in Chicago, sure as anything.

7

NOTHING

I WAS itchy all day long. I couldn't sleep. Not with inchoate thoughts scampering through my mind like mice, not with Mort coming into the room to stoop and fart on us in bed, not with Elsie and Evelyn standing in our doorway with held hands wearing matching jumpers, silent, waiting for me to notice them in a horror scene that I swore Stanley Kubrick would later steal for *The Shining*, not with Irene breaking into the room after I'd closed and locked it again, throwing bacon at us for some reason. For the most part, Irene was the most stable of them, but every once in a while we were treated to a reminder that Celeste's glamour hatchet job hadn't spared her. Most hosts don't throw bacon at their guests and demand that they eat something because they're too skinny. Usually Irene didn't. Today, she did. And also eggs. And toast. It was fine. I was awake anyway.

I got out of bed early and, on a whim, decided to have dinner with the family. We were usually able to escape meals (I'd glamoured them into thinking we'd perpetually "just eaten"), but that day I was hungry — not for food, but for the presence of other beings. My system barely tolerates human food, but I forced myself to pick in an attempt to quell the roiling of my belly. I'd hunted and eaten abundantly last night at the end of my shift, after smelling all that intoxicating blood in Sammy's truck, but still I was famished. Once the sun set, I might just rush out fast enough to leave a Maurice-shaped hole in the door on my quest for another neck to suck.

Celeste didn't wake. Mort's swamp gas had either knocked her out or, conversely, woken her enough at the time that she needed to make up her sleep now. I sat with Irene and Henry and the kids, glamoured nobody, and tried only to act normal. To act human.

I didn't even have to bring it up. Once Elsie and Evelyn went for their bath, Henry folded the evening paper back to a page he'd been saving and began talking about the incident at the docks. And some other brutal murders that the police now thought might be related, given the way the victims seemed to have been vivisected.

I wanted to ask questions, but there were none to ask that would tell me more than the paper was volunteering. Irene didn't have any tolerance for it anyway. She seemed determined to protect my apparently-15-year-old ears from the world's horrors, and so kept cockblocking the topic. "It's that madman Capone," she decreed. Mort lasted for a while, then got up, announced that he loved unicorns, and left the table. Dammit, Celeste.

So I went to work. My hunger vanished; the news had stolen every emotion from me other than nerves. I woke Celeste before leaving and kissed her with what I hoped was apology for last night's fight. I understood; I really did. And in the dark of night, I supposed I could admit to myself that I did have some self-hatred. The same had been true of my human teenage years. I hadn't liked teenagers even when I was one — *especially* when I was one. Same for vampires. As with any group, there are good vamps and asshole vamps. But as a species, we tend toward decadence and drama, and I'd left Europe with the firm declaration that I was done with both. In New York, those we'd found had been even more elitist, even more pinky-in-the-sky superior. But still I truly did get it. I hated our kind, but Celeste had never been the loner I'd been. She'd been weird, yes, like I'd been weird. But a loner? Never. Like most beings, she needed the comfort of warm bodies. Or cool bodies, as it were.

I had a bit of time before my shift, so after leaving home I spent that time searching pointlessly for whatever I'd sensed in Celeste's blood-thoughts at the end of our argument. I didn't know what she'd seen or heard or sensed or smelled, but I know it'd been *something*. For some reason, in some way, she'd come across evidence of our kind. I meant to beat her to it. Maybe I could find them first, get their feel, convince myself to get over my prejudices and try to accept them. If I could do that — and with advance planning and intention, I felt sure I could — then finding us some like-kind friends might be the best gift I could give my wife, who'd been so patient with my moods, my whims, and my obnoxious insecurities.

But because I had nowhere to start, I naturally found nothing. I ran through alleyways when I knew nobody was watching, to cover ground faster. I entered abandoned spaces, smelling the air. The entire time, I felt an unknown presence breathing on the back of my neck. I turned around five or six times, sure I was being followed. But despite the prickling sense of presence and foreboding, I came up empty. I found nothing at all.

So when 9pm came, I went to The Bomber. I helped Daisy unpack the boxes from last night, which I'd simply stacked in the storage area beside those three 20-gallon barrels of beer — which, maddeningly, still smelled of the blood from Little

Sammy's murder truck. It was mindless work, and we talked little. Daisy was quiet as usual, with her peculiar mood as thick as always. But from time to time, I'd say something that amused her and she'd give me her rare, sweet smile. It always struck me as innocent. Frail. Sweeter than this horrid world deserved.

The speakeasy's doors opened after that, for those who knew the password — including the local cops, with whom we were as friendly as we were vaguely threatened. If we kept them in booze and bribes, everyone got along. They didn't ask much. I didn't even begrudge them the cash we gave them. They were poor immigrants in an ethnic ghetto, same as I was supposed to be. Their wives hung their wash out on the same lines and their kids walked the same streets as the Flynn kids. If letting them wet their beaks kept them on the job, it helped to keep the streets safe. The Organization was respectful back then. They killed each other, but the rest of us were their customers. The customer, any good businessperson knows, is always right.

The night's energy rose as the clock ticked on. I stayed out front, keeping my eyes open.

In this town, you never knew what you might see if you just paid enough attention.

8

SPECIAL DELIVERY

IT WAS JUST after midnight when I heard the scream.

I was behind the bar at the time, besieged by customers on the front end and Timothy on the back end. It wasn't at all hard for me to keep up, but I tried my best to look harried. In truth I could have served at five times my best speed, while singing and dancing. But doing so, while fun, might raise more eyebrows than drunkenness could explain.

"Maurice," Timothy said, emerging from the back room with a clipboard in one hand and a pencil in the other, "did you tally bar tips from last night?"

"Yes, sir."

"And you entered them into the register?"

"Yes, sir." We had a system. Since the speakeasy wasn't a legal business, tipping above and beyond asking price was really just part of the single income stream we were skimming off society's top. It was easiest to drop it into the register, then take a percentage of the overall profits for everyone. I found it more than fair.

He vanished. He was back five minutes later.

"Did you unpack all of yesterday's delivery?"

"Just before we opened today, Mr. Reys."

"And it's all back there?"

"Why, is something missing?"

"No, no. I just can't get something to square. If anything ..."

I didn't get to hear what had happened "if anything" because he returned to the back room without finishing the sentence. His mood was confused. He knew I was honest. This was something different from thinking an employee had his hand in the till.

"Maurice?"

I was serving sixteen people at once. One had vomited on the floor. Interestingly, one of the other customers had cleaned it up. I liked that about the speakeasy. I was busy at the bar; Daisy was washing glasses and opening bottles in the back between serving as best she could in the crowd; Timothy was doing ... well ... whatever this was. The puke wasn't being tended, so someone else had handled it. They were all in this together, after all.

"What?"

"Do these order sheets look right to you?"

I came over and peered at his clipboard. On the top sheet was yesterday's list of items delivered, and beneath were prior orders. I flipped, but it's not like I'd memorized what I'd unpacked. *Two cases Canadian whiskey, one case gin, forty gallons of beer, twenty bottles of wine ...*

"I guess. Why? Is something ... ?"

But a baseball team had just come through the back door. I didn't understand at all. It was nearly midnight — what, had they played an ultra-late game? Sunset came around seven. But although baseball had never been my thing, I'd noted how obsessed humans were with it. The game wasn't over until it was over, and sometimes that meant a very long time, provided the field had lights. The players were all thirsty. I got to work serving, and Timothy returned to the back. After that, I forgot about him. He kept to his place and I kept to mine, as the night and revelry and music and impromptu dancing wound into high gear.

The ragtime ensemble played louder, encouraged by the crowd. Several well-dressed men I'd handed drinks told me I was doing a bang-up job, kid, and three of the women engaged me in distracted conversation, asking if I had a girlfriend. One, too old for me but still flattering, said I was cute.

A scream pierced the barroom noise, sharp as a needle through flesh.

Heads perked up. But the front room was loud, the revelry thick. For a human, it would have been very easy to lose the unpleasant shriek in all the pleasant ones. The closest patrons grew curious expressions — the kind a person gets when he thinks a situation might need his help, but would love an excuse to believe he'd heard wrong and it actually didn't. I had to remind myself that with my vampire hearing, I might have been the only one who'd heard the scream for what it was:

Terrified.

Horrified.

The kind of scream that rips flesh, that comes near dying.

I rushed after it. I didn't explain or excuse myself. Less than a second later I was in the hallway that led to Timothy's office on one end and the door to the storage area on the other. I stopped, scenting the air like an animal. And I smelled it again: that horrible, wonderful odor.

The door to Timothy's office cracked open. He'd been away from the front room's noise, closer to the scream.

"Did you hear—?"

"Close the door," I said.

"What's wrong?"

"Do it. *Now.*"

Timothy must have heard some of the raw terror in that scream and the authority in my voice, because he obeyed without question. As far as he knew, I was just a kid — a kid in his employ, at that. I was supposed to call him "sir" and do exactly as he said when he said it. I'd never before told him to *just do* anything. But things were different tonight.

My brain filtered out sound from the front room: the band, the drunken cheering, the baseline babble of conversation. My eyes must have dilated, because the hall seemed brighter. My heart beat harder, pushing my vampire blood through each capillary. The feeling was at once terrifying and erotic.

And the smell. The positive *reek* of that falsely silent hallway.

It was so strong that when the screaming resumed — a few bleats, then cut off sharp — I barely heard it. My hands made claws. I began to salivate. My hypersensitive vision saw every nail in the hallway's panelboard walls, every mote of dust beneath the bulb in its center. The wash of scent was so intense that I could actually *taste* blood in the air.

From the storeroom. The room that doubled as the taproom, where Daisy had been working.

Beneath the door: a crimson welcome mat of blood. It was viscous enough that the leading edge formed a liquid wall, thick like a pancake. As I watched, it spread like flattening dough.

I forgot the door opened outward, into the hallway. When I struck it pushing the wrong direction, the thing practically detonated. It became splinters and hinges, two sad flaps swinging back to bang on the rebound.

Daisy was on the floor, absolutely covered in blood.

At first I thought she was face-down and dead — artery severed, bled out like a pig in a slaughterhouse. Only after a fractional second did I realize she was actually on her back; the uniform coat of red had made her just a *thing* without obvious sides. Only a fractional second after *that* did I see that she was very much alive. In the same moment I found I could smell her even over the deluge of blood: her human flesh, the unique scent that was *her*. Usually, Daisy's scent wasn't something I noticed — or at least something that warranted mention. But the horrorshow facing me had given me a vampire's full-body erection. And in the haze, I saw and heard and felt it all.

The beating of her heart — too fast, its rhythm tachycardic.

The darting of her eyes, visible only once tears washed the blood from her corneas.

Her breath, which I couldn't just hear. I could actually *feel* it. I felt its wash when she turned toward me, but even beyond that I could feel the way the rise and fall of her chest pressed the floorboards beneath her, its rhythm telegraphed from my feet to my legs.

There was blood *everywhere*. It was far too much to have come from one person, which explained how Daisy was still alive. It wasn't her blood; I'd figured that out just from scent the moment I'd entered the room. This blood was ... *richer*, somehow. It generated fumes. It made me want to sway on my feet. I felt drunk. Dizzy. Because of the dizziness, at first the other thing I saw didn't make sense: the wooden cylinder not far off, cracked like an egg shell. Then it did.

It was a keg.

The keg that hadn't smelled like blood because it had been in Sammy's truck. No. All along, it had smelled like blood *because that's what someone had filled it with*.

I knew what had happened.

Daisy had been moving the thing, maybe preparing to tap it. The keg had fallen, possibly because she'd been alarmed. Even a human could smell that much blood once the cork was popped. It had slipped from her hands; it had hit the floor; it had broken and Daisy had slipped, screaming in the puddle.

Too much to wonder. Too much to solve for now.

So first things first.

"Daisy ..."

I extended my hand and moved a step, but something in her eyes grew hard. They flicked one way, then the other. Her terrified lips pressed harder, white where blood hadn't coated them. She looked like she might be about to say an M sound, maybe to begin my name, but before she could another scream escaped her.

I didn't realize why in time.

It was because we weren't alone in that bloody back room, and never had been.

9

BLOOD AND GLORY

STRONG ARMS TOOK me from behind. They were too strong. Far, *far* too strong.

Vampire hands.

My first instinct was to thrash and break free, but it was instantly replaced by a second instinct: to go still and play possum. Given my mechanical disadvantage, it wouldn't be quick to break free of someone with any degree of vampire strength, and in the time it took anything might happen. With all this blood on the floor — and such *pungent* blood at that — they probably couldn't scent us well enough to tell the difference, to know I wasn't the human they'd surely assume. I was wearing long sleeves. The vampire's hands weren't touching my skin, so he wouldn't know how cold it was. If I didn't make a fuss, he'd think I was just some dumb kid who'd stumbled through the wrong door. Assuming, of course, that he hadn't seen the door explode, or think too hard about its state now.

So I gave him just a tiny bit of fight, like a human would.

"Stay cool, kid," a voice said. "Nothin' to see here."

Then there was a laugh: two other vampires, coming from behind a row of shelves. Both were dressed like Sammy and his ilk: expensive tailored suit, fine silk tie, fedora, long overcoat, gangster's polished shoes now covered in gore. Neither was wearing a gun, though. There'd be little point in that.

The vampires looked at me, then at their companion holding me. One of them — one with blue eyes so sharp, they shone from his face like diamonds — looked right at Daisy and lingered way too long. I knew the look because before Celeste, I used to give it to human women I found when I was hungry. Nowadays, I stuck to feeding on men out of respect, and glamoured them into forgetfulness when I was done. It only seemed polite. But the primal part of me, in the middle of this blood-bath, throbbed with sympathy. The way that blue-eyed vampire was looking at Daisy, it was clear he wanted to drain her. *Ravage her. End her.*

But he broke his gaze and licked his lips — his fangs — and his eyes turned to the door. He approached it, touching the splinters. The third vampire looked on.

"What happened to this thing?" Blue Eyes asked.

"Dunno. Who cares?" said the one behind me.

The other moved to stand in front of me. "Hey kid. Anyone with you?"

I tried to play dumb. What would a human do? Meanwhile I watched his neck. There are a few ways to kill a vampire, but the one I wanted most right now was to rip his head off with my teeth.

"You hear me?" he demanded.

I was about to open my mouth and tell him that nobody else was coming, but then I remembered my fangs. If he saw them, I'd lose my advantage.

I shook my head.

The vampires shrugged.

"Go check it out, Sal," said the one behind me.

The third vampire left the room through the broken door.

It took a few minutes. In those minutes, I couldn't look at the vampire holding me so instead I looked at the blue-eyed one and at Daisy. I tried, with my eyes, to tell her everything would be okay. They hadn't told her not to scream, and I wished they had. If they'd just gone ahead and glamoured her, she'd have gone docile. Without it, she looked on the verge of doing any of a dozen things that might get her killed: screaming again, running, or God forbid trying to fight.

Sal returned.

"Just some guy in the office down the hall. I took care of it."

I fought the urge to flinch. "Took care of it" might mean he'd glamoured Timothy or that he'd killed him. But either way, I couldn't change whatever he'd done now.

"What about the people out front?"

"I peeked out," Sal replied. "They're all fucked up and loud. They ain't heard nothin.'"

Still he licked his fangs, and I heard the one behind me do the same. If they moved to slaughter those out front, I'd have to break free and take my chances. A lot of the vampires in Europe thought nothing of killing humans, and we'd found the same in New York. It made me a pariah to consider human lives worthwhile, but what the hell — I was a pariah anyway.

"Looks like it's just you and us, cupcakes," said the vampire holding my arms. "What do you think? If I let you go, can you be a good boy?"

"Of course," I said. I did my best to sound servile and afraid, but given my fury it was far from easy.

He didn't let me go. The vampires looked at each other. I realized all three were probably related — maker and made, or a trio of brothers. They were talking without speaking. Without related blood, I heard none of it. I could probably tune in if they tried it again (most vampires are related if you go far enough back, and sometimes you can hear it if you're as good at blood ties as I am), but they stopped before I could focus, returning to using their mouths.

"Tell me something," said Blue Eyes. "You don't seem real surprised to see all this blood."

The only response I could think of sounded more macho than I intended: "I've seen blood before."

"Yeah? Where."

"In the war."

It was a dumb thing to say. When the war had been on, a human who looked like me would have been in diapers.

"I could *make* him good," said Sal, moving to glamour me. But before he could, the one holding me broke my arm. I didn't have to fake a scream of pain. We feel pain just fine, even if we heal right away.

"I'm gonna let you go now, kid," he said. "But you just remember how easy that was for me to do before you decide to try something funny. Okay?"

My arm was knitted before he spun me away, the pain gone with it. I almost slipped in the blood and fell, joining Daisy on the deck. Instead I skated twin tracks in the crimson, then watched the tracks bleed closed once my feet had passed. It was nearly impossible to think. I was drunk with bloodlust.

I looked down at Daisy. I wanted very much to help her up, to speak to her, to touch her, at least — anything to erase a tiny bit of her fear. But I was also trying to read the situation, playing human, searching for an advantage. There were three of them and only one of me. I'd have to choose my time carefully even with my head dizzy, and that meant keeping my focus on them, not her.

I let my arm hang as if it were broken, faking a wince. Then I asked what I thought a human might ask in this bizarre situation.

"Are you going to kill us?"

"Thinkin' about it," said the one who'd been holding me. He was, as I suspected, dressed in the same gangster threads as the others. All three looked mid-thirties, dark like Italians. I don't like to stereotype, but these guys were doing it to themselves.

"What, you maybe *ain't* gonna? Dumb, Vince," said Blue Eyes.

"There's gonna be blood all over even after cleanup," said the vampire who'd been holding me, apparently named Vince. "If there's not a body and a killer to confess, it could raise questions. We don't need the publicity. Not after the docks."

My brain lit. *The docks.*

"I think she dies," Vince said, thoughtful. "Crime of passion, maybe. Then you glamour him into sayin' he did it."

"Woah. I'm not gonna glamour him."

"Why the fuck not?"

"You know I can't do a job like that!" said Blue Eyes. "The cops are gonna ask questions about where he was, what he done, what happened ..."

"Just do what you did for the guy in the office!"

There was a pause. Sal looked sheepish. Seeing it, I felt furious. Furious enough to almost make my move. He couldn't glamour Daisy like he'd glamoured Timothy. Because he hadn't glamoured Timothy at all.

"Wait. You *killed* the guy in the office?" Vince said.

"I told you I did!"

"You said you took care of it!"

"Not by tellin' him stories! Who you think I am? Shakespeare?"

"Jesus Christ."

"What?"

"*Now* how we gonna explain this? Why did this kid go in and kill that guy after killing his girlfriend?"

The vampires considered. I was about to spring when they turned to me. It was Vince who met my eyes. The moment vanished.

"Have a seat, kid," he said, giving the others a long-suffering look.

He took my arm and tried to pull me away from Daisy. I resisted. That was a mistake. The vampire half-frowned, then cocked his head, knowing something wasn't right about me but unable to say what it was. The way he'd taken me this time, one of his fingers was touching my wrist. Had he noticed my skin was cold?

I made my eyes glassy, like I'd seen in humans I'd glamoured. I let my muscles go slack, adopting a vacant facial expression. Reluctantly, I let him lead me away from Daisy. But she hadn't moved and I could reach her in an instant. She'd be fine while I tried my best to play possum.

I sat on a wooden crate of whiskey bottles while he knelt before me.

"Listen to me," Vince said, staring into my skull. "You and the girl here, you were lovers. It was true even if people didn't know. But tonight you found out she was fuckin' someone else. You got that so far?"

"Yes," I said, making my voice distant.

Now he took me by my upper arms, so he could stare more intently. I could tell just by watching, he was as bad a glamourer as his buddy. It shouldn't take acrobatics to do what he was doing. It shouldn't take so much striving to focus.

He was so intense, I could feel his hands compressing my biceps. It almost hurt. But what he hadn't realized was that one of the places he was holding was over the bone he'd just broken.

His brow furrowed, again sensing something amiss. He looked at the other vampire, who was still near Daisy.

"What?" asked Blue Eyes.

"Am I forgetting something?"

"I don't know, dummy."

The clock was ticking. I could feel his fingers moving over my sleeve. Some part of his brain had remembered my arm should be broken, yet clearly wasn't. I'd missed my chance to wince and pull away when he'd grabbed it. We were all foggy here.

He countered the doubt by turning me a bit, focusing hard. I heard something behind me, from where the other vampire was standing.

"She was fucking someone else," Vince repeated. "And when she told you, you just lost it. You ... you beat her to death with one of those pieces of wood on the floor. And you ..." He looked past me, then nodded. Whatever was going on back there went further. "You slit her throat."

I blinked.

You slit her throat.

Why would he give me that bit of drama? Forensics and autopsies were shit back then. A bludgeoning would explain the scene better than a slit throat, and chances were nobody would think otherwise if my confession said that's how it'd gone down.

Why, unless there was something on her throat the vampires wanted hidden.

It hit me. All of it: the way they'd both looked at Daisy, the *hungry* way they'd sized her up. Vampires in devoted relationships fed on their non-preferred sex, but macho fucks like these two would never take Timothy for sustenance — and they'd never lick spilled keg blood from the floor. No. They'd need a girl for that, and the more shy and innocent she was, the better.

In a fractional second, many things happened.

I blinked. My head started to turn.

The vampire holding both of my arms lit with recognition of what was wrong: He'd been holding an arm that was supposed to be broken, yet no longer was.

His nostrils flared. With a new reason to wonder, he could smell me just fine.

Eyes wide.

But I was already up. Already standing. As Vince came toward me, all I had time for was to strike him hard. I knew I was probably older, probably stronger, but I didn't realize by how much. My would-be glamourer smashed through a row of boxes and hit the brick back wall, sifting red dust. The sharp smell of liquor joined the blood like a chemical haze.

I turned to find Sal with his mouth on Daisy's neck. He'd already used sharp fingernails to rake her throat most of the way open. These fucking alpha-vamp types get turned on when the girl is already dying by the time they start to feed. Daisy's eyes had gone to glass, her head lost to a miasma of delirium and pain. She was looking at me while not looking at me at all. Her lips moved sluggishly. She had minutes, at the very most.

I knocked the obvious threat back. Blue Eyes crashed through one crate and fell backward over the next, giving me seconds to face the others.

Sal had been too lost in ecstasy to register the tumult right away. He rolled his eyes up with his fangs still in her carotid artery, surprise more than anything dawning as I flew at him.

My leap caught him in a tackle, and together we rolled away. A chunk of Daisy's red flesh came with him, sinew caught between his fangs. Blood spurted, but the geyser was weaker than it should have been. She'd been mostly drained already, or her heart had already begun to fail.

"WHAT THE MOTHERFUC—?"

Sal stopped talking when I tore his jaw from its hinge.

Given a few minutes, it'd have grown back. But it didn't, because I did just as my fantasy demanded: I sunk my fingers into his neck as he'd done to Daisy's and pulled. His spine separated with sickening ease. How old could he have possibly been, for his body to be so weak?

And he began to burn.

Blue Eyes was still recovering, likely dazed by the intoxicating blood frenzy. But Vince was already up, coming at me hard. I didn't think. I just reached out and found a large chunk of the door I'd shattered. All I had to do after that was aim. Thrusting was not required — Vince did that part for me.

As his weight fell on me, it also fell on the makeshift stake — right into his black heart, where I'd so carefully set it.

I stood and faced Blue Eyes as he straightened. But now that he could see and smell me, he had to be realizing what I was. I wasn't some American vampire: soft and pretty and new. No. I was from the first batch, two millennia old. He was no match for me. I was a redwood tree, and he was only a twig.

I flinched. He ran. Out the door, into the nighttime streets.

The scent of charring flesh filled the air as the remaining vampires burned. It took longer than it should have — more evidence of how young they were. But still within thirty seconds, there was smoke in the air, no more fire. And we were alone.

Enough smoke, I learned later, that someone in the speakeasy shouted *Fire.*

The Bomber emptied. The streets filled. And then, knowing nothing else to do, the patrons dispersed and went home.

I didn't notice.

I was too busy doing what had to be done.

10

MADE

DR. ANNABEL RICE waited for the vampire to elaborate —
to say what it was that he'd needed to do. She knew, though; of
course she knew. She let him have a few seconds of quiet
contemplation. Then she spoke.

"You turned her," Annabel said. "You made Daisy into a
vampire."

Maurice nodded.

"It bothers you," Annabel said.

"Does it?" Maurice asked nobody in particular.

"You've gotten so quiet."

A beat. Then: "Yes, I suppose I have. I was just wondering
if what I did could have been avoided."

"You said you turned the other two — Reginald and
Celeste — because if you hadn't, they'd have died. It sounds
like the same was true for Daisy. Could she have been saved, if
a doctor had gotten there in time?"

Maurice laughed. It was a bitter laugh, devoid of humor.
"Not in the 1920s and not today. Her throat was opened, front
to back."

"Then you've answered your own question. If it was the

same for Reginald, Celeste, and Daisy — if they'd have died without you — then why do you blame yourself for what you did?"

"They didn't train first. They didn't know we existed before they became one of us. I didn't give them a choice."

"You kept them alive, so there'd be a choice to make," Annabel said.

"Is that your professional opinion?"

Annabel realized she'd been sitting forward. Once she'd begun believing that Maurice was a vampire and that his story was true, she'd found herself on the edge of her seat, literally.

"I suppose I can only take your word for it," she said.

Maurice didn't reply to that, probably feeling it rude to tell the psychiatrist her business. But still, what he was implying was right. She hadn't been there, and the events in question were now close to a hundred years in the past. She didn't know Reginald, or Celeste. If Maurice's subconscious had had other reasons for driving him to do what he'd done, of course she wouldn't hear the real story so plainly.

Maurice laid back. Looking at the ceiling, he went on.

"I don't regret any of them," he said. "I suppose I should make that clear. For humans, even if a child is mistake, few mothers love those 'mistakes' any less. All three of my progeny were unplanned, but I've loved them just the same. It's just that … it's not like you may think."

"In what way?"

"I told you that maker and progeny are bonded in blood. We're always a part of one another. It's like a joining of souls."

Annabel thought about her husband. She'd entered into marriage expecting a magical "joining of souls," but instead she'd ended up with a deadbeat who thought foreplay meant starting sex while she was asleep. "Sounds nice," she said.

"You say that now, but that's because you haven't experienced it. You don't just join your progeny's or maker's blood; you also join *their blood's* blood. When you got married, you inherited in-laws, right? Well, imagine carrying those in-laws with you everywhere. Having them right there inside you, every moment of every day."

Annabel imagined. She shivered.

"It's not like that for everyone," Maurice said, "but it's always been like that for me. Given what I've seen of Reginald and the way he's already surpassed my ability to glamour, it'll almost for-sure be true of him. Some of us are born better at the mental half of vampirism than others. There are vampires who only ever feel their makers, not their makers' makers. Not me. I feel them all. It's a problem even when I'm not trying."

"What happens if you try?" Annabel asked.

Now Maurice was the one to shiver. "I don't," he said. "Only a few times in my life have I really focused on my blood-line, seeing how far I can extend myself. It's the only thing worse for me than deep glamour. I don't like being inside others' heads. It's unnatural. When I look through blood, it feels like an intrusive act. Like a violation. When I do it to vampires, I feel their lust and the frenzy they feel when they go out to kill. And when I look into humans—"

Annabel cut him off. "You can look into *humans?*"

"Oh yes. Blood is blood. There's an intelligence in all of it. Vampires are just far more attuned to seeing what blood has to say, similar to a vampire's enhanced senses of sight, smell, and hearing. But every time a human has 'just gotten a feeling' about her sibling's joy or pain, that's blood talking. It's a bond that's not widely understood, even by us. But it crosses species. It goes up and down. If I focus into Celeste, it's not just her I can sense, or just the other vampires she's touched. I can still see through the eyes of her human relatives, who were born many generations after she was turned. Human-vampire,

vampire-human. Before, after ... it doesn't matter. Blood is blood. What one experiences or feels is echoed in all who share their bloodline, or have *ever* shared it."

Annabel sat back, feeling strange. *Blood is blood.*

"It sounds overwhelming," she said.

"Now you know why I don't like to do it," Maurice replied.

After a quiet moment, he sighed.

"So yes. I turned Daisy. It was a very near thing. She was, by then, unable to swallow. I bit my wrist and squeezed all I could into her mouth. I even dripped it into the hole the other vampire had ripped into her neck. For a while I was sure it couldn't be done. She didn't have the mechanisms, anymore, to swallow what I gave her. I didn't know how it worked, other than by drinking the blood of a vampire, freely offered. But: Did it need to go to her stomach? Could it be absorbed directly into her blood? I didn't have a clue. All I know was that for a while, Daisy went right on dying. All the ragged holes in her stopped moving and breath left her. I'd taken her head in my lap. For some reason, all of a sudden, it meant everything that I succeeded. She *had* to wake up, or it'd kill me. I'm not even sure why. I barely knew Daisy, but her murder struck me as all that was wrong with our world. All that had soured as it'd begun to change."

"Change how?" Annabel asked.

"Vampires used to be monsters: the days of villagers and pitchforks and Nosferatu. Hundreds of years ago, our current leader, Logan, took over the Vampire Council. He told us that humans were waking up and becoming enlightened. He said we wouldn't be able to hide and rely on their fear and belief in mysticism much longer. It was a slow boil. By the 20s, we'd gained new openness and mainstream lives, especially in America. Vampires started refusing to live in the shadows. We were gods; humans were put here for prey — that's what some, like the so-called Annihilist Faction, began to say. But still they were the minority. Still they were on the fringe. Because humans had evolved, sure. But they were nothing yet like they've become today. The beginning of the new way, in truth, began during Prohibition in Chicago, though I didn't know it at the time."

"How so?"

"I'll get there," Maurice said. "It's all part of the tale. But ... I didn't want to be part of it, you see. Not part of the underground trade, the propaganda, the fear-mongering, the well-timed grabs for power. I'm apolitical. I'm socially disinterested. I'd say I was a conscientious objector, if I'd ever cared enough to object. What made me an outsider in life made me an outsider in undeath. We'd left Europe to get away from the rampant decadence of vampirekind there, only to find a new and growing kind of decadence here — one that, given time, became so much worse than anything I'd fled in France. I wanted nothing to do with the vampires we found. *They* came to *us*. It was *them* who started this, not me."

"You mean the vampires you killed," Annabel said.

"At first, yes. I was just solving a problem in the moment. Somehow, we'd been given a barrel filled with bootlegged blood by mistake — our kind's mirror to human Prohibition. Daisy discovered it just as those who'd lost it came looking, then tried to clean up the mess and tie us both up as loose ends. That's what happened at the dock massacre, I think. Because at the time, Chicago was a city at war. That's what made it the perfect cover. With so many humans firing guns and so many bodies turning up dead by human hands, who was looking for vampire claws?"

Annabel wanted to ask a thousand things.

But instead, she kept her mouth shut and let Maurice go on.

11

―――――――

AWAKENING

I JUST TOOK care of her. That's all I did.

However it happened, my blood found its way into Daisy where it was needed. The wounds the vampire had inflicted in the back room of The Bomber healed, but her old scars, from before the attack, remained and would remain forever. Daisy was locked in time after that, just like any new vampire. And I was father to another misfit, for whom I'd become responsible.

I carried her, as I carried Reginald decades later, to a high point so she'd wake to a view of the city. She coughed and woke, her wounds still seeping, her body dying so it could once again come to life.

When she awoke, I explained. She tried her new gifts. Everyone, it seems, goes through the same phases. There is disbelief, and then when acceptance comes, there's a mish-mash of bargaining and mourning. She'd seen her last sunrise, and life at home was about to become very different. In a way, it was good that her father was gone and her mother was losing her mind. It meant there'd be few questions asked about young Daisy, and why she so carefully remained in her room during the day and sneaked out each night.

On the surface, her appearance did not change. But just beneath the surface, it changed a great deal. If I'd taken a photo of Daisy before and after the turning, it's doubtful anyone would have seen the difference. But in person, the alterations were strong — stronger than the natural increase in magnetism that normally comes when a person is turned.

She became radiant in a way that was impossible to quantify. Magnetic in a way no watcher would ever be able to put a finger on, but could not deny. Before, she'd been pretty, but acted plain enough to hide it. After the turning, that was no longer true. Her eyes stopped looking down and became things of beauty. Her posture straightened, and suddenly the world could see her face.

But all of that was expected, if more significant than I'd imagined. What surprised me most were the changes in Daisy's personality.

Every vampire has their story of finding something new after turning. The agent that makes us what we are is selective in its way, plucking genes and abilities and tendencies from our personal back catalog and shining a light upon them. The gifts that vampirism gives us from our own grab bag are not random, I don't think — but they are often surprising. I learned cunning and stealth. Celeste could suddenly solve complex puzzles. Both of our personalities changed: some traits magnified, some shortcomings diminished. My new progeny Reginald is too new to say what his sure-to-be-short vampire future holds, but he and I did a little test not long ago and I discovered something fascinating: He lacks almost everything physical that modern American vampires value, but has an extraordinarily advanced mind. He can't run fast enough to catch prey, but his newly enhanced brain is second to none.

For Daisy, her turning was like the opening of a bud that had lived its life balled. She raised her face to the nighttime sun and bloomed into something entirely new. It was an awakening the likes of which I'd never seen.

I took her home. At the time, she was both confused and highly articulate. Before we arrived, she was able to describe her neighborhood in far more detail than I needed in order to find it, down to the number of nail heads visible on each building along her walking route. We were side by side. I held her hand because she seemed unsteady on her feet — woozy from blood loss, I assumed — and as we moved she told me all she imagined happening inside. She knew by then, of course, and believed. She knew what she was and had accepted it fully, with less resistance than I've seen before or since. That knowing and acceptance had made her curious about the process. She seemed to be watching her own thoughts, noting as they brightened around the edges with new vampire intelligence. She imagined new connections inside her brain. Neurons forming nexuses. A labyrinth inside her skull, growing newer and more complicated turns.

"Was it like this for you, Maurice?" she asked.

She was leaning on me. Her hand was in mine, but she'd put enough weight on that side that I felt like I was holding her upright. We must have looked like a pair of drunken lovers, strolling hand-in-hand in the moonlight. She was taller than me. I was stronger by far, but her tall frame made it awkward. It was a fight to keep our feet on the sidewalk.

"It's different for everyone."

"I feel ... *warm.*"

Something about the way she said "warm" told me she wasn't referring to temperature. Or at least not to temperature all over her body. It was localized. Throbbing, perhaps, in one specific spot.

"You need sleep."

"I want food."

"Human food no longer nourishes you, Daisy. You only think you need food because habit—"

She giggled in a way that wasn't exactly Classic Daisy. It was a sexual sound — the kind you expect to be accented with a lollipop or an over-the-top innocent expression.

"I don't mean *human* food, silly."

"Your body will remain mostly human for a few days," I told her. "You don't need to feed tonight. Your vampire nature will get all it needs from your human blood."

"Well, yes," Daisy said, "but I didn't say I *needed* food. I said I *wanted* it."

Her hand was working in mine, squirming like it had a mind of its own. Her skin wasn't paling as much as I'd have expected. By contrast, she had a full-body blush. She seemed uncomfortable, her voice wet, her eyes distracted. I'd never seen her like this before. Or *wanted* to see it. I was a married man. I'd spent our few months in Chicago making human friends on my own terms, and Daisy was one of them. Even if I'd been single, I don't think I'd have been attracted to her. We just weren't that way.

"And I think I shall like to fuck it," Daisy went on, now putting her free hand thoughtfully to her chin, irises rolled to her eyes' corners. "Yes. I would very much like to find someone to eat, and fuck him at the same time."

"Daisy ..."

"Would *you* like to fuck, Maurice? I'd never really thought about it before, but maybe that would be okay."

"Daisy, I'm your—"

"Oh, is it weird? Like incest for us now? I'm sorry. If you'd prefer, I could call you Daddy."

That actually made me look away. I let go of her hand. If she'd fall without me, oh well. She'd heal.

"I don't want you to ..." I began. But she'd already

dismissed it, her mind moved on, thoughts scattering like disturbed mice.

"I've done it before, you know. Just once. I wanted to know what all the fuss was about, so I let this nice boy do it to me. It wasn't terribly interesting. I think I'd like to give it another try." She put her hand up her dress, bunching the fabric. This did not appear to be conscious. "And I think I should like to start wearing hats," she said. She turned to me, excited. "After work, I've usually just gone back to sleep. Are you saying I can stay out all night now, Maurice?"

I didn't want to draw attention to her underwear-bound hand, which was actively working. I forced myself anyway. Best confronted now.

"Daisy. You may need your hands to steady yourself."

She saw how awkward I was, then turned to her buried hand as if she hadn't realized it was there. She yanked it out immediately.

"Oh! I'm so sorry. I need time to adjust, I think. Maybe you're right. Maybe I should sleep. Would you take me home?"

"That's where we're going." And where we'd been going the whole time. It was as if she'd forgotten.

"Will you stay with me?"

"It's best that I don't."

"My bed isn't large, but I'm sure we could squeeze. I wonder if my family would object." She shrugged. "I suppose I could bleed them if they do."

I forced myself to turn her to face me, my hands on both of her upper arms. I'd never seen such a shift in personality. I've always wondered why it happened, and at first could only conclude that Daisy was always wild inside but had been repressed by her upbringing. Since, I've realized it was the blood. The strange blood she'd lain in, while she'd come back to life.

"Daisy," I said. "I know this is all confusing. I know so much is new. You probably feel like the world is full of possibility, and very eager to try it all out at once."

"Oh, yes," Daisy said. "For instance: two men at the same time. Or a *girl*, Maurice! Girls are so pretty."

"But I need you to remember that this is all part of the change. The most intense of these new feelings will pass as you become fully vampire. For now, I need you to keep reminding yourself that this isn't you, that you're basically on high-test drugs. It's important that you lay as low as you can and wait for this first phase to end. Stay quietly busy. Try to be boring. I know it will be hard."

She took it in. Then she nodded. Once, curtly. It was a nod of decision, as if she was drawing a line.

"All right. I will *be boring*, Maurice. You don't even think I should feed?"

Not in this state of mind, I thought. She'd suck whole families dry like juicy fruit.

"No. Wait at least until the weekend."

"That long?"

"Yes." Then I said something totally made up, but that I thought I could own: "I command it of you, as your maker."

"You can do that?"

Lies. "Yes."

"Well. Okay, then. I suppose you could also demand that I do many other things. Degrading things."

"Yes. But I won't."

"Perhaps just one," she said. Her hand was back under her dress. I pulled it out by the wrist.

"Oh," she said, noticing. "I'm sorry."

"It's okay."

"Take me home?"

"And leave you there," I clarified. "Without me."

"Yes. That's best. Hold my hand?"

It was the hand she'd sent spelunking. Without a word, I moved to her other side and took the unfouled one.

As we resumed walking, Daisy nuzzled her face against my shoulder. I could feel her fangs. They'd come down the instant she'd awoken and hadn't retracted since. I could feel her breathing: hot, excited, full of new vampire adrenaline.

"I'm sorry for tonight," I said.

I don't know why I said it. So much had happened so fast, I hadn't had time to consider my own thoughts. I'd been forced to put Daisy front and center, and because of it I'd back-burnered the rest of the night's troubling new discoveries. There was blood in bootlegger's barrels, smelling so strong I half wondered if it was normal blood at all — a scent so powerful it'd nearly driven me mad while I'd been cleaning it up. Then there were the vampires who'd shown up to retrieve the barrel, acting for all the world like members of a syndicate. And then there was the fact that I'd made someone new. Someone whose change already had me on edge. She'd almost died because of my kind — because vampires existed. Somehow, that felt like my fault. Although, who was I kidding with "almost"? She *had* died. I'd just given her something that kept her upright after the death was over.

Fangs still against me, Daisy said, "Don't be sorry. I think I'm going to like being one of you."

From the beginning, I believed her.

12

DOGHOUSE

I GOT HOME LATE, almost sunrise. Celeste was already asleep. Something told me to wake her up, but despite knowing better, I didn't. Creating progeny is a draining experience. You'd think for a vampire, the act would be no big deal. Our hearts still beat; our lungs still breathe; our fingernails and hair still grow. The reason we're nearly immortal is the same reason we can't change much physically: We just heal phenomenally fast. For all those reasons, losing blood isn't traumatic — but giving it to another being is, for some reason, different. I'd dripped maybe a half cup of my essence into Daisy's mouth and open throat, but you'd think I was human; you'd think I'd lost gallons. Our blood has intelligence. I think that when it wakes another, it's not *we* who are tired. It's the blood that, afterward, needs its rest.

So I was physically drained, even more mentally drained. I'd gone to work that night expecting to serve drinks, observe humans, and feed before returning to bed. Instead, my life had forever changed in a blink — maybe in the time it took for the vampires to arrive, maybe in the time it took for Daisy to break that blood-filled barrel. Either way, I'd left my wife as a husband, but returned to her as a father.

I curled into bed behind Celeste and let the sleep of the dead take me.

I don't usually dream. That day, I did. It was a confused vision with no clear narrative. There was no timeline. No consistent characters. All I remember was a sense of needing to reach a place, yet finding my feet unable to move. The harder I tried to run, the slower I went. I was trapped in tar. The day seemed to stretch for weeks before I woke to greet the night.

Celeste was already up when I opened my eyes. She was facing the blacked-out window, her back to me, naked from the waist up.

"I smell someone on you," she said. "A woman."

I rubbed sleep from my eyes. "It's Daisy."

She looked over her shoulder, but really looking into my blood.

"You turned her."

"It happened fast. It wasn't planned."

"You should have woken me, Maurice. You should have told me."

"I was tired. *You* were tired."

"I see."

She was still looking away. I had no idea what she knew. If she wanted to pry, she'd have it all. So far she'd probably just gotten a sense — the tip of something that broke her slumber. She'd want me to tell her the rest, using my lips.

"Are you angry?" I asked.

"I'm confused."

"What are you confused by?"

"You won't associate with other vampires. Yet last night, you created one."

"Others came, Celeste. They were going to kill her."

"Going to? Or did?"

I wasn't sure what to say.

"I want to see her," Celeste said.

"You will. In time."

"Now. Tonight."

"Why tonight?"

"Because something's wrong. I can feel her on you. I can feel her *through* you."

I was still groggy. I rubbed my face. "Celeste, you know you're not good at blood ties. No better than you are at glamouring." There was no way she, of all vampires, could feel Daisy. Not so soon, with Daisy still mostly human. Not with me between the two of them.

"*I can feel her,*" Celeste insisted. "Her blood is strong. Different. Was she okay, when you left her? After the turning?"

I thought of how Daisy had been. No, she hadn't been okay. She hadn't been normal.

Her blood is strong. Different.

It made me think of the blood in The Bomber's back room. The blood I'd cleaned up feeling so high I could barely stand it, so aroused it was impossible to focus. The blood Daisy had been lying in as she'd died, before I'd brought her back to life.

Was it like this for you, Maurice?

No, Daisy, I thought. *It wasn't at all.*

"Give her time," I told Celeste, pushing my unsettled feeling from her prying internal eyes. "I'll introduce you later. A few days."

"Why?"

"She needs to process. She needs to find how she fits into her new life."

Celeste rose without reply. She left the bedroom. She closed the bathroom door and I heard the shower begin.

"Celeste?" I said through the door.

"I'll see you in the morning," she told me.

I didn't like the sound of that, but truth was that part of me was relieved. I suspected I was in the doghouse, but staying there was easier than working through the exhaustion I still felt. The only way I can describe it is this: Something had changed, and not just with Daisy. We have a sense, like animals have a sense. Mine was prickling like an unscratchable itch.

I passed Mort in the hallway. He was in his pajamas, but he seemed to have fashioned himself a unicorn horn out of stiff paper, which he'd tied around his head and painted in bright colors. He said something to me about leprechauns too, I think. I was about to try and see what had gone wrong in his mind — to erase the problems in Celeste's glamour — but then he tripped me and I hit the floor. After that I decided he was more or less okay.

I walked into the kitchen, bleary eyed, yawning through a persistent stupor. When Irene saw me, she dropped the bottle of milk she'd been holding. It detonated on the tile floor like a bomb.

Henry looked up at Irene, then me, then Irene. Then he returned to his paper.

That's when I realized I hadn't changed clothes after my crazy night, and was still covered in blood.

"We were painting," I explained.

"You don't say," Henry said, eyes still on his paper.

"Maurice, honey," Irene said, "did you go out last night?"

"Yes."

"To the store?"

"Yes, of course."

"Oh, honey. I'm sorry." She tried to hug me. I was so confused, I actively pushed her away.

"Sorry about what?"

"We didn't know. We just found out."

"Found out what?"

Henry's voice came from around his paper.

"Your boss is dead."

I forgot to act shocked. Irene was fawning all over me. Looking at the blood. "This doesn't look like paint," she said.

"Says here," Henry announced, "that Tim Reys was gutted in his office. Found when they went in to clean it up that he'd been running a speakeasy out of the back room."

"Gangsters," Irene said.

I kept my mouth shut. It was hard to organize my swirling thoughts. Last night, before Daisy and I had left, I'd cleaned up with vampire speed. But in the rush, I'd forgotten all about Timothy. About everything but that blood-soaked taproom, actually. I'd had too much on my mind. I figured the customers would head out but had forgotten all about what that vampire had done to my boss — or where Blue Eyes might have run after leaving. I'd locked the place front and rear, and the only person with a key was Timothy. So how had anyone found him? He hadn't had a family to report the fact that he hadn't come home, and as far as I knew our packed house had been too loud for them to hear the goings-on in the rear. In some part of my mind I'd planned to handle things at The Bomber — including Timothy, I suppose — tonight. It was tops on my list of errands.

"Says here," Henry said, "he was hung from the ceiling with his own intestines."

Irene gasped.

"Doubt it was suicide, though," Henry assessed. He put the paper down and looked me full in the face. "Maurice, how much weight do you suppose your average colon will support before it rips?"

"What?"

Henry tapped the paper with a single finger. "Well, it says they found the intestines, but not the rest of the body. I guess it broke. Only the intestine was left behind."

"Wait. The body is *missing?*"

"Gangsters," Irene repeated. It seemed to be all she could say.

Henry was still watching me and waiting, probably for my thoughts on the tensile strength of a human colon. When I didn't answer, he returned to his paper. In the silence, the twins entered the room, again in matching pajamas, and then left without word. Irene was still frozen with her hand over her mouth, milk all over the floor. Henry, apparently tired of the subject and heedless of the fact that I was covered in blood, started complaining about the White Sox' lack of performance lately.

"I need to go," I told them.

"Where?" Irene asked.

"Work."

"Take a sponge," said Henry.

I was halfway out when Irene said, "Maurice?"

I looked back.

"Everything okay?"

Because she'd realized that of course there *was* no work anymore. I'd need to—

I turned to answer, but she was already throwing bacon at me.

Yeah. Maybe I wouldn't need sensible excuses with this family after all.

13

———

PUKE

WITH THE POLICE making things at The Bomber a lot more complex (I peeked as I ran by; it was surrounded by cop cars), I moved "clean up" down my priority list and instead moved "check in with Daisy" to its top.

I meant to climb the fire escape, tap on her window, and ask for permission to enter. The rules in this situation struck me as fuzzy. Last night it'd been easy enough for Daisy to move through her own front door because the house was her own. I'd wanted to get her situated, but she hadn't invited me in. Now, Daisy was a vampire, and I shouldn't need permission to enter a vampire's home. Except that might be wrong. She still had a human mother and a brother, and it was their home, too.

But I didn't get that far. I had to change my plans. The fire escape was half off the building, its bolts rusted and torn from the mortar. I could climb the building itself, of course, but the ghettos weren't always dark at night, and I didn't want to be spotted. So I went through the front and, despite the hour, knocked on the door.

I looked down at my watch. It was almost 1am. *Sorry, Mrs. Farley.*

Nobody answered.

I knocked harder. I must have been agitated, because this time my strikes broke the lock. The door sighed inward.

"Daisy?"

Nothing.

"*Daisy?* It's Maurice."

I walked through the door before realizing what I'd done. Only once I was inside the family's apartment did I look back at the threshold I'd crossed without effort. I guess this counted as Daisy's home after all, given how easy it was to enter.

The lights were on. All of them.

Only then did I realize I wasn't alone.

A bland woman was standing in the corner of the kitchen. She'd been there all along. She was staring right at me. She was also holding a loaf of bread and a frying pan. What she planned to do with them, I couldn't imagine. It didn't look as if I'd shocked her into stillness. Based on what I was seeing, she might have been standing in that same place, catatonic, for hours.

"Mrs. Farley? I'm sorry to intrude. My name is Maurice. I work with Daisy at the—"

She opened her mouth and yelled: "*DAISY!*"

I jumped. I waited for more, but the woman hadn't flinched. She still looked ready to make French toast.

Daisy emerged from a bedroom.

"Oh, Maurice! I'm so glad you stopped by."

I eyed her mother, who'd returned to being a statue. There was activity in an adjacent room: her brother moving about despite the hour, apparently. The vibe was wrong. Way wrong.

"What's going on here, Daisy?" I asked.

"I've been so busy. Do you like what I've done with the place?"

I looked around. I hadn't seen the apartment before and

couldn't say for sure what was different, but some of the window dressings were either new or *avant garde* beyond what even the French had ever seen. She'd nailed the kitchen table over the main window, its legs now horizontal and pointing into the room. The remains of a couch were scattered around, and if I had to guess I'd say the rest of it was what she'd used to barricade the other windows in the other rooms. One was a mess of springs and stuffing and cross bracing, as if the couch had tried to escape lengthwise but instead had splatted against the glass like a cartoon character into a rock face.

"It's …" I began, but stalled out.

"Come!" She took my wrist, her mood bright. She didn't just seem energetic; she seemed downright manic. I didn't precisely go with her. I was more accurately dragged. All of it was wrong. The day after turning, she should have been weak as her body literally ate itself alive. She should, by all rights, have been a zombie.

"I'm getting hungry again," she told me.

"Wait … Did you feed?" I asked.

"Oh, yes. Of course."

"How … *Who?*" There wouldn't have been time after I dropped her off the night before. The sun had almost been up by then, and there'd been nobody around. Besides, new vampires never fed so soon after turning. For one thing, their instincts took a while to kick in. For another, it usually felt like cannibalism.

"Mom and Chuck," she said.

"You fed on your *family?*"

"They say blood is thicker than water, right?" She laughed. "Of course, they're no good now."

I thought of the strange woman in the kitchen and something lit in my mind. I didn't like what I was beginning to suspect.

"Daisy ... I just walked right into the apartment."

"Oh, that's fine. Mom doesn't mind."

"I shouldn't have been able to pass the threshold of a human home without an invitation."

"Well, it's not a human home anymore, now, is it?" she said.

So it was true.

"You *turned* them?"

"I had to. I was so hungry, I practically sucked them dry. Chuck about died on me."

She didn't give me time to absorb this. I was inside her room a moment later. It looked like a little girl's place, all pink and soft dolls.

"You remember my friend, right?"

She gestured to the corner, where Timothy Reys had been propped with his insides dangling like eels. I jumped. This made Daisy laugh again.

"You stole his body?"

"Of course! They were going to try and pin it on you. No body, no evidence, right? You heard what those vampires were planning."

"But they're dead! They can't frame me if they're dead!"

Daisy put a hand on her hip. "Oh, come on, Maurice. One got away, remember? Besides, just the fact that they killed him framed you. There were just the three of us working with him last night. Tons of cash went through that place, and of course the cash is missing, too. Who else could it have been, other than the employees?"

I skipped right past her contradiction — the idea that I was already framed, yet stealing his body somehow cancelled it out. Instead I focused on the most recent revelation: "The cash is missing?"

"Either missing, or in that box over there." She pointed. I could see the ends of bills around the closed box's edges.

"You *stole the money?* Daisy, what the hell do you think you're—?"

She swatted the air. Clearly I was being a killjoy.

"Oh, *lighten up,* Maurice! Timothy didn't need it anymore, and the cops would just stick it in their own pockets. I got my throat ripped out and you had fend off three zoot-suit blood-suckers. After all that, who deserves that money more than us? We might as well have some fun!"

At this point, she took a flower-decorated man's hat she for some reason had on a shelf and put it on Timothy's head. She also had a pinwheel, which she stuck in his dead hand. When it fell to the floor, she picked it up and stuck it in his guts instead. Then she put her hands on her hips and inspected her work, judging it for aesthetic appeal.

Feeling lightheaded, I sat on the bed.

"What should we do tonight?" Daisy asked.

"I need a minute."

"How many of us are there in the city? How many vampires, Maurice? Do they have a club? Where do we all get together?"

I pressed my thumb and index finger into my temples. Timothy's corpse smelled like a meat hamper. Daisy flitted from place to place: around the room, out of the room, to the room's other side. I could feel her energy. It flooded the room like a physical presence, but it was also pressing out from within me, from the blood ties we shared. Its presence was cloying, like too much cologne.

"I guess we should talk," I said. "All of us."

"Good idea," Daisy said. "Call your friends. I want to meet them."

"I meant all of us here, in this apartment."

"You mean Mom and Chuck?"

I pressed my temples harder. I hadn't looked up. Beside me, Timothy slumped forward and hit the floor. The sound was like a giant anus pooping wet hamburger.

"Yes, Daisy. I mean your family."

She sat beside me, bouncing the springs. I could feel her pout. "They're *boring*. Chuck has been throwing up blood since I turned him and Mom won't stop cooking. Except that she's not doing it right. I think she's confused. She keeps putting pans on the stove, then pressing her palm flat into them when they get nice and hot. It's smelled like ham all day in here."

Until it started smelling like Timothy, I supposed.

"Is that normal?" she asked. "For a new vampire to be confused?"

"Yes, it's very normal. Sometimes new vampires act crazy. Sometimes they do stupid things like steal bodies, raid cash registers and—"

Now that Timothy was taking a nap on the floor, I noticed the twin wounds above his carotid artery.

"Did you try to feed on him?" I asked.

"I was *hungry!*"

I heard someone stumble into the room before looking up to see who it was. I expected the crazy mother but saw the crazy brother instead. He looked like something out of a horror comic. He was pale as paper, eyes translucent, blue veins mapping his skin like miniature highways. To this day I'm still not sure what went wrong, except that people say turning works a little like inbreeding. If new vampires make new vampires, they get tons of defects. I'd have warned Daisy, but it never happens. My other progeny were half dead the day after turning, then had to be goaded into feeding after a week of starving. Creating is the farthest thing from a new vampire's mind. Again I thought of the blood in the storeroom, wondering if it had a role in all this oddness.

"I don't feel so good," Daisy's brother said, one hand on his stomach.

She snapped at him like a brat. *"Get out of my room, Chuck!"*

He answered by vomiting blood like a geyser. Only it wasn't normal barfing. It was like he'd turned on a fire hose. His ralphing defined physics. Not only did he manage to generate impressive pressure from nowhere; he also regurgitated far more liquid than his body should have been able to hold. The room became a horrorshow in seconds, every surface running with crimson rain. A row of little toys and framed photos took a gusher and fell from a shelf. This made Daisy furious. And so, soaked with gore herself, she stood and whacked him with a pillow until he took his sickness to the front room, where he vomited on his mother. Mrs. Farley did not seem to mind.

"I'm sorry," Daisy said, whipping her long, dripping hair behind her and then beginning to squeeze it dry. "He can be so *rude!*"

I wiped blood out of my eyes. It was everywhere, including in my mouth. I spit it away, revolted. Vampire blood doesn't nourish us, and we really only bite each other during sex. But I did at least know what vampire blood was *supposed* to taste like, and Chuck Farley's tasted nothing like it. His was more like beets left in the sun, mixed with pureed fish.

"You were saying?" Daisy said, returning to the bed.

I didn't know where to start. I'd come to check on Daisy and do my duty as her maker, telling her about herself and her future, doing my best to prepare her for her new immortal life. Now I supposed I had to do the same for her family, but it was clear they were damaged beyond saving. I'd heard about vampires like her brother before. They never healed, because other than stitching wounds made immediately before turning, change isn't something our bodies are good at. Or even capable of. If he was throwing up now, he'd probably be doing it past his thousandth birthday — assuming he didn't run into the sun to end it all tomorrow. Her mother might just need time to mentally adapt, but something in me doubted it. If the brother was that bad, Mrs. Farley's problems were likely due to damage inside her brain. Physical damage, like Chuck's blood fountain, would be permanent.

I had to think triage. The time for ideal solutions was long past.

"You need to come with me," I told Daisy.

She brightened in an instant. "To meet some other vampires?"

"To take a shower. Then to my place. You can't stay here. You can stay with me."

"Your wife is into that?"

"To you *staying with us,* yes." Or at least, she'd *have* to be. In truth, I was probably moving both of us into the doghouse full-time. Celeste had said she wanted to meet my new progeny. But would she really want to meet the strange thing that progeny had become?

Daisy's expression fell. She seemed to have had something more intimate in mind. "Oh." Then: "What about Mom and Chuck? Can they come, too?"

I allowed myself a half-second to enjoy that preposterous idea. I could move Chuck in with Mort. It would be hilarious.

"No. They have to stay here. They can ... sleep."

Which was just me biding time. They were new enough that I should still be able to glamour them, and in doing so I could probably even get Chuck to stop puking as he fell unconscious. But it was a few-day reprieve at best. Within a week, they'd need to feed, if they were able. By then the last of their human blood would be gone and my glamour would stop working.

I had no idea what I'd do then, but for now I could only focus on one problem at a time. Even focusing on Daisy left so much of my recently-promising Chicago life in ruins. There was still the matter of my dead boss, my lost job, and a probable murder investigation on my doorstep.

Most troubling of all, even if Daisy and the rest of it settled, there was still the matter of the blood barrel and the vampire gangsters who'd come to claim it.

Chicago's underbelly, I feared, had only begun to reveal itself.

14

DADDY

WE BARELY MADE it home before sunrise.

After an hour spent chasing Daisy's brother and mother around their apartment — an hour filled with puke assaults and her mother trying to brain me with her frying pan, which she could almost do because she'd inherited impressive speed — all I wanted was a quiet journey home to rest.

I was beat. Thank God I'd already fed; I needed the physical and mental fortitude to corral the two ruined vampires and convince them to sleep, then to clean up the worst of their mess. I had to do that part alone because Daisy was no help. She kept tugging on me, trying to get me to take her out on the town. She also kept quizzing me about vampire miscellany — things she'd decided she needed to know to be part of our shared species, laced with enthusiasm for the whole "great dark gift" that I found hard to stomach. And if she wasn't tugging, she was pouting that I was a killjoy with all my order and cleanup — not any fun at all. We had hundreds of The Bomber's dollars, she told me, and should be out there living it up in Timothy's memory. All while refusing to help me dispose of Timothy's corpse, which by then had broken into two separate pieces.

I did my best. And "my best," which I concluded as first light kissed the sky, would have to do. Crime in the 20s was a whole lot easier to get away with, and being from a species of murderers I was uniquely equipped to do it. I incinerated the body and the worst of the blood-soaked linens, then took plain old human cleaner to the rest of it. I didn't come close to getting all the blood, but I thought it might pass if anyone came calling. Until they got a warrant and discovered the blood caked in every little corner ... and, of course, the sick vampires nestled snugly in their beds. That wouldn't necessarily point to the murder of Timothy Reys, but it'd get the right folks thinking that *something* was amiss.

I reminded myself that I couldn't solve the problems all at once. All I could do was solve its pieces. *One day at a time,* as the saying goes.

With the apartment and relatives handled for the time being, all we had left to clean up was ourselves. Unfortunately, the shower didn't work in Daisy's apartment. It looked like someone had, for reasons unknown, banged the living shit out of the plumbing within the last 24 hours with a blunt instrument — like, for instance, a frying pan.

I'd been telling Daisy to clean herself the entire time I was cleaning her mess, and if she'd tried, we might have discovered the lack of facilities in time to do something about it. Instead, we realized we had no way to clean up with dawn at our heels. I wanted to run home in what remained of the shadows to shower there, but Daisy kept trying to run away even in the coming light. She was crazy with vampire energy; she either didn't understand she'd need to spend the day indoors or refused to give up her fun to do so even if it meant dying. So we couldn't run. I had to hold her tight, and together we had to ride the streetcar.

Covered in blood, reeking of gore.

I glamoured the driver into acceptance and glamoured prospective passengers into taking the next car, but I didn't like the increasingly obvious footprints we were leaving between us and what we were supposed to be fleeing. Celeste and I have always been good at laying low. Even as a human (and a misfit even then) I'd known how to blend into the background. We'd come to America on the down-low, settled into New York on the down-low, moved to Chicago on the down-low, and for three months had lived in peace and relative happiness here on the down-low. Now it was all changing. Less than 36 hours ago, we'd been free. I couldn't shake the feeling that every moment since that barrel had broken in The Bomber's back room, I'd been drawing a map to my front door, for anyone to find us and unravel all we'd built. With at least one escaped gangster in our recent past, that map felt like a problem waiting to happen. Anyone might come calling ... and I swore more than once, I caught someone lurking in the corner of my eye. *Santori? Little Sammy?* I had no clue. The mob might be after us to settle Timothy's bills, or it could be a league of vampires dressed just like the two goons I'd dispatched. The world used to feel safe and comfortable. Now, it felt like a deadly game of Hide and Seek.

The old feelings were back, stronger than they'd been since Europe. Old tendrils, wrapping my neck like cold, dark hands.

Daisy and I entered the Flynns' building and began to climb the stairs just as the sun peeked over the horizon. Her enthusiasm blessedly began to wane with the day's arrival. She plodded slower, both of us summiting the steps like climbers at the end of a very long journey. We ran into nobody in the building's lobby, nobody in the stairwell, nobody in the hallway as we dodged the sunbeam from the window at the hallway's end.

When we arrived at our apartment, I realized I'd lost my key. I knocked on the door until Henry opened it. He was dressed in slacks and a cardigan, smoking a pipe. He looked us over for long seconds, scanning our blood-soaked bodies from head to toe.

"Well then," he said. "Come on in. Your mother made pancakes."

Then he went back to the kitchen, leaving the door open.

"'Your *mother*'?" Daisy asked.

"That's new," I told her. "They usually think I'm a cousin."

Irene, as things turned out, wasn't making pancakes so much as hitting roaches with an unlabeled tin can. She did not look up when I peeked in, nor when I called her name. Mort was walking repeatedly into a wall inside the shared bedroom. I could only assume that Celeste had tried to glamour them all again, or that her first glamour was still working its way through their minds like cancer.

Daisy shrieked from behind me. She'd turned to find Elsie and Evelyn in the center of the hall between us and the bedrooms. They were again wearing matching outfits and were again holding hands, moveless on the ratty carpet like a pair of vacant-eyed dolls.

"Come and play with us, Maurice," they said in unison.

Daisy was having none of this. She squeezed by them, pressing her back to the wall so she wouldn't have to get closer than absolutely necessary. She left a huge blood smear on the paint. The girls' eyes rolled up to watch her, but they didn't turn their heads.

"For ever ... and ever ... and *ever*," they told her.

"Go eat breakfast!" I barked.

They dropped hands and walked past me without comment.

I peeked in on Celeste, who was already asleep. I knew this time I couldn't drift by on the technicality of her slumber, but I could at least delay waking her until we'd made ourselves presentable. I told Daisy to shower first, and after trying to get me to join her she complied with the door left open, probably as an incestuous invitation. I ignored it, but Mort did not. He was not subtle. He found the open door, then stood before it like a man paralyzed by the sight of something holy. I had to close the door at that point, and tell Mort in a very glamouring way that he was extremely interested in counting checkers in his room right now. I hated glamouring him again. Hell, I hated glamouring at all, but especially Mort, especially then. He'd been born dumb, and our mental intrusions couldn't be helping. Delving into his mind felt like plunging my hands into rotting mulch.

Daisy emerged dressed in the clothes I'd given her: Irene's, because Celeste was way too short for her wardrobe to fit. She'd done something remarkable with her hair, given the short time she'd had and the meager beauty supplies in the Flynns' cabinets. I suppose she was trying to entice me — not because I was particularly appealing, but because I was the only male vampire she'd met who wasn't her brother. I had to keep reminding myself: *It's the change that's arousing her.* I still wasn't attracted to Daisy and she wouldn't be to me under normal circumstances, but vampires are strange. Sex is mixed into everything with us. It pops up out of the blue in all sorts of circumstances, like a miner unexpectedly hitting a vein in ore.

Still, I had to admit: The change suited her.

"Where are your old clothes?" I asked.

"I put them in the trash can, like you asked." Then, too lascivious for comfort, she smirked and added, "... *Daddy.*"

I'd been sitting on a chair in our bedroom, atop a thread-bare sheet I intended to put with the other clothes and burn. I had a handful of clean clothes, but still I paused before leaving the room, knowing I'd have to lock the bathroom to keep her out, seeing the way she sat on the bed beside Celeste. The way she reached out, and touched my wife's hair.

"Let her sleep," I warned.

Daisy smiled, intending nothing of the kind.

15

GIRLS

UNDER THE SHOWER'S SPRAY, I began my intensive course of rationalization. I knew exactly what I was doing and why it was bullshit, but I wanted very hard to believe that it wasn't going to fall apart. I wanted very hard to believe things would work out fine, that everything would quickly return to normal.

Between assurances that I could clean up my mess, my mind served up penny dreadful horrors of all that could easily go wrong, or had perhaps already gone wrong.

I'd think: *Daisy is fine. Many new vampires are high-energy and full of lust, and she's young. Whatever you sense amiss with her, it will pass.*

And then I'd think: *But her family. Her family will be a problem.*

I'd think: *We did nothing wrong at The Bomber. And beyond that, we cleaned everything up.*

And then I'd think: *But who's a better suspect, in the eyes of the police, than the immigrant kid who worked for Mr. Reys for just a few months — long enough to see how much money went through the place, to make friends with the mafioso who came and went with the shipments of liquor?*

I didn't like how Daisy had returned to a scene we'd vacated cleanly, to retrieve a corpse. I didn't like the way she'd propped it up in her room. I didn't like her mania, or the frenzy with which she'd turned her family. I could rationalize it all (it was my fault, for instance, for leaving her alone and worked up without knowledge), but still my mind returned again and again to the worst possibilities. What if something was truly wrong with Daisy? What if I'd opened a box that now couldn't be closed?

It made me anxious. It made me rush through my shower, knowing I'd fail to get off all of the blood. I kept thinking of Daisy beside Celeste in our room. What might she do to my wife while she slumbered?

I practically broke the door off its hinges when I returned to the bedroom, my hair wet and uncombed. I must have looked crazy. And, as if to verify it, both women on the bed turned at the sound, staring at me like I was a maniac.

"You woke her," I said to Daisy.

"I woke myself," said Celeste.

"It was the strangest thing," Daisy said. "I just kept looking down at her." She touched Celeste's arm, probably as silent apology for sleep-watching. Celeste shrugged it away. Something they'd already covered as they'd been chatting, I supposed. "I had all these thoughts in my head, but they weren't mine. I started to think they might be hers, that we might be connected somehow. And I watched, and I watched ... and I kept thinking, 'I wonder if her eyes are brown?' And then she opened them, and they were."

"I could hear her," Celeste told me. "I could hear her in my dreams."

"Is it always like that?" Daisy asked me.

I didn't answer. I hadn't spoken. I was still in the doorway, hair in wet curls, legs bent and broad as if I expected to take a tackle. But the answer was no.

Celeste laughed. "What's wrong, Maurice?"

"You aren't mad?"

"Why would I be mad?"

My eyes ticked to Daisy, then back. Then to Daisy. Then back.

"We had a little fight last night," Celeste explained, turning to Daisy.

"About me," Daisy said. It wasn't a question.

"In part."

"He's silly."

"*So* silly," Celeste echoed.

"He's worried about us."

"As he does."

"It's sweet."

"Until it's a bit too much." Here, Celeste broke away from Daisy and looked at me. "Isn't that right, Maurice?"

I had an answer to that, but for some reason didn't know to whom I should address it. I could feel both of them in my blood, same as they could feel each other. It was stronger than it should be, just as Daisy's blood, in the blood-ties-sense I always did my best to avoid using, was *louder* than it should be. My vision wanted to double. The bond had enough energy to confuse my eyes. I kept wanting to see them as one person instead of two.

I tried to give Celeste an update, given that we'd been at odds the night before and she didn't know most of what had happened in one of the longest 36 hour spans of my life. But I couldn't speak as freely in front of Daisy as I'd have liked, and nobody seemed to feel like talking about it anyway. The two of them had bonded in the handful of minutes I'd been showering and were already best friends. I was suddenly the odd man out, unable to get a word in edgewise.

Honestly, it was a relief. I was bone-tired, and the last thing I wanted was to spend hours rehashing the barrel incident, the vampire gangsters, my dual killings, Timothy's murder, Daisy's turning, and all the ramifications thereof. I was already worried about what the human authorities might do or who the vampire escapee might tell about our adventures, so I didn't particularly want to go deep with Celeste on any of that, either. I'd gotten comfortable with the Flynns and I knew she had, too. I didn't want to go on the run and I didn't want to leave.

I needed sleep, not discussion and high emotions.

So I rationalized silence, just as I'd rationalized everything during my shower. My only real concern was staying in Celeste's bad graces. So I persisted just enough to shove some words in between their chatter, making sure Celeste knew that I was ready to be forthcoming and that *she* — not I — was the one who didn't have time to talk. Hell, Daisy had already told her the colored versions of the worst parts already anyway.

So I laid on the bed and closed my eyes, sure that sleep wouldn't come. I was too agitated, too emotionally unsettled. Add to that the chattering ladies across the room and I figured I had a ready-made recipe for insomnia.

But I didn't last ten minutes. I slept like the dead, without dreams.

16

SLEEPLESS DAY

WHEN I OPENED MY EYES, I had no idea how much time had passed. I don't normally sleep so deeply. Part of being a vampire is heightened awareness, so my sleep is normally the half-slumber of a napping cat. Waking from such depths was disorienting. At first I didn't know where I was. Awareness came slowly.

The room was quiet, dark, and still. Beneath the door, I saw, was a line of faint yellow light. Beyond that, I heard the low chatter of somnolent voices, audible only once I laid very still.

We'd done a supernatural job of blocking sun from the apartment, so not a pinprick of it intruded. It might be midnight or high noon; I hadn't a clue. So I rose, but I couldn't find my watch in the dark. It didn't matter. The Flynns, it seemed, were gone. That meant the sun was still up. They all left during the day. The children went to school; Henry went to work; Irene went to social engagements and the excessive errands we'd glamoured her into feeling were necessary, just to give ourselves solitude.

I knew the house was empty of humans during the day, but

experiencing it was strange. Despite sleeping lightly, I seldom woke and pretty much never got out of bed. It gave my steps a surreal feeling, as if I was somewhere I shouldn't be.

The line of light led me to the door. When I opened it, the volume of voices bumped up. Looking right, I saw that the women had set up camp across from each other in the kitchen, across the Flynn's chipped table.

I walked closer, neither turning to see me. I saw that in the table's dead center was a bottle of red wine, the cork replaced only slightly, leaning at an angle. Celeste and Daisy each had glasses. Wine — along with cigarettes and a few other human indulgences — were tastes we'd retained. I am French, after all.

I could tell right away that the mood had calmed from the previous night's high — or low, as it were. Without asking, I could tell that neither had slept. It was written on their faces, audible in their voices, feelable in their blood, and palpable in their energy.

Celeste saw me. Smiled. And patted the chair beside her, with Daisy on its other side.

"Celeste, I—"

"Shh." She patted the chair again. "Sit."

I did as I was told. They'd been talking a moment earlier, but I hadn't heard what about. Now they were quiet. The kitchen was as still as a grave. It was strange to not see Irene by the sink. It was strange not to see Henry with us at the table, his paper open and rustling.

My eyes found the clock. It wasn't 2pm, as I'd thought. It was after eight. The sun had gone to bed already, and they'd burned the entire night in conversation.

"Is that really the time?" I asked.

"Yes," Celeste said. "How did you sleep?"

But that question didn't interest me. I said instead, "Where's the family?"

"They decided to spend the night with friends."

I looked at my wife. "Celeste, we've talked about you glamouring—"

"It wasn't me. It was her." Nodding at Daisy.

I turned my head. Tired, Daisy seemed completely different. Not manic at all. There was no lust — for blood, sex, or greed — on her face. She was like an entirely different person. Or, perhaps more accurately, like the girl I'd known before I'd changed her.

"But she's brand new," I said.

"She's still very good at glamouring," Celeste told me. "What's that you've said? 'What vampirism doesn't give us in brawn, it gives us in brains.'"

I nodded. It seemed to be true. Especially as Logan's regime focused more on vampire evolution, training, and the enhancement of our species, the quiet and intelligent ones among us seemed to stand out more and more. As a culture, we were even then growing stronger but dumber. Outliers weren't yet looked upon as they became in later years, but "strong and fast" was already becoming the norm. Daisy would make people wonder, for sure.

"You've been up all night?"

Daisy nodded. "This isn't our first bottle of wine."

I picked up the bottle. "Did this come from The Bomber?"

She shook her head. "The Flynns had a few bottles. They aren't as law-abiding as you'd think."

I looked at Celeste, Daisy, Celeste. Without intending it, my blood sent a question into the ties we shared across the table, as maker and dual progeny. It was perhaps intrusive, but the women let the answers come to me. I saw their whole night's talk in the span of seconds. I no longer had to ask if Daisy had told Celeste about the money and Timothy's body. I knew she had, along with everything else. Everything except for the creeping fear of it all — the certainty that something bad was coming, that some loose end would be all of our undoing. That rotten thought was mine and mine alone.

"You told her about your family," I said to Daisy.

"I told her everything."

That gave me a flash I wasn't expecting. I saw an avalanche of secrets they'd already shared: my experiences with Celeste, Daisy's rough childhood, Celeste's abusive father, Daisy's single sexual experience and the baby she'd given away after, Celeste's regrets and hopes, Daisy's latent fears. Daisy was at once fragile and strong — at once the shy girl I'd thought, and also a broken girl I couldn't have imagined. They'd shared a lifetime, and yet it'd only been a night.

"*Including* about her family," Celeste said.

We shared a look. I already felt guilty for leaving Daisy alone with virtually no educational talk, and Celeste knew she didn't need to twist the knife. She also knew, same as me, that there shouldn't have been any danger from my not telling Daisy about the Vampire Birds and Bees. New vampires don't make new vampires. Period.

"Are you feeling better?" I asked. "I mean ... you seem calmer."

"It's strange. Yes. I feel almost like I'm sobering up."

"It's that way for everyone," Celeste said. "The agent that makes us vampires is like a drug. We all adjust differently, but even after all this time I remember that sensation of 'coming down' over the first few days."

Like a drug. Inside my mind, I saw the broken barrel of unusual blood.

"They'll get better too, right?" Daisy asked. "Chuck and Mom, I mean? They'll 'come down' too, right?"

Celeste and I shared a glance. The answer was yes and no. Like any new vampire, the agent would spike in them and then decrease to baseline. But I'd seen those vampires in person, and Celeste had seen them in Daisy's memory, shared over the sleepless day through blood ties. She knew as well as I did that what had happened was unusual, mostly unprecedented, and that baseline itself would have to take a new meaning. We both knew that when a vampire is damaged in the turning, it's the kind of damage that cannot heal.

"We'll just have to see," Celeste said.

Daisy could read her voice, though, and she could read my body language. Though we were both doing our best to bury our thoughts, she'd gotten a least a whiff of our deception. She seemed like she wanted to pick at the issue, but then she backed off. Afraid of what she'd hear if she dug deeper, probably. As she should have been.

Still she opened her mouth, but we never learned what she'd planned to say.

Because that's when the knock on the door came, and the first of the new ones entered our lives.

17

ENVOYS

SOMETHING WAS PLAYING my nerves like an instrument in a big string band. I didn't have any specific idea who was at the door, but the air itself screamed that all was not well. It might be the police, come to ask me about Timothy's death. It might be vampires, upset about the death of their fellows at my hands. I figured it was best to be safe, never sorry, so I grabbed the most universal weapon I could find: Mort's wooden baseball bat from the front closet. I snapped it in half like a twig, and what remained was sharp enough to deal with whoever might need dealing.

I didn't bother with the chain. Instead I put my shoulder behind the door and set my feet, opening it with one hand while the other held my makeshift stake at the ready.

Two men stood beyond the door. One was broad-shouldered and ugly. The other was thin, pretty like a woman. Both were dressed well, but the small one wore his suit much better. On the big man, the same garb looked utilitarian, as if he didn't know how to set his body within it — as if someone else had dressed him to make him presentable. The thin one looked like a men's clothing advertisement, proof of the expression that says clothes make the man. He even wore a hat, tipped perfectly.

The big one said, "Are you Maurice?" He had a slight accent. Irish? Scottish? I've always had a tin ear.

"Maybe. Who are you?"

"Maurice Toussant, of Marseille?" the same man asked.

My grip on the bat tightened. I hadn't been to Marseille for a very long time. Nobody knows my roots. Nobody in America, anyway.

"Who is it, Maurice?" Celeste asked, trying to see around me. Daisy was beside her, both women now visible to the outsiders. I'd told them to stay put, but of course they hadn't.

"Is that your wife, Celeste?" said the big man.

"I think it's time you tell me who the hell you are. If you're cops, let's see your badges."

"We're not police, Mr. Toussant. We're envoys."

"Envoys for what?"

"May we come in?"

The thin man pushed forward, past the big one. He put his hand on the door. I could smell cologne on him, assertively strong. His lips parted in something pretending to be a smile, and behind them I saw fangs. Of course. Now I could smell what the cologne was masking.

"Please," he said.

The standoff was pointless. I stepped back and let the door open. The home was the Flynns', not mine. We'd been invited, but these two hadn't. Even if I wanted to invite them in, I couldn't. Didn't they know the rules?

Even without an invitation, the pretty vampire tried to enter when the door opened. An invisible wall held him back, his feet moving uselessly beneath him. Murder crossed his face as he looked back up.

"Or perhaps you could come out here," said the big one.

Also a vampire, I had to assume, or he'd have come in after the thin one's display.

"I like it this way," I told them, putting a few feet between our two parties. Then I repeated: *"Envoys for what?"*

"My name is Malone. This is Isaac. We're here from the CVA."

Isaac nodded and adjusted his hat, but he looked irritated by this need for civility.

"What's the CVA?" I asked.

The big vampire looked both ways down the outer hallway, then said in a lower voice, "The Chicago Vampire Alliance."

"Not interested," I said.

"It's not a matter of interest," said Isaac. "You can't just show up in town without letting us know. This isn't France. This is *Chicago.*" No accent on this one. He was American through and through.

Malone put a hand up, moving himself between me and Isaac. "What Isaac means is that we have a network here. For everyone's protection."

"I don't need protection."

"Actually," Malone said, "you do. You just don't know it yet. You work at The Bomber speakeasy, right?"

"We both do," said Daisy. She'd been behind Celeste, but now she took a step forward. Isaac looked her over with what struck me as quiet appreciation. Worse, Daisy looked Isaac over, too.

"We *did,*" I corrected. "What of it?"

"Do you know a regular drinker named Ricardo?"

"Short. Spats. Likes his martinis dry."

"That's him. I don't imagine you could smell him, with all that liquor to confuse your senses?"

"Are you saying he's a vampire?"

Malone nodded. "It's not just the liquor. He also wears a special cologne that mimics human musk."

"Why?"

"Because we've been watching you."

"You've been *watching* me?"

"Before you get too upset," Malone said, "I should tell you that we're not the only ones. I believe you've also met our friend Santori?"

That set me back. I had to think. But yes, it made total and complete sense. Something had bugged me about Santori the few times I'd seen him, though I'd never been able to put my finger on what it was. Nobody but Timothy was ever allowed close enough to Santori for his vampire scent to register, but there was something about the way he moved. He was feline, graceful in a way the eyes refused to register.

"Tall guy," Isaac said, as if I hadn't understood. "Dark hair. Usually drags around a little pissant to do his bidding who they call—"

"I know who Santori is," I said.

"Now, he's not watching you like we were, but rest assured he knows who you are. It's his business to know."

"Liquor?"

"Don of the vampire mafia," Malone countered. "He runs the whole damn thing."

"He wasn't watching you," Isaac repeated, "but I'll bet he is now."

Malone shot him a look. The idea was apparently to gain trust, not scare us.

"Look," Malone went on. "It's like I said. We keep tabs on the comings and goings of our own, as best we can. We always meant to get in touch with you, but certain events ..." He eyed Daisy. He had to know she'd worked The Bomber with me, and had to know she was a vampire now. Whether he knew how those two things connected, I wasn't sure. "... have acceler-ated our timeline. We're friends. This would be much easier to discuss if we could sit somewhere comfortable."

"Of course." I looked at Isaac, who'd again shoved his way up front like a man desperate to win a pissing contest. "Come on in."

Isaac walked forward, his gait conveying annoyance at needing to ask permission. He struck the same barrier as before, feet sliding again as if on ice. This time, though, it really pissed him off. His fangs returned.

I shook my head. "'*Friends*,'" I sneered. "'*Here for our protection.*' How, exactly? You don't even know how the simplest things work. How old are you, anyway? This is a *human* home. I couldn't invite you in if I wanted."

Malone, at least, had seen the trap coming. I'd watched his eyes widen as Isaac had stepped forward, too late to stop him. Now he just looked exhausted by his partner's idiocy.

"Maurice," Malone said. "May I call you Maurice?"

I shrugged.

"Cards on the table. I've lived for fifty years as a vampire. Isaac has been just a few months. We know, from the European network who told us you'd emigrated, that you're nearly two thousand. We know your wife is half that. There's not a chance we could overpower either of you. So please. Man to man. You hold all the cards. Can we please sit down some-where like gentlemen, rather than standing like enemies?"

"You don't need to overpower us," I said, looking at a spot just below his left armpit, "when you're carrying a gun."

"Afraid of guns?" Malone said, opening his jacket to reveal a shoulder holster. But uncharacteristic to his big, broad face, he was smiling in a way that was clearly a nudge, clearly risking a joke.

"Of what's in the clip, yes."

Malone did the last thing I expected. He removed the gun from the holster and held it out to me butt first. When I hesitated to take it, he nodded. "We're friends."

I took the weapon, then depressed the release and removed the clip. Inside were wooden rounds in brass jackets. I don't know why the slugs don't burn and shatter when they're fired, but they don't. Knowing such things was my brother's purview, not mine.

"Why," I asked him, "would you walk around with vampire-killers?"

This time, Malone was the one who shrugged.

"It's like I said," he told me. "This is Chicago."

18

―――

FEAR

"SO DID YOU GO WITH THEM?" Annabel asked her patient.

Maurice nodded. "Yes. I didn't like it, but it was the only thing I could do. I'd tried my best to stay away from Chicago's vampires, but now here they were at my door. I suppose I could have refused, but what would have been the point? They'd confirmed what my gut already knew about Santori, and learning that he was vampire mafia got my mind connecting dots. The vampires I'd killed at The Bomber had sure looked like gangsters. If they'd worked with Santori and Santori already knew what I was, the vampire mafia might already be on our trail, wanting an eye for an eye. So I figured I'd hear Malone out, knowing I could outmatch him if he wasn't telling the truth. Better to have allies when you have enemies."

"Just Malone?"

Maurice nodded. "Isaac stayed behind. To 'protect' Celeste and Daisy."

"You say that like he didn't really mean to protect them."

"Oh, I imagine he did," Maurice said. "Daisy, anyway. I

saw the way he looked at her, and the way she looked at him. I trusted Celeste to keep them in line, and at first she did. But while I came to like Malone, I never trusted Isaac. I wish I'd reacted without thinking, and killed Isaac back then."

"'*Back then*'?" Annabel clarified.

"I waited over eighty years too long," Maurice told her, "but our score was settled in the end."

Annabel opened her mouth to ask more — about what Isaac had done wrong, about what had happened between him and Daisy, and most curiously why Maurice had apparently killed the same Isaac just recently according to her math — but Maurice went on before she could.

"The women stayed inside the apartment," he said. "Isaac waited outside, unable to get in. I know they talked, for as long as we talked. Afterward, Celeste and I compared notes. We covered a lot of the same ground, but whereas Malone gave me an official explanation, Isaac gave Celeste the street-level version. He was new then — arrogant like all the 'official' new vampires of the time. He was so sure he was better than others ... and that his species, more to the point, was better than humans. I've lived a very long time, and in that time I've come to think of humans as partners. They make the planet run and we protect it. If we feed without killing them, the system works. And that's how it had been for thousands of years, until Logan's regime started to show its true colors. Vampires like Isaac saw humans as an infestation. They think the planet is supposed to be ours."

Maurice shifted on the couch, sitting more upright.

"I went with Malone, both his and Isaac's pistols tucked into the back of my pants. I didn't trust him yet, so we sat opposite each other in the park. Then as the night wore on, we moved to an all-night cafe. We ordered coffee so they'd let us stay, but Malone just kept pouring his into a plant beside our table. By sunrise, that plant was wired enough to dance the Charleston."

"You said the CVA was watching you," Annabel said.

Maurice nodded.

"Why, though? Couldn't they just spy on you through that psychic thing, with the blood?"

"It doesn't work that way," Maurice said. "Blood ties only form between related vampires, not all vampires. Most can only feel the maker-progeny bond."

"Not you, though, right? You said 'blood is blood.' If I were a vampire with ties to you, you said *you'd* be able to sniff out even the humans in my family tree."

Maurice made a face. It was hard to believe a vampire could be so repelled by such an intriguing vampire skill.

"It's supposed to be a two-way bond — a mutual sharing," he said. "And there are ... well ... ways to abuse it. Preventing that are some of the few vampire laws I actually agree with."

"How can you abuse blood ties?" Annabel asked.

"You'd have to ask psychopaths. Supposedly if you know enough about a person, you can crowbar your way in even if it's blood you're not usually able to touch. It's like mind rape, and the subject usually knows you're there. As far as covert surveillance goes, it's pretty far from ideal."

Annabel was both intrigued and disappointed. She wanted to ask more, but Maurice clearly found the whole thing repugnant. She was fascinated with what he'd told her so far, wanting to learn as much as possible. Unfortunately, she'd drawn a vampire who didn't seem to enjoy being a vampire. It was a wonder he was able to bring himself to feed.

"So they sent someone to follow you?" she asked. It was such a little downer of a question. Vampires were fascinating and powerful, and yet they resorted to peeking around corners?

They should be able to transform into bats to do their spying, at least.

Maurice looked back up at the ceiling and nodded. "They'd sent their guy Ricardo as a spy, to keep an eye on me at the speakeasy. Only, that's not fair; I guess he was 'on reconnaissance.' Turns out, I hadn't stayed under anyone's radar. They'd known we were in Chicago the minute we arrived. New York, too. Only, New York didn't care that we'd come. Chicago did."

"Why?"

"Fear."

"Fear of what?"

"Of humans, ironically," Maurice said. "We're strong; we're fast; we don't die when we're stabbed or shot or burned or crushed. But humans outnumber us a hundred thousand to one, and for half of each day they're able to move around when we're not. Any vampire who tells you he's never feared waking to a stake in the heart is lying. Literally all it takes is knowing that we exist and knowing where to find us when the sun is shining. If humans have that, there's nothing we can do to stop them."

"What's that got to do with the CVA?"

"Nothing, directly," Maurice said. "But I had a lot of perspective that the younger vampires didn't — and a lot more now, with the benefit of hindsight. The CVA was, looking back, a direct result of the paranoia that Logan's Vampire Council was trying to create."

"Wait ... the Vampire Council *wanted* paranoia? They were *trying* to make vampires afraid of what humans might do?"

"Of course," Maurice said. "Fear has always been a tool for powerful people looking to become more powerful. We're always willing to give up freedom, privacy, or control to someone who we think will make us safer. The Chicago vampire network — and later, the entire American network — spread a very specific breed of propaganda. And of course, the rich were getting richer. Money helped them buy power. Power helped them earn more money."

"I'm not sure what you mean."

Annabel found herself sitting forward. If she perched any more on the edge of her seat, she was going to fall into his lap.

He went on, but didn't really answer her implied question.

"Most of the vampires in the CVA had good intentions. They worked kind of like a neighborhood watch. Guys like Malone had decided it was better to *act* than just sit around waiting for the things the Council was working so hard to make us afraid of: humans getting smarter and stronger and less afraid of the dark. The rise of Capone made it easy to fear; Chicago's streets were becoming war zones. So the CVA kept watch over vampire neighborhoods, and they carried guns that would kill both species, just trying to keep the worst of it from where we laid down at daybreak. But by the time Malone and I talked, they'd run up against something a whole lot bigger than just keeping eyes peeled for trouble on the block — something that outmatched their little 'neighborhood watch' by a long shot. And by chance or fate or shitty old Maurice luck, I'd stumbled into the same exact thing."

"What do you mean?" Annabel asked. "What had you stumbled into?" Annabel asked.

She could sense Maurice's thoughts churning. Feeling foolish, she tried to reach her mind out to his — to do a version of the vampire trick he'd described. But of course nothing came. She was human. She wasn't special at all.

Finally, Maurice broke the office's dark silence.

"The blood," he said. "In the end, it was always about the blood."

19

THE BLOOD

"THIS," Malone said, "is why we need your help."

By the time he showed me the facility, I'd known Malone for almost two weeks, just like I knew his closest friends at the CVA — a nucleus in the larger group that simply called themselves the Crew. We'd grown tighter with them than the old me would have been comfortable with, but at the time, it felt safe. I knew Isaac and Daisy were getting too close, and I saw it for the poisoned breed of "close" that so many of the young ones believe passes for affection.

As Daisy spent more time with Isaac, I spent more time with Malone and the Crew. I found a way to justify letting her go. Daisy, I reasoned, was young and wild. Vampirism had unleashed something within her that, it turned out, had only slightly dampened after the first days of her turning. She was a girl with her eyes newly opened — and to me, as an old man, that made her both hard and frustrating to handle. So I did the easy thing. The cowardly thing. I let Isaac do a lot of the handling, even though I knew he was trouble.

Given our new familiarity, I didn't immediately balk at Malone's mention of needing my help. We'd been over and over it. Truth was, the CVA *had* been planning to contact me and Celeste simply to get us registered, and to show us the ropes in Chicago's vampire community. But beyond that, they'd seen the fact that a powerful vampire of the old guard had come to town as kismet. Chicago had a growing problem, and fate had sent Maurice Toussant to help solve it. I wasn't even close to interested in vampire affairs, but as I looked across the open space Malone showed me with all its machinery, I was definitely intrigued.

"What is it?" I asked.

"They call it a distillery."

I didn't know much about such things, but it wasn't like any distillery I'd ever imagined. There were enormous wooden casks that looked like barrels laid on their sides, twice as tall as me, and there was the general feel of a mad scientist's lab — complete with metal-jacketed orbs connected by tubes in one of the warehouse's corners. Beyond that, the comparisons to a liquor distillery stopped and a strange new intelligence seemed to have taken over. Along two of the walls were two-tall rows of chambers with glass fronts, each around seven feet tall and three feet wide. Inside the chambers was dangling stained rubber tubing tipped with long metal needles, plus some sort of measuring device both inside and mounted to the front. Long tubes ran overhead, from end to end. The place had high windows like a factory's — the kind that let in light, but don't expose what's inside — but all were blacked out, boarded, and covered again in heavy draperies nailed all the way around the edges. There was no ventilation that I could see, and I'd heard that kind of thing was essential for distillation, if for nothing else than to keep the whole works from blowing sky-high.

Malone led me to one of the huge casks. Someone had cut a big hole in the front, big enough for a person to walk through. Before entering, he handed me a flashlight. Then he looked at me, while we were still a dozen feet from the entrance, and said a strange thing.

"You hungry?"

"Not particularly."

"You fed tonight already, then."

I figured this was so redundant as to be rhetorical. But no, Malone was waiting for an answer.

"I fed tonight. Why?"

"Have you ever heard humans say it's a bad idea to go grocery shopping while hungry? Same reason. Come on."

That didn't make sense until we got within five feet of the empty cask. That's when I started to smell the blood. Although it wasn't precisely *blood*; I could see that now. In the back of Sammy's truck — and then again in The Bomber's taproom, even before Daisy had broken the barrel — I'd thought the smell was blood, but after seeing the facility and all its chemistry, my mind opened to the possibility of it being something else. Or perhaps more accurately, something *more*.

By the time we ducked inside the cask, I knew why Malone had asked if I'd eaten. Once in the intoxicating reek of the place, I grew absolutely ravenous. And also a little woozy. If I wasn't already sated, I'd probably have been hungry enough to think it worthwhile to feed on Malone — just because he was there, because he had a neck.

The inside of the cask was stained an impervious, unwashable red.

"Hungry now?" he asked, laughing.

"Jesus. I won't lie. I'm thinking of eating *you*."

"Exactly. Normal blood do that to you?"

"Not like this."

He nodded. His flashlight played around the cask, turning red to orange wherever the brightest of the beam touched. "They call this shit 'Thrilloglobin,' or 'Thrill' for short. From what the lab can tell, it's mostly blood. You saw the bleeding chambers?"

The seven-foot tubes with tubing and needles hanging inside. Now they made sense. It gave me chills, to imagine them all filled with humans, drained as fast as they could produce new blood. Human cows, kept inches from slaughter.

"The blood funnels to a mixing vat, where they either add something or do something to it. Nobody's sure. The chemistry set you saw in the corner? We think that's where they create whatever's added."

"You don't sound very certain," I said.

"We're not scientists. We're just a bunch of people with eyes and guns. Oh, we've asked for some eggheads to help figure it out, but the Vampire Council doesn't really seem to care enough to send anyone. We've got an audience with the Council and Logan himself coming up, but to be honest I'm not hopeful. Not about finding the formula, anyway."

"Why?"

"Because the formula really doesn't matter. All that matters is the end product, Thrill, hitting the streets. And the fact that it comes off like a Chicago problem, and our problem alone."

I'd had a question, but my brain could no longer find it. Just being in the empty cask was making me dizzy. I could only imagine what drinking the real thing would do to a person.

"Is there somewhere else we can go?" I asked.

"Oh. Sure. Keep forgetting you're new to Thrill. Come on. Stuff to show you this way, anyhow."

20

———

THRILL

MALONE LED me out of the cask. We crossed in front of a line of identical wooden structures, up a set of metal stairs, and past a conveyor lined with empty wooden barrels that looked a whole lot like the barrels our beer used to come in — or, more on-point, the barrel of Thrill we seemed to have received by mistake.

At the end of the conveyor was another short set of stairs leading to a glass-walled office that perched like a crow's nest above the factory floor. We entered and Malone shut the door.

"Any better?" he asked.

My head was spinning. I was hungry, horny, a little euphoric, and stupid amounts of confused. I didn't know if I wanted to eat, fuck, dance, or just fall down until I stopped twitching.

"Not really."

Malone laughed again. "Take deep breaths. It'll pass in a few minutes. And think, you just breathed in what we couldn't scrub off. The kids drink this shit by the shotglass, then they party 'til dawn."

"You busted this place?" I asked.

Malone shrugged. "As much as a bunch of meathead vamps can bust anything. We don't have Council support, so it's not like we have troops or Guards. But hey, man, listen. I got kids. Real *kids*, turned the same time as I was. Plus one that stayed human, so now I got *grand*kids. Maybe it's a cliche, but I don't want shit like Thrill on the streets, messing them up."

I looked out across the factory. As promised, my head was clearing. I remembered my question from earlier.

"Why did you say it's a Chicago problem?"

"Near as we can figure, all the distilleries are here. The Council don't care. They got bigger fish to fry, I guess, with a whole nation to look out for."

"Wait ... there are *more* places like this?"

Malone gave another chuckle — a jaded one this time. "Shit, Maurice. This is a drop in the bucket. Near as we can guess, there might be ten or more. But the Council won't be able to ignore us for long, 'cause truth is, it's actually *not* just a Chicago problem anymore."

"What do you mean?"

"That's what I wanted to show you. Look. When we knocked the doors down, they didn't have time to clear their shit out."

He set an oversized leather-bound book, like a ledger, on the desk and flipped it open. Sheafs of paper fluttered from the bindings: quality test results, signed certificates of receipt, and something sciency-looking all about security and "three chemists." I wanted to read them all, but Malone was still flipping, not yet finding what he was looking for.

Finally he stopped. His dirty working-man's finger — indelibly blue-collar — scanned the page. "Look. They've got a whole logistics chain."

"What do you mean?"

"Trucking," Malone said. "They're shipping it out. Thrill is a Chicago treat right now, like deep-dish pizza. But soon it's gonna be in every shithouse burg, lighting up vampire parties like nothing else."

I scanned the page. Something didn't quite make sense.

"These times," I said, running my own finger down the timestamps in the shipping log. "Looks like they're working in the daytime?"

"Right," said Malone. "And that right there's the bigger problem. See, this factory can work all hours. No big deal; it's light-tight. And in some ways, no worry about working right under the city's nose, 'cause the folks running this place glamoured the neighbors. But what *can't* always run at night? *Trucks. Shippers.* The clubs that serve Thrill, they *operate* at night. That means they need to stock up during the day."

It sounded familiar. The Bomber had been small enough to take deliveries at night, and I'd insisted on that much if Timothy wanted my help unloading. But bigger speakeasies, like pre-Prohibition bars, worked just as Malone was saying: You stocked when the place was slow or closed, so you could raise the rafters when rush hour came.

"How is a vampire business doing this much logistics while the sun's up?" I asked. And, as I kept scanning the page, I saw how *much* business was truly being done. The book was just a log, not a shipping map, but it still painted a vivid picture. I wasn't looking at a small network. The distillery, when it'd been running, had made a ton of product to move to a ton of places.

"Like I said, that's the problem," Malone said. "See, there's a reason these Thrill 'distilleries' are thriving right now. *Right now.* Get what I'm sayin'?"

Right now.

Meaning: During Prohibition, while another illegal business with a lot of similar customers was already booming.

"Oh, shit," I said.

Malone nodded. "Exactly."

21

PARTNERS

THAT'S what Malone and his buddies at the CVA wanted my help with: stopping the trade and putting an end to Thrill. Not many vampires got on ocean liners to cross the sea, and that meant that most of America's vampire population at the time had been made here — a few hundred years old at most. There were only a few as old, strong, and fast as Celeste and me in the States, let alone in Chicago. For what they were facing, the CVA would need the all the strength and speed it could find.

The problem, you see, wasn't just vampires.

Vampires had invented Thrill, but they couldn't distribute and sell it alone. For that, they needed partners. They needed folks as interested in money and power as Thrill's makers, but who were able to move around during the day. They needed a network, plus a shipping system with the necessary bribes. They needed trucks and drivers and muscle and accounting of a very specific type.

To get those things, the makers of Thrill had gotten into bed with the human mafia.

Al Capone ruled Chicago in 1929. The Mob had built a masterpiece of commerce, serving the needs of millions upon millions of people who didn't want to give up what the government had decided to make illegal. Santori didn't need to build his network in parallel; he could just piggyback off what the Organization had built. There was more than enough profit in Thrill for the vampire mafia to give the human mafia its taste ... and for its part, the human mafia liked the intimidation it gained from its vampire partners. New muscle who couldn't be killed by lead? It scared disorganized crime out of town, greasing the wheels for the liquor trade.

Everything fed on everything. They all got richer, and as they got richer, they bought everyone they needed on the way up. The police were bought; town hall was bought; the whole vampire culture gained all it needed to become the officious, elitist state it's since become.

Malone told me all of this — the stuff through May of '29, at least — as we stood in the office and looked across the empty floor of the distillery his ragtag crew had managed to successfully raid. Only then did I sense the truth behind Malone's situation. When he'd told me they'd shut the place down, I'd mistaken the emotion in his voice for pride. In truth, it was terror. The distillery raid wasn't a feather in the CVA's cap. It was a target. Malone's Crew had begun something without realizing what they were getting themselves into, and now they either had to finish it or die trying. My bet, given the forces allied against him, was on the latter.

"No way," I said.

"Maurice ..."

"There's a chance, if I'm not kind of an asshole right now, that you'll look back on this later and decide you might have been able to convince me," I told him. "I don't want to be an asshole to you. I like you. But I can't have you thinking there's a speck of possibility here. I'm not a do-gooder, Malone. There's a reason I worked in a human speakeasy instead of becoming a night-beat cop sent to bust one."

"You could make a difference here," Malone said.

"You're missing the point. It's not that I don't believe in myself, or think it's too difficult. It's that I don't *want* to make a difference. My 'friends' back in Europe told you I was here, right? Those people know me. They know who I am. They must have told you what kind of a citizen I've always been."

Malone didn't reply to that. Yes, they'd told him.

He said he respected my decision, and I think he actually meant it. He was a reasonable guy, and that meant he had to know what a bleak picture he'd painted. Joining his cause was the worst item on the menu. He'd already dug his grave, but only fools would voluntarily hop into it with him.

Making myself an enemy of the mafia?

No thanks.

I was a sideline sort of fellow, just trying to get by.

22

BATHTIME

BESIDES, I had my own problems.

I returned that evening to learn that Daisy hadn't come home. She'd been staying with us at the Flynn's, which was looking like a hostile sanctuary as the human cops started asking questions. Still, it was the lesser of evils. The situation at Daisy's old apartment had disintegrated; her mother a basket case and her brother so sick he was literally falling apart. And it was a cruel kind of sickness. Chuck kept losing organs in his puke — but because he was a vampire, they grew right back. It gave Daisy agita that she wouldn't admit. She buried her emotions by turning away like a teenager. She buried it by spending all her time with Isaac.

And it got worse from there. I'd been afraid to glamour the cops until I had to, because I didn't know what evidence they had or what their investigation entailed — or, to Malone's point, if they'd been bribed by the town's two mafias. I got the impression that the extreme nature of Timothy's murder (*presumed* extreme; they only had the fragments of him that Daisy had left behind) had linked The Bomber case to the slaughter down at the shipping docks a few days earlier. I didn't know if they knew about the broken Thrill barrel, the presence of three other parties at the speakeasy that night, or anything else. I could see it going either way, and either way glamouring might earn unwanted attention.

So I didn't really worry too much about Daisy and her acting out. She was safer with Isaac, ironically, than she was with us — which, in turn, was safer than staying with her family. I hated that her relationship with Isaac (and my relationship with Malone) had dragged us right back into the vampire culture I'd left Europe to avoid, but it was just one item on a long punch list of problems.

I couldn't make a plan. All I could do was get by night to night.

With The Bomber closed, I no longer had anything to occupy my time. I didn't want to get another job; doing so might raise attention. Mostly I just hung back with Celeste, whose own work and hobbies were disturbed by my constant presence.

So when Celeste asked me, on the night of the distillery, if I'd seen or heard from Daisy, I shrugged but didn't let it bother me. She spent the day with her asswipe boyfriend. So what?

And the next day.

And the next.

Life was becoming a monotonous drone of waiting. At any moment, the police might come back with more questions, or maybe to try and arrest me. At any moment, vampire mafia might come knocking on my door as Malone had.

And as to Malone, I started to avoid him. I couldn't afford to encourage him. Our circles — with both Celeste and Daisy making vampire friends — began to overlap. I'd hear that Malone was working on his case and that his Crew was learning more and more about the trade, getting in deeper and deeper. I wanted nothing to do with it, but Malone practically begged. He said they needed me, for the good of the Vampire Nation. I told him, *Fuck the Nation.* What had the Vampire Nation ever done for us?

Daisy finally came back, reeking of Isaac's cologne. Worse, she came back reeking of Thrill, which Isaac had a fondness for despite his group's mission. Its scent impregnated her clothing like smoke and befouled the entire apartment. I threw her clothes into Irene's wash and glamoured Irene into spending extra time working them clean.

One day Mort came to me and said, "I like our new brother."

Then, to prove glamouring hadn't actually made him sweet, he said, "... you stupid frog" and walked away.

At first I figured this was just Mort being what Celeste's glamour-job had made him. But then Elsie informed me that there was a strange naked man with a boo-boo in the tub and that she was no longer interested in taking baths, ever.

I'd been in our room all day, trying to pass the time. Occupying myself without associating with vampires outside my own family had become nearly impossible, so I spent a lot of time reading. The books in the Flynns' library were all terrible pulp and I kept forgetting to go out and get more. Laziness built on laziness, and although Elsie's announcement intrigued me (or alarmed me), it still took me a few tries to get up and decide the matter was worth investigation.

Elsie was wrong. There wasn't a naked man with a boo-boo in the tub. There were two. The one on the bottom was dead, and I was able to ascertain this by the fact that there was water in the tub and the second was on top of him, back to back. The guy beneath was either past his expiration date or extraordinary at breath-holding.

The water was so red, it was opaque.

I later learned that the dead man on the bottom was more or

less an unfinished snack. Daisy had started feeding on him, gotten blood all over, and put him in the tub to clean him up. She'd been high at the time, whacked out on the Thrill she and Isaac had been doing the entire day over at his apartment. She'd passed out, and while she'd been unconscious the man had bled out in the tub. The second man was a drunk she'd picked up at a hybrid speakeasy, and he'd apparently not noticed the tub was occupied when he'd decided to get in and draw himself a bath. By the time I found him, the only reason he hadn't drowned was because the corpse beneath him was keeping his mouth above the water.

He saw me, though, and turned out to be far more awake than you'd figure a man floating in blood would be. Kind of an asshole, too.

"Who the hell are you?" he demanded.

"I'm the guy who the hell's home this is," I said. "Who the hell are *you?*"

"Daisy!" the naked man shouted.

Instead of Daisy, Henry arrived at the bathroom door. He was dressed for work, smoking his pipe. It was 2am.

"Say, Maurice," he said, seeming not to notice the bathroom's other two occupants, "who do you like in Tuesday's game?"

"What?"

Henry bit his pipe's stem. "I favor the Cubs myself."

Daisy, also naked, shoved past Henry. Henry apologized.

"Oh, bother," Daisy said, seeing the tub. This made no sense to me. Judging by her lack of attire, she looked ready to party. How long had it been since she'd seen her guest? What had she been in another room doing, while he'd been lounging in here?

Daisy knelt by the tub's side, perhaps to reach in and pull the plug. But she was unsteady on her feet and slumped into the porcelain edge, opening a scalp wound that healed within seconds. The man in the tub — who, I noticed, was also bleeding copiously from the neck — must have misinterpreted her intentions because he began to grow an erection. It immediately deflated like a ballon, as if it his body had just realized all the blood needed for full mast was leaking into the water around him.

Daisy fell to the floor. Not unconscious. Just really, really high.

"Good talk, Maurice," said Henry. He bit his pipe again and turned around. Moments later I heard him open a newspaper in the kitchen. Irene passed holding an iron and a bag of flour. It was still 2am.

I heard the door, realizing with relief that Celeste had just come home. I called to her. Within seconds she was where Henry had been standing.

"What happened here?" she asked.

From the floor, to nobody in particular, Daisy said, "You're so sexy."

"I don't know. I just found them."

I'd indicated the tub. She knew I hadn't meant Daisy. "'*Them*'?" she echoed.

"There's a dead guy under this one," I explained, nodding at the man with the deflated boner.

"Who the hell are *you?*" the man demanded of Celeste. But his eyes were glassy, and I knew he was losing track of reality by the second. He was paler already. The bathwater was warm, and he was bleeding like a rain barrel with the bung removed.

"Help me," I said, taking the man's arm around my neck.

Celeste took his legs. We were moving him to the tiles beside Daisy, who immediately began to manipulate his flagging member with her hand, when the second body bobbed to the water's surface and Daisy said, "Well, that's ..."

I looked. She was holding up an arm. Both of the naked men already had two. I began to wonder if there were other parts stuffed here and there: the rest of a third man we'd find over time, like the world's worst Easter egg hunt.

"Daisy." I slapped her face, then turned her onto her side when she began to retch. I'm not sure why I bothered. Vampires can't drown, either in water or their own vomit. "Daisy, wake up."

Daisy was still tugging the dying man's penis. "Come on," she said. "Come on, and fuck me like a real man."

"*Daisy!*"

She blinked. Her eyes opened, and for the first time she actually saw me.

"Jason," she said.

"I'm actually Maurice."

"No. Jason. Where is Jason?"

"Is Jason ...?"

She went limp. Out cold. Then the guy on the tile beside her died.

"Oh, goddammit," Celeste said.

I was too preoccupied to really hear her. I kept wondering if "Jason" was the guy in the tub, the guy on the floor, or the owner of the disembodied arm. Option #4 was the worst of all, suggesting that maybe there were more of Daisy's bled-out suitors hidden around the apartment like sweets stashed by a kid for later.

I hauled the man out of the tub, then pulled the stopper to drain the tub. Irene came through the hallway again and said that she had Borax. Celeste took the second man and the arm. Because Suitor #2 had died more recently, he was bleeding more rapidly. Mine, had he not been waterlogged, would have been a desiccated husk. But Celeste was taking a waterfall down her front, resentment clear on her face. Another of her favorite dresses ruined.

"I can take them down to the incinerator," I told her.

She gave me her wifely look. "You do that," she said. She walked to me, then tossed the second dead man on top of the first. My burden was a little too wide to fit through doorways without turning, but Celeste clearly cared more about making a point than making my errand easy. "I'll mop."

"Irene can mop."

"Irene has done enough, Maurice. She was a normal woman once. Remember that? Remember normality, before all this unpleasantness began?"

I've known my wife for a millennium. I knew she wasn't just referring to Daisy, though Daisy was the recent worst of it. More, she was referring to the choices I'd forced upon us, in the name of xenophobia. *I'd* been unhappy in the vampire culture of Europe, not Celeste. She'd had friends. *I'd* made us leave; *I'd* made us come here. And look what had happened? Of course the problem hadn't turned out to be Europe after all. Of course my issues had followed us across the ocean. Of course, I'd brought Good Old Antisocial Maurice with me.

"I'll deal with it," I told her. "You go clean up."

She didn't answer. Instead she just exited the bathroom, leaving me to do what I'd promised.

23

———————————

SLEEPLESS

WHEN IT WAS DONE — the bodies and arm (I never did find its owner) incinerated, the clothes gone, the bathroom cleaned, Daisy's groggy body dressed and put to bed — I got beneath the sheets well after sunrise to find Celeste still awake.

"Maurice?" she said.

I was gun-shy. I tried to find her tone before answering, but came up empty.

"Yeah?"

"I'm sorry about the way I acted."

"You had every right."

"It wasn't your fault. Daisy did that. She killed those men."

"She didn't mean to."

We were quiet for a few moments. In vampire logic, the argument makes sense. Murder is just sort of how a lot of us roll.

"I'm not mad at you. I'm not mad that you turned Daisy."

"Oh. Good."

"I love Daisy." She paused, collecting. Then: "I think that's why I was so mad."

"You were mad because you love her?"

"I was mad because I was afraid. Afraid of losing her. She's in trouble. It's that stupid *drug*. She was born addicted to it, and it's the drug that makes her do bad things, not Daisy herself. You know that, right?"

I thought about denying it. Then I said, "Yeah, I know that."

"We have to help her."

"I know."

"She's a good girl — or at least she would be, if she could stay away from Thrill." Bitterness entered her voice. "It's Isaac who keeps her in it. It's fucking *Isaac* who's the problem."

That was perhaps a bit simplistic, but I wasn't going to argue. Truth was, I'd been reckless in turning her, then negligent as a mentor. Truth was, there'd been psychological damage in Daisy when she'd been human, and vampirism had magnified and unleashed it like an animal breaking free of a cage. Isaac was just the most recent problem. Isaac was gas thrown on a fire that was already burning. He made what was bad worse. But also, fuck Isaac. Fuck him with his pretty face and cocky manner and stupid stinky cologne.

"*Tonight,*" Celeste said. "Tonight, we need to fix this. We just use tonight, and tomorrow night, and as many nights as it takes, and we look at all the ways we can make life better for her. For all of us. We've waited so long, Maurice. God gave us an angel, and I intend to protect her."

My heart sank a little. For the first time, I saw with clarity what this was for Celeste — what it'd been all along, though I'd been too preoccupied with my own problems to see it. The entire time we'd been in Chicago, I'd made life about me. *I'd* been dissatisfied with my place in the vampire community; *I'd* taken a job in society's underbelly to scratch my subversive itch; *I'd* been inconvenienced when my creation went wrong, then made excuses not to deal with it because *I* was too busy with "more important" things. But while I'd been so self-absorbed, I'd missed the fact that my accident had opened a door for my wife. She'd wanted children before she was turned, but it'd never happened. I knew it was a hole in her heart. I'd known that about Celeste forever.

God gave us an angel, and I intend to protect her.

It wasn't God who'd given us Daisy, and nothing we made could be called an angel.

But in the end, it didn't matter what Daisy was to me.

To Celeste, she was the daughter we'd never had.

24

WE SEE YOU

SO WE DID what we could. We waited for her to wake and when she did, Celeste sat with her and held her hand and patted it while she came around. The drunkenness of the night before was gone. She was hung over like a human after liquor, her vampire body wracked by vampire drug in a way that no normal drug would be able to harm her.

As it passed, she asked what she'd done. Her memory of last night was mostly missing. She remembered feeling very good and very strong and very confident, and in that fugue she remembered going with Isaac to a string of vampire speakeasies, drinking enough Thrill to keep the night moving. After a while she remembered leaving Isaac behind. Maybe there'd been a fight; she had no clue. In the corner of her mind she seemed to recall thinking he wasn't very fun after all, and she'd hit a human speakeasy after that, finding some strapping young men who were very interested in her in ways they'd never been interested before her change. Vampire Daisy was sexy; Vampire Daisy was desirable. She remembered dancing and laughing and not a lot else. Only when she saw the blood on Celeste's sleeve did she start to get a hint of the rest. Then the remorse came, and the person who laid in Daisy's bed after that was more like the human girl I'd known than the vampire she'd become. I thought she'd cry. She came close, and Celeste did, quietly, and after a while I just had to leave the room. I've never been good at sentiment. I have my feelings, but they're so much more comfortable buried inside.

I had no work to go to, and even though seeing the scene between the women made me want to find Malone and his small clique from the CVA more than ever, I remembered my promise and stayed put. While Daisy was busy feeling temporary remorse and Celeste was busy feeling maternal and proactive, I went ahead and let myself feel guilty. The last thing I should have done in that moment was to distract myself. I'd done that enough already, and it was time to stick around, to pay attention to someone who wasn't me, to do right by Daisy as I'd sworn to Celeste the night before.

Celeste found me in the kitchen. The Flynns were all asleep.

"Get your shoes on," she said.

"Are we going somewhere?"

"We need to go get her family."

"Wait ... you mean her mom and brother?"

"You know of any other family?"

"But they're vampires. They're best on their own."

"Or with their own kind."

"I ... I *did* tell you about them, didn't I?"

Meaning: wanton creation by my own wanton creation. Messed up in the worst sort of way.

"Get your shoes on," Celeste repeated.

So we went across town. The three of us, all in a line. Celeste kept her arm interlocked with Daisy like girls on a playground. The streets were mostly deserted, except by troublemakers. Four of them came toward us, flanking to mug us or worse, and I tensed to dispatch them. I never got the chance. The two in the lead went for Daisy first, and Celeste practically ripped their head off. All four ran, concrete chipping under their heels.

We listened at the door of Daisy's old apartment before knocking. There was nothing. I imagined Mrs. Farley standing in the kitchen with her frying pain, moveless since the last time I'd been here.

Daisy was looking at us, sheepish.

"No matter what," Celeste assured her, "we will take care of them. Because we will always take care of you."

Still Daisy looked like she wanted to run. I wasn't the only one who distracted myself to avoid feeling. In that moment, I felt sure that if Celeste hadn't interlinked their arms at the elbow, Daisy would have sprinted right back to Isaac, right back to the scene she'd left the night before. To my knowledge, she hadn't been here since the night I'd retrieved her. Afraid, probably, of how much worse her brother might have become — or how much unlike her old mother Mrs. Farley had become.

But when we opened the door after thirty responseless seconds, we saw that the Farleys weren't unwell at all. They were dead.

At first, I was the only one who knew it. I had five seconds of clarity before Celeste picked it up, and at that point we should have dragged Daisy out into the hallway and made an excuse to come back and "see them later." But that was also the moment Daisy's reticence broke, and she pulled free of both of us. She marched into the apartment, its farther-in walls speckled in blood and gore, and called for them.

"Mom? Chuck?"

"Daisy," I said. "Maybe we should—"

But Daisy called louder. *"MOM? CHUCK?"* Walking

forward, shoes squishing in carpeting now strewn with half-clotted cells. Seeing that, my mind was already turning to something else. Something worse. The layer of gore on the ground was fresh enough to squish, and that meant it'd been ejected there — probably from Chuck's mouth — within the last twelve hours or less. Yet I could smell ash and sulfur in the air. Vampires don't bleed when we die. We burn. All the evidence told me that whatever had happened here, it'd happened recently. Whoever had done this, I thought, might still be here.

Daisy severed my thoughts with a scream. She'd been halfway through shouting her brother's name, yet dropped that syllable like something hot.

Celeste and I rushed to her side. She was staring into the second bedroom, to the bare wall with its single window in the corner.

Across the wall, written in blood and guts, was the message: WE SEE YOU.

Below the message, sitting on the floor with backs against the wall, were two charred forms. They looked like spent firewood crushed into human shapes — or vampire shapes, as the case may be. There were stakes through each of their chests, half-burned with the wooden ends still pristine. I'd been afraid of this since we'd walked in, knowing it was likely the bodies would remain. Old vampires like me, when staked, practically explode into flash and dust. Younger vampires burn like logs, leaving evidence behind.

The blood on the wall, though, wasn't black. Daisy's family's murderers had either taken it from Chuck's copious mouth — or (and this struck me as far more likely) from their middles, sliced with the blade of a knife before dying.

Daisy hadn't stopped screaming. She ran to the corpses, tripping, falling into what I suspected had once been her mother's lap. The body crushed to cinders. We both rushed to pick her up — to help, yes, but more pressingly to get away. As we did, I caught the slightest whiff of warmth from the place where Daisy had smashed the burnt body. The embers weren't cold and the blood on the wall hadn't dried fully, from red to brown. A picture was already in my head, along with a timeline.

"We have to go," I said.

Daisy tried to grab one of the corpses, then the other. In her embrace, they crumbled like frozen sand. She was half sobbing, half shouting. Half despair, half rage.

"*We have to go!*"

Because the message was clearly from those we'd wronged at The Bomber, from the vampire mafia. They'd followed a trail, reaching the home address of the woman who worked for Timothy first. The kid who worked the bar would be harder to find; nobody knew we lived with the Flynns. I'd left no formal address at the speakeasy, or anywhere else. Daisy, on the other hand, was a normal citizen. Her residence would be easy to find.

I only knew a little about the vampire mafia, but I'd heard plenty about the regular one. It wasn't a group I wanted to cross further than I already had.

WE SEE YOU.

Which might not be figurative. It might mean they were on distant rooftops right now, watching us with their supernatural vision. I knew Daisy had covered all the windows before the last time I'd visited, but now all were open. What other reason could there be, if not to surveil and wait?

An animal instinct prickled the back of my neck. I was sure that I could actually feel someone *right behind us*. The presence was palpable. I kept looking back even as I knew nothing was there. I was sure, each second we waited, that assassins to our rear were raising stakes, aiming their wood-filled tommy guns.

I didn't ask again. I dropped decorum and simply grabbed them both, Daisy over one shoulder and Celeste over the other. The door had swung closed behind us. I didn't stop to open it. I just ran through, down the stairs, and through the door at the stairwell's bottom. I continued to the lobby and blasted through the lobby doors with a bang.

As we hit the streets, my sense proved true. Five suit-clad vampires rushed from the distance, closing fast.

Then more, from the other direction.

Surrounding us.

Not with stakes in hand, but machine guns filled with wooden death. They wouldn't have to get close enough for my strength and speed to make a difference. All they'd have to do, within a partial second, would be to open fire.

I didn't think.

The oldest of us, in extreme, adrenaline-laced situations, are sometimes able to fly.

A good thing. Because if I hadn't taken to the air with my burdens on my back — something I could never plan, something that took me by surprise the few times I've been furious enough to make it happen — they'd have killed us for sure.

The building vanished beneath us as we took flight, our would-be killers buzzing like a nest of angry bees.

25

CRASH

WE LANDED IN A HEAP. The vampire agent responds to adrenaline, like the muscles of a human mother forced to lift a truck to save her child. But adrenaline doesn't live long in humans or vampires, and by the time we were soaring free, I'd already begun to feel it wane. I headed for the outskirts, trying to force myself to stay at the heights of fury and fear. With a park in sight, my flight began to sputter like an engine running out of gas. I put my head down to set our trajectory, gritted my teeth, and took a breath.

We were on the ground moments later with limbs broken, faces bloodied, and a strong tree branch splitting Celeste's skull hard enough to show her brain.

Daisy screamed. I looked over to see her staring at her legs, both of which had bent the wrong way with heels behind her ears. The contortion of broken legs and back made her more or less round, so I could wheel her away if I wanted.

Celeste shook her head. She spattered me with blood and pieces of prefrontal cortex. When she saw grey matter flying, she set her head still. For a few seconds she was brain-damaged and vacant, but then new brain filled the gap and bone and scalp healed, hair growing back into place over the mess. On the ground between us, the discarded bits were already melting into ash.

"Damn," she said, using her left hand to straighten a break in her right arm. There was a crack, a pop, and a wince. Then the pain departed and she put a hand above her eyes.

"You okay?" I asked.

"I have a headache.

Daisy was still screaming.

"They were waiting for us," Celeste said.

I nodded. I'd just been trying to get away. In a sense, the panic of flight had been easier than the safety we now found ourselves in. Now, I had to think. Now, I had so many new things to worry about, so much to fear.

"Who were those men, Maurice?"

"*MY LEGS OH GOD MY LEGS!*"

"Walk it off," I snapped at Daisy.

"Maurice ... ?" Celeste asked. Even if she didn't know specifics, she knew I was hiding something. I'd kept so much of what Malone had shown and told me from both of them. No reason to cause alarm. I wasn't going to get involved; I had as much of it as we'd see under control.

Celeste repeated herself. I almost snapped, but held my composure. I wanted to tell her that I knew *she'd* seen vampire activity in Chicago before all of this had begun and hadn't bothered to tell me, but I knew it'd just be for spite. *Of course* there were vampires around. It was probably Malone and his friends that she'd sensed, keeping tabs and deciding how to get in touch.

"*IT HURRRRRTS!*" Daisy bellowed.

Celeste stared me down for another second, but then rolled her eyes, said, "Oh, for Christ's sake," and turned to Daisy. She stalked over, yanked Daisy's legs straight, then pulled out the post of a metal park sign I hadn't noticed had impaled her and tossed it away.

At each action Daisy shrieked again, but then all of a sudden she seemed to realize she was healed and was only yelling out of habit. She stopped, stood, brushed herself off, and moved to join us. Halfway, I think she remembered *why* we'd run — what exactly those vampires had done to make their point. She turned, walked to the closest thing the park had to an overlook, and went silent with her back to us.

"If they came for her family, they'll come for her," Celeste said. Her frustration with my secrecy was gone, replaced by a mother's pragmatic wisdom. She spoke with a no-bullshit tone. What came next for her would be whatever best protected Daisy, whether I wanted to be part of it or not.

I saw it in my wife's eyes. I didn't consider fighting. I nodded, looked to Daisy, and was just about to speak when Celeste beat me to it.

"What are we going to do, Maurice?" she asked.

In the moment, I had absolutely no idea.

26

LAVENDER AND HONEY

"SO WHAT *DID* YOU DO?" Annabel asked the vampire.

Maurice got up, went to Annabel's desk, and sat behind it. She was about to ask why when he turned in her chair and opened the mini fridge against the wall. He straightened with one of the several bottles of chablis she kept for when the day got too tough, or when her terrible husband threatened to be particularly terrible — a little lubrication for the ride home. More than once, she'd skipped driving and taken an Uber. He never noticed her semi-drunkenness, but it made the evenings more tolerable.

"How did you know I had wine?" she asked.

"Doesn't everyone?"

She wasn't sure whether he was joking, whether he actually believed everyone had wine at all times, whether he'd read her mind, or whether he'd somehow smelled it from across the room. It seemed not to matter. She did feel like a drink right now — now more than ever. The vampire had a way of spinning his tale that didn't quite lull her into sleep, but certainly lulled her into a trance — a downright immersive one. A skill akin to glamouring, she supposed.

He opened her drawer and found the corkscrew. Glasses were on the back counter, near a still-full pitcher of water. He pulled the cork and poured for both of them, then returned to the couch and handed Annabel one of the glasses. She sniffed the wine inside — something she didn't usually do before gulping down its sweet intoxication. The mood and dim beyond the windows seemed to call for extra senses. The wine's bouquet was floral, perhaps lavender, and kissed with honey.

"We did the only thing we could," Maurice said. "We ran. We hid."

"You didn't fight?" She tried to keep judgment out of her voice, but the spell of his story had dulled her objectivity. Seemed to Annabel, Maurice had a simple problem: Thus far in his story, he came across as someone who's self-effacement makes him self-important. He was so insistent on staying uninvolved that the whole world was forced to revolve around his apathy. *Be a man,* she wanted to say. *Be a man, and for once stop trying so hard to pity yourself.*

He seemed to take the mood of her question and gave her a look. A hard, borderline angry look. When he spoke next, it really was as if he'd read her mind.

"I suppose it sounds simple," he said. "The vampire mafia was the problem, so I should have just decided to fight the vampire mafia. Easy, right? Except that you're forgetting one thing: *It's the fucking mafia.*"

"They were coming after you anyway. You couldn't escape."

"You're right. Turns out, we couldn't. But at that point, we hadn't even tried. We were still in the same apartment, living with the same family. We hadn't so much as ducked. The mafia wasn't my business. I hadn't bothered anyone. I'd just been trying to live my life. *They* came to *us.* They sent a barrel of

Thrill to The Bomber by mistake; *they* came after it, killed my boss, then tried to kill Daisy and blame it all on me. I didn't ask for anything that happened."

"But Malone and the CVA—"

"—picked a fight they wished they hadn't started, and *wouldn't* have started if they'd known what it was. They thought they were busting up a gang of thugs with one glorified meth lab, nothing more. Malone told me himself that he'd never have gone after the mafia. So why, with all this nice, easy hindsight, should *I* have?"

Annabel sat primly, hands folding in her lap. She wanted to be indignant, but instead felt chastened. Whatever he'd done to keep her quiet about his nature and his visits, it seemed, did not extend to the rest of Annabel's mind. She was quite clear, listening to him, that she'd overstepped her bounds. A therapist was supposed to be objective. She hadn't been there, when all of this had happened. She didn't know how it was.

"You're right. I'm sorry." She paused. Then:. "So you left Chicago?"

Maurice watched her for another second, probably deciding whether he wanted to let her off the hook. Finally he sipped his wine, looking away.

"I wanted to. Malone talked me out of it. He said that the vampire mafia seemed to have a way to use blood ties to track vampires they wanted to hunt down."

"The thing you mentioned earlier? The psychopath's solution?"

He shrugged. "Maybe. I believed him; that's all that mattered. His argument was that there was strength in numbers."

"But they wanted to take on the vampire mafia, and you didn't."

"He probably thought that by keeping me around, I'd eventually change my mind. I had no such plans. But they had their own little neighborhood, so sure, I decided to join it. Their fight wasn't my fight, but we couldn't stay out in the open. I'd protect us. I'd make us a home, and I'd stand guard at its gates. I didn't have to take the fight to anyone else. I just had to keep it from coming our way."

"So you left the Flynns."

"I wanted to, but it would have been cruel. If vampires came looking for me, Celeste, and Daisy, they'd end up at the Flynns' — and we'd already seen what happened when they'd found Daisy's apartment. The Flynns hadn't asked for any of this, either. So I had to take the risk and glamour them one more time, then get them to move into a new apartment next door to ours. Considering the challenges of such a glamour, I think I did pretty well. They were suddenly living in an all-vampire community — who I had to convince not to feed on them, by the way — but had to not notice that those around them were vampires. Henry had to stop going to work; Irene had to stop seeing her friends; the kids had to stop going to school. They had to accept all of that as normal, just like they had to think it normal that in their new neighborhood, there were no open windows and people only came out at night. But it worked. They adjusted, and nobody bit them. Although plenty of the neighborhood kids were tempted. More than once I sat outside their apartment door, waiting to chase hungry vampires away with a broom."

Annabel sipped. She realized her glass was already half empty, and found herself wondering where it had gone.

Maurice, seeing this, took the wine bottle and refilled her.

"What about your family?" she asked.

"We stayed in, like I said. Went a little stir crazy, but that was a price I was willing to pay."

"Did it work?" Annabel asked.

Of course it hadn't. He shook his head.

"What gave you away?"

"Daisy," the vampire answered.

DAISY DIDN'T OBEY. Daisy refused to lay low.

Celeste, unlike me, was fooled by Daisy's latest turn-around, convinced that the murder of her family had scared her into behaving. She believed that after two strikes, Daisy had finally learned her lesson and would kick Thrill and the vampire speakeasy scene for good.

For a few days, she was right. Immediately after the Farleys were murdered, Daisy fell into a funk, refusing to leave her bed. She cried, she slept, and she stayed sober. She wasn't the bright and happy daughter Celeste wanted, but at least she was clean. At least she was safe.

But not long after, Daisy's defenses kicked in. All at once, she was up and awake, buzzing around the apartment with a smile on her face. When Celeste asked if she wanted to talk about what had happened, Daisy said no. She was fine with it, she told us. Right as rain.

But then she called Isaac, and before I could stop them, they left together. They came back wasted, then screwed loud enough that we could hear everything through the walls. She kept asking him to choke her, beat her, cut her with his pointed fingernails. The next day their sheets were covered with blood. When we complained, she asked what our problem was. If we wanted clean sheets so bad, no big deal. She'd just go out and fucking buy some more, *geez*. She didn't come back from that errand until 24 hours later, again with Isaac but without any new sheets, even higher on Thrill than before. Without sheets, that night they stained the mattress instead.

On and on it went. Daisy told us that we weren't her parents. She was an adult and could do what she wanted. She *wanted*, it seemed, to party with Isaac. They went out and we couldn't stop them, short of silver handcuffs. She came home every few nights high, laughing, and horny. When she was alone, we'd hear her crying. She refused our help. She told us she was strong enough, that she could handle herself on her own.

"She's young," Malone told me. "That makes her stupid."

The one saving grace after our move was that we finally had a place to be social that didn't require going outside. Malone's entire Crew lived in the building, and we usually met at the big apartment owned by Sally and Madge, the lesbian couple who'd adopted two kids, Walter and Lucy. They'd been made vampires at ages 15 and 7, respectively, but each was at least twenty years older than that now, given their time as vampires. It was a nice little family. And as long as I could ignore their constant hints that I should join the cause, it was a nice little Crew to hang with, too. Malone's wife Inez wasn't a soldier, but there were quite a few who were: Sally and Madge, big and strong Dexter, his wife Lenore, and shy accountant-type, Rolf. Rolf wore little round glasses and was bald up top, with a ring of hair circling his head's equator, around the back from ear to ear.

We were all at Sally and Madge's place, drinking beers. I hate beer, but every other member of the Crew liked it. Social reasons, perhaps, despite the way the yeast made vampire systems rebel. Celeste and I stuck to wine. They laughed at us for it, but it was a kind laughter. At least we were all giving Prohibition the finger together.

"Walter and Lucy are young," I said, to counter Malone's assessment.

"And they're stupid," said Madge.

The room shared a laugh.

"But they stay in line," Celeste said.

"With effort."

"But they *do,*" Celeste repeated.

Sally shrugged. "Their parents were killed when they were turned, more than two decades ago. Lucy was only 7. Their scars have more or less healed."

She didn't mean literal scars, of course. She meant the kind of scars that, in Daisy, were still fresh and bleeding ... despite what Daisy's plastered-on smiles wanted us to believe.

I wished they'd stop discussing it. Celeste seemed to be fishing for an answer to our situation, but in reality she was fishing for a specific *version* of that answer. *She's young and dumb* wasn't the right answer because it explained rather than fixed, and neither was *This phase will pass* or any version of *She had issues long before you met her.* Celeste was determined to fish until she got them to say, *Daisy's just fine and will come home tomorrow perfect and clean, and will stay that way forever.* Unfortunately, that answer wasn't coming. We both knew it, but Celeste kept trying to believe otherwise. The conversation had nowhere to go but down. It was depressing.

A waiter circulated, carrying appetizers. Except that it wasn't actually a waiter. It was Mort. And he wasn't actually carrying appetizers, though he probably thought he was. His serving platter was filled with wads of balled-up aluminum foil.

"Freshen your drink, sir?" Mort asked Inez.

"I'm a woman," Inez replied.

"Very good, sir."

Mort left without touching Inez's drink, giving her a foil-ball appetizer, or acknowledging her gender.

Rolf was watching Mort go, licking his lips. His fangs were down.

"*Rolf,*" Malone warned.

Rolf huffed. We'd been through this, but that didn't mean he had to like it. My bringing humans to live in the building was like frat guys renting their spare room to a stripper, then never being allowed to hit on her. The only reason the Flynn family hadn't been sucked as dry as walking oranges was out of respect for me — which, in part, hinged on their respect for Malone. Despite my constant rebuffs, Malone seemed to think I'd one day come around. He'd learned how good I was at diving through blood ties, but not how much I hated it. He said it'd make me a good spy, in addition to a strong fighter, if I could be convinced to walk the blood roads lightly. I told him to piss off. It was our thing.

As if to infuriate the vampires further, Henry entered the room after Mort left. He sat down in our midst as if part of the discussion, pipe between his teeth and a newspaper on his lap. We wouldn't let him out to get a new paper, so he kept re-reading the one from two weeks earlier. I'd glamoured him into believing it was fresh each day, but the collision of my glamour and Celeste's original was making them all feeble. Irene wouldn't stop baking tarts. The twins roamed the halls of the building hand-in-hand in identical outfits, equally tempting and freaking out their vampire neighbors.

"Ah," Henry said around his pipe, reading the sports page. "Clowns."

I didn't mind his presence. We'd gotten used to the Flynns

— both their oddities and their human scent. As far as predator and prey went, we and the Flynns had long ago gone platonic. Besides, with Henry in the room nobody wanted to talk about vampire matters. That was just fine with me.

So the room broke up. Celeste and I went back to our apartment and the others went to theirs. I had to admit, it was kind of nice living in an all-vampire building. I hadn't wanted to be around others like us, but with Daisy in crisis their presence was sort of welcome. I liked not having to sneak around, glamouring someone every second. I liked the fact that our neighbors knew our nature and lifestyle because they shared it. It wasn't terrible, I decided, not to be alone.

The sun was preparing to rise, so we decided to go to bed. Daisy wasn't home. We were getting used to that, too.

Before she closed her eyes, Celeste asked me, "Do you think she'll be all right?"

I lied.

I said yes.

28

DREAMS

THAT DAY, as I slept, my mind moved between dreams and visions. Even asleep, I could tell the difference.

Nothing like it had ever happened to me before, and it's barely happened since. Like my occasional ability to fly, it wasn't something I expected or would have been able to control. It happened, I think, because of instinctual adrenaline: my gut-level need to protect my family. I've always had an affinity for blood intelligence, but that night it rose a notch. My mind drifted out and borrowed sight from other vampires in the city — distant cousins of cousins of my cousins. It was blood ties without the effort. It was my mind in theirs, without anyone noticing my presence.

I was in the mind of the vampire I thought of as Blue Eyes.

Running from The Bomber, covered in Thrill.

I didn't need to see him in the mirror to know whose mind I'd entered. I was in his head — in this memory of not-that-long-ago — and knew my borrowed identity as sure as I know my real one. I could smell the reek of synthetic blood soaking my fine suit. I could feel the squelch of real blood in my shoes, thrown upon me when the other me, Maurice, had begun cutting his companions. My (Blue Eyes's) other memories were inaccessible, though. As Maurice, I could only see this one.

In Blue Eyes's memory, I was suddenly back at his origin point, at a gentlemen's club surrounded by a fence with a gate of ornate scrolled ironwork with rosettes on the end. Then through the front door, whereafter the walls were the red of sunset and an enormous fresco of a lion, done in gold, dominated the foyer.

Before me, I saw a kid. Only *not* a kid. Just a small man, made smaller by his reputation around here as a footstool upon which the true players could rest their feet. I knew who he was, through the minds of Blue Eyes and myself. The small man had come to The Bomber a few times, taking notes and opening doors for Santori. They'd called him Puffed Wheat. Poor bastard.

What happened to you? the small man asked. It wasn't a demand. Around here, only men of status made demands. Besides, you couldn't demand anything with that voice. Not if you wanted to make any S sounds and be taken seriously.

Where is Santori? my borrowed mouth asked.

He'th playing poker in the lounge.

I need to see him. Tell him I need to see him right away.

Ith that what you really want me to thay to him?

I felt Blue Eyes hesitate. No. Blue Eyes had status, but not over Santori. Demands were never the way to get Santori's attention, unless you wanted it in a very unpleasant way.

Did you get the mithplathed barrel of Thrill back? Puffed Wheat asked.

A girl broke it. Then I felt myself blurt: *Sal and Vince are dead.*

How?

There was a vampire. Old. Very old. He killed them. But the girl ...

What?

She was almost dead. I think he may have turned her. But before that, she was ... she was lying in the blood.

Eyes wide, looking like the punching bag he was, Puffed Wheat just gaped. He said the same thing again, but now its timber was different, filled with fear and foreboding:

WHAT?

Hands, pushing him aside to trip over one of the benches in the lobby, almost hitting the floor. My hands. Blue Eyes's hands.

Through a velvet lobby, past the enormous lion fresco, its stolid gaze now seeming to stare through Blue Eyes's (my) soul, to see right through me, until—

Big oak doors, padded in red leather, the kind with buttons puckering the leather in a pattern of staggered diamonds. In the vision I saw the other vampire's hand out, pushing them open. And then—

Santori in front of me, on the opposite end of the round table with its chips and green felt and cards face-down in a pile in the middle. Santori always sits at the back, every single time, never in a corner and never with his back to the door. I knew this because Blue Eyes knew this. He met the vision's eyes, annoyed at my intrusion even as the room stilled with the seriousness of my message. Blue Eyes repeated his story, adding more details, and when he was done Santori was quiet for a moment until he said, *Check with our guy. There's supposed to be a new vampire in town. From Europe. A Frenchman. Find out everything about him. Find him, and I might forgive your mistakes tonight.*

And then Santori said, *Find out everything about* her, *too — about the girl you think may have been turned after you fucked this up. Find the girl, then put an end to her.*

My mind separated from the other vampire's mind. In the

way of dreams I was suddenly neither here nor there but was somehow in both at once, and then fantasy took over — no longer real, no longer blood ties delivering truth through means unknown and uncontrollable, but now just the product of my own nighttime worries.

It came in shotgun blasts: nightmares that hit me in the very core of my being.

In those nightmares, I saw Daisy, out with Isaac, unprotected, now dead in my morose fantasy — but not dead like a vampire dies; no, my mind still wanted to see her as the innocent human flower she'd been before I'd made her something unholy. I dreamed of her throat ripped open as it had been that night at the speakeasy, except that this time the wound would kill her. I watched the light leave her eyes. I wouldn't be there to save her.

A graveyard of bodies, vampires this time, burned to cinders: Malone, Sally and Madge, Rolf, all the others.

I dreamed of swimming in tainted blood. Of taking it in. Becoming an uncontrollable thing myself — dead to the world as Thrill addicts became, my churning feet unable to escape a relentless treadmill.

I woke covered in sweat. Vampires sweat. Oh, yes.

"Maurice?" Celeste asked, waking beside me, seeing the way I sat up with the covers pooling at my waist, staring into the distance.

"I have to find her," I told my wife. "And if I have to chain her in silver to keep her safe, I will."

29

GLAMOUROUS

IN THE GRIP OF NEAR-SLEEP, I believed everything the vision had shown me. I figured that as I woke and dressed and waited for the sun to fully set so I could leave the building, that feeling of dread and certainty would wane, but it didn't. Not one iota. I remained sure that what I'd seen was genuine: a real memory plucked directly from Blue Eyes's cortex, made the night I'd killed two vampires at The Bomber and turned Daisy. I should have chased him, I realized. I should have caught Blue Eyes so he couldn't report back to Santori. But I'd been caught between two impossibles that night: If I'd gone after our loose end, Daisy would have died. Stopping to turn her had saved her ... and yet doomed her because Blue Eyes had been able to run home and tattle. The vampire mafia, then, had known about us for weeks. They'd seemingly known about *me*, like the CVA had known about me, from the very beginning. Some-how, we'd eluded them for this long — all but Daisy's family, that was. But a clock was ticking, and we couldn't last much longer.

Malone caught my wrist as I moved past his apartment door.

"Not now, Malone," I said.

"You're going after her, aren't you?"

I didn't reply. I didn't need to. Malone nodded.

"You can't just run," he said. "They'll keep coming."

"I won't fight the mob. I just want our girl back."

"It's the mob that's threatening your girl."

I didn't feel like having this argument. There was a difference between protective hunting and proactive hunting. I could keep her away from Santori without *confronting* Santori. I figured it was like dealing with hornets: If you don't make problems for them, they'll leave you alone. But if you fuck with the hive? Well. Then you'd better watch out.

"I don't need to take on the mob," I told him. "If she's not out there making a spectacle of herself, they'll let her be."

Malone looked like he wasn't sure he believed that. I could relate. Some part of me wasn't sure it believed, either. It was the part that kept replaying the interaction between Blue Eyes and Puffed Wheat, before Blue Eyes had shoved past him.

She was almost dead. I think he may have turned her. But before that, she was ... she was lying in the blood.

Worry in that voice. And worry in the peon's reaction.

She was lying in the blood.

It made me wonder things I'd wondered before. About the differences in Daisy from the start: her mania on day one, the way she'd turned her parents, the way her blood's voice, in my internal ears, was so much louder than the rest. It was as if her hemoglobin's volume was turned up to ten, vibrating on a higher frequency.

What did it mean, to turn a vampire who'd been born in Thrill?

"Maurice ..." Malone said.

"Help me," I spat, "or get out of my way."

But when Malone went back into his apartment — for

wood-filled guns, maybe — I took off. I didn't want his help; I'd just wanted him out of my way. If he came with me, he'd never let it go. *They'll keep coming,* I kept hearing him say. *Best to join the Crew. Fight the Thrill trade. Cut off the head of the beast that threatens to devour you.*

But fuck that. I wasn't looking for more trouble. I wanted my family safe; that was all. I didn't mind running — right out of town, if I had to. So what if they could track us? They were tracking us already, and last night's vision proved I could see right back into them if circumstances were right.

I was almost outside when I ran into someone's back. Irene's back.

"Maurice!" she said. "We see you so seldom these days. How are you?"

"I'm fine, Irene." I moved to slip past her, but she moved to block. I didn't want to bowl her over, but urgency was on me like a pall. I knew the vision I'd seen was weeks old by now, but I still felt the press of time. The sword of Damocles couldn't hang above us forever. Sooner or later, the string holding it would have to break and let it drop.

"Have you talked to Henry?"

"No, Irene."

"He misses you."

I almost laughed. Henry missed nothing but his newspaper.

"He was so proud of you," she told me, "getting that promotion."

Right. The promotion I lied to them about, way back before all of this had gone to shit.

She was smiling at me. It was suddenly too much. I'd held everything inside — pretending, as Daisy pretended, that all was well. But it wasn't well. I hated that we'd come here; I hated that I'd brought Daisy into this life; I hated the mob for what it had done and threatened to do. I hated that my marriage was strained, that I'd created someone new to fear for, that for the first time in forever a part of me was out there in the world, high on Thrill and totally beyond my ability to control.

But here and now, most of all, as I met Irene's gaze, I hated what I'd done to the Flynn family. They'd been normal before we'd entered their lives, living unremarkable human lives. Irene had been proud of the way she held their little, poor family in as high a station as they could hope to achieve. Henry had been proud of his work, of the way he always aspired to more. They were proud of their children — even Mort. We'd taken that from them. We'd made them into ... well, into *this*.

So I put my hands on Irene's shoulders. I looked deeply into her eyes. She flinched.

"Maurice?"

"Where's Henry? Where are the children?"

"Henry and Mort are upstairs. The girls are staying overnight with friends."

I looked into her. Although her mind had been scrambled, what she'd just told me was true. There were humans in the adjacent building, and Elsie and Evelyn had made friends of them in the courtyard. It was safe enough. The twins were glamoured into keeping our secrets.

"When you see them next, tell them to come to our place. Do you understand me?"

"Yes. Of course. But ... ?"

I could see confusion in her. Confusion was good. It was better than the dazed, zombie look she usually had.

"I have something to tell them. All of them, one at a time. So just send them, okay?"

I'd fix them. One by one, I'd take the time. I hated glamouring, second only to my hatred of delving deep into blood ties. It was so ... *vampire*. I'd always glamoured on a surface level when the need arose, doing the minimum to get what I needed. But I could do better. I could repair the damage Celeste (and I; let's be honest) had done. I could make it so that, when all of this was over, I could release my hold on them and they'd go back to the way they'd been.

"Okay," she said.

I looked into her eyes. I felt my glamour going deep.

"Watch me very closely," I told Irene.

I could afford the few minutes it took to fix her, even as hurried as I felt. I owed Irene that much.

She watched me.

"Listen to the sound of my voice."

She listened.

I began.

Even a vampire can do good, if he tries.

30

FOUR ASSHOLES

"WHAT THE HELL DO YOU WANT?" Isaac greeted me.

"Where's Daisy?"

"How should I know?"

"She's not with you?"

"No. Fuck her."

I heard laughter behind him. That made me put my hand on the door and push it away from Isaac's grip. I saw that he wasn't alone. Three poshly dressed vampires were in chairs in his living room, all with sleek cheekbones and expressions like they'd bitten into a very superior lemon.

Clockwise: Moira, Penelope, and Charles. I'd met them all. They were ostensibly in the CVA, if not part of the sub-group that comprised Malone's Crew. But if they'd ever done anything to advance the vampire cause, I'd yet to see it. Lounging around like players and flappers without a club to call home was about the limit of their community service.

"Lost your little girl, Maurice?" Charles asked.

I didn't want to reply. It could only serve to distract me from what was important.

"She went out with you," I said, focusing on Isaac.

"When?"

"Tuesday."

It was Saturday. Isaac shrugged as if to say, *Oh, you mean way back* then.

"Yeah, well, when you're done riding the whore, you don't stick around to see who she fucks next," he said.

I picked him up in one fist, gripping the fabric around his throat hard enough to choke him. His shirt was sturdy as hell; I was able to slam his head into the ceiling without so much as a rip.

Charles startled to his feet. The women remained seated, bodies writhing and faces smiling as if this were a mating display for their benefit.

"Put him down," Charles said.

He had to be the one to say it. Isaac sure couldn't. His larynx was crushed.

Charles stepped closer.

"Touch me," I said, "and I'll break you backward and shove your head up your ass."

I hoped he'd try anyway. I was pretty sure I could do it. You can fit anything into anything if you're not afraid to rip and are willing to tolerate the mess.

Charles made a face. All show, no balls.

Above me, Isaac squeaked. I loosened my fist so he could speak, but increased the upward pressure bending his neck. Any harder, and I'd pop the floorboards of the apartment above, introducing him to his neighbors.

"Where is she?" I asked.

He squeaked, "My maker's maker is in the vampire mafia, you know! I could—!"

He wasn't getting it. I squeezed harder and tried again.

"*Where is she?*"

"I told you! I don't know!"

"You spend every night with her. Every day. I've never been able to get rid of you and I've really been trying ... so why should I believe we're so blessed that it's happened without me?"

"She dumped me, man! She told me to piss off!"

"And you did? Just like that?"

"What was I supposed to do? She was fucking half the club!"

I pressed harder upward. Isaac's vertebrae began to snap, and he screamed in pain.

"FUCK! It's true! What do you want me to say?"

I dropped him. He fell in a heap. I must have severed his spinal column, because for twenty seconds or so he seemed unable to move below the neck. Then he healed and mobility returned and he stood to face me — except he didn't actually face me so much as come to his feet three yards back and let Charles shield him.

Coward.

"He's telling you the truth," said Moira. "Daisy has ... a *reputation.*" She put a finger between her lips, as if she needed to bite it to keep from saying something unladylike. It was probably supposed to be sexy. Under the circumstances, it was anything but.

"Look," Isaac said, still behind Charles and straightening his rumpled collar, "Tuesday night, we went to Frenzy. We both drank, but she put it down faster than usual. She always gets ..." He stopped, probably on the verge of saying something that'd cause me to break him again, and chose a better word. "... '*friendly*' when she's high, but this was another level. She drank like a girl with something to prove."

Yes. We'd seen that. It walked hand-in-hand with her penchant for self-destruction. She'd sometimes lock herself in her room and break her fingers, over and over again. She used to take Irene's kitchen knives, rest the butt of one on her bed, and lean onto the point until she passed out from the pain. The murders had changed her, sure — but more and more, we had to admit she'd been broken to begin with.

"She started hooking up with guys right on the dance floor," Isaac said. "And ... more. I told her to knock it off. I grabbed her arm to drag her out of there, because she was doing it just to piss me off. But she told me to just go away, that she was done with me. The others in the club? Well, let's just say that they were glad I was leaving, and could do what they wanted. What she said *she* wanted."

Penelope gave a sexy little giggle. I shot her a look and she stopped. They all stopped.

"Frenzy," I said, returning my attention to Isaac.

"Frenzy," he confirmed.

31

FRENZY

FRENZY WAS in the basement of the Farmer's Bank building, half the city away. I was there in less than a minute.

"What's the password?" the bouncer asked me. They didn't have a cool sliding drawer like we did, to see through. At Frenzy, they just asked you through the door.

"Let me in," Maurice said.

"That's not the password."

"Open the fucking door."

"Also not the password."

"Listen, I—"

"Fuck off."

I stood before the door, hands in fists. The night air was still and damp, tinged with rain that wouldn't quite come. I could feel the blaring of jazz music through the club's walls more than hear it, bass telegraphing across the walls and up the columns of my legs. I'd run here in a frenzy of my own, and as I stared at the closed door it took all I had not to rip it off its hinges. Logically, there was no reason that my dreams meant Daisy was in trouble right here, right now, this very second of this very day. The memory I'd borrowed was weeks old, and even our escape from the mobsters at Daisy's building was no longer new. The urgency felt new to me, but it was a grudge the mob had been sitting with for some time.

Still, as much as I tried to turn away from blood ties, it was one of my best gifts and I knew it. The memory might be old, but my mind's subconscious decision to crawl through the vampire family tree and find it wasn't. There was no reason for the mob to be after Daisy right this minute — but there *might* be a reason for me to have started thinking about it just last night. I can't predict the future, but more than once I've sensed the intentions of the people around me enough to guess what was likely to happen. This was like that.

I was sure Daisy was in the club. I had to get her.

Still, causing a scene would be a mistake. I had no idea what the inside of Frenzy looked like, and I had no idea how hard the bouncers would work to keep me out. I didn't know who frequented the blood speakeasies — and if they were supplied with Thrill by the vampire mafia, it seemed like the vampire mafia might hang out there. So far, they hadn't found us. If I barged in, they might.

No. It was smarter to enter quietly, if I could.

I circled the building. Doing so didn't improve my mood. The Farmer's Bank, being a bank, wasn't built for easy access. There was just the one entrance from the outside, and given the fact that the access I'd tried was to the club instead of the bank itself, I had to assume they were guarding the stairwell. It's not like I could sneak in through a window.

That's when I saw a group of people approaching the door. There was one slim, perfectly fancy looking man in pinstripes and a woman wearing full flapper regalia. With them was a group dressed in street clothes who looked like they were part of the world's most boring city tour. A few even had cameras around their necks.

I sneaked closer and sniffed the air.

Humans.

By the time they'd reached the door and knocked, I'd decided what I was seeing. The man and woman were vampires, and they'd brought snacks to the party.

I saw my chance. The vampires were talking to the door and the humans were pressed into an obedient knot, obviously glamoured. I pushed myself into their center.

"Who are you?" one of them, a little fat man, asked. "Are you Jim?'

"Yes. I'm Jim."

"Then where are my ball bearings?"

I took a shot: "Poughkeepsie."

He shifted on his feet, as if the answer frustrated him but was not unexpected.

"Next time, Jim. Next time, we talk about this in advance."

The door opened. The tall, pinstriped vampire began waving us in.

"Move it!"

"I'm not happy about this side trip, either, Jim," the man told me.

I decided he hadn't seen the half of it. The really fun part of their side trip was just about to begin.

I slipped away from the group after we were down the stairs, down a hallway made of unfinished concrete blocks. Ahead, the hall opened into flashing, thrashing melee that I'd have thought was a fight if I hadn't known better. The tour group of humans turned right before reaching it, but I didn't move with them. The guy to whom Jim owed ball bearings watched me go, annoyed that I was getting away. He *needed* those ball bearings.

The club's dance floor was loud and chaotic as hell. They had a live jazz ensemble on a small raised stage, but something about the room's acoustics created a natural amplification that no modern speaker could have matched. The musicians all appeared to be vampires, so maybe their vampire bodies were able to blow, strum, or strike their instruments harder without losing tune; I had no idea. All I knew was that I wanted earplugs.

Into the crowd. I was immediately consumed by it, like an amoeba taking a foe into a vacuole for digestion. All around me were vampires who were totally out of their minds. I don't think half of them saw me — or if they did, they saw me as one more thing to lean on, to drool over, to try to fondle and kiss. This was long before raves, but as with many things, vampires were ahead of the curve. They even called scenes like this "blood raves," as if in premonition, and the vibe was exactly the same.

It was all sweat, scent, gyration, hunger and naked lust.

I pushed my way through, unsure how I even meant to find her. The basement must have held three hundred vampires. It was large and there was plenty of room, but they'd self-crushed into huddles thick as packed sardines, eager for the press of bodies. The ceiling was higher than I'd have expected for a basement, the walls farther out. But even with my eyes peeled and my attention sharp, all I could see were glazed-eyed partiers — and none of them mine.

Then, I saw her.

I wouldn't have, except that she'd climbed atop the bar. The crowd cheered in a way that struck me as familiar, as if they'd seen the same girl do this same thing before. As if Daisy had been here for straight days and nights, as Isaac had implied, and become this place's party queen.

She slithered in the bright and cycling lights, hands on hips, hands on breasts. Queen of the club, my little girl was.

I began to move. Hands reached up; hands grabbed her.

She went willingly, circled by what I now saw was a gang of suitors. They took her to a second hallway, at the rear, off of which I could see rooms. I pushed faster. The music crescendoed, then ended. The crowd hooted and cheered, and a new song began — faster this time, hot like a precursor of swing.

Then the ceiling opened up. The vampires had installed a primitive sprinkler system, but not to quell fires.

From those sprinklers, it began to rain blood.

My adrenaline spiked. I could smell the Thrill dappling my clothes, soaking me and nestling against my skin. So could the others, it seemed; the frenzy (appropriately named club, this) multiplied.

Mouths open in ecstasy.

Fangs down.

They fed. On each other. Sex and food, together as one.

I pushed through the haze threatening to subsume my brain. The reek of Thrill was strong, almost overpowering. I was already having a hard time focusing, recalling what I'd come here to do. But hearing Daisy scream — in fear or delight, I couldn't tell — woke me.

Into the back hall. Into the only room with a closed door.

Inside were six men and one woman, Daisy, who I could hear but not see. A muscular vampire at the rear saw me enter, then pushed back when I pushed forward.

"Hey man," he said, "wait your turn."

This was not a wise thing to say to me.

It took nothing to throw him away. He stumbled, fell, and then came back at me. Also unwise. This time I knew he meant business — and that was fine, because I just needed an excuse.

I heard his ribcage collapse when I struck his chest with the butt of my palm. There's a way to do it where the ribs, when they try to knit, sort of tie themselves in a knot. It takes a guy out of commission for longer than normal, and in the meantime they panic, unable to suck air.

The others turned. All but the one with his hands on Daisy's tits.

"Who the fuck are—?"

One, two, three, four. They broke like kindling. I felt like I was lying on the beach, lazily swatting flies. How old could these assholes be, to be so slow and weak? A few months at most? One tried to fight back; I fended him off with all the effort of flipping a light switch. The others — either too high to care or not interested enough to try again — rushed out the door. The one whose chest I'd collapsed stirred last, but he just looked at me and ran.

Daisy sat up, seeing me before her consenting molester. *"Maurice?"*

It's rude to punch someone down before they even raise their head to acknowledge you, but I gave less than a fractional shit. I hit the last vampire hardest of all, breaking his skull against the wall enough to show his brain. It must have been intact enough for a survival instinct, though, because the second he hit the deck he scrambled out on all fours, dripping brains like a creature from a horror show.

"Maurice, what the hell?" Daisy said, blinking.

That's when the gunshots began.

32

MASSACRE

I HEARD it before I felt it, felt it before I smelled it, and I smelled it before I saw it.

By the time I retreated a few steps and peeked into the melee, I'd already decided what I'd see. I didn't know who or how or why or even really what, but all that mattered was that vampires were dying. The guns being fired *rat-a-tat-tat* on the dance floor shot birch rounds, and every time they struck a heart the burning began. The reek of Thrill, both from the sprinklers and the partiers below, was finally losing to the acrid odor of sulfur and brimstone. The sound of vampires running was like flapping leather wings.

I could feel their terror in my blood.

"Maurice? Maurice, what's going on?"

She was high as hell. Out of her fucking mind. Daisy, unlike most of the dying beyond, wasn't as afraid as she should have been. She'd been drinking Thrill nonstop for days and nights, probably never really coming down. Her tone of voice was curious at best, petulant at worst. She wanted to know why the party had stopped, and Captain Downer had come to stop it.

"Come on," I said. I'd already decided what we were facing. There was just the one exit: up the stairwell through which the killers had come. We couldn't run out a back door or slip through a window. If we were in the country I might have been able to break through a wall and dig, but this was New York. Nothing but concrete beyond. By the time I got us out, they'd be upon us.

"I don't want to go," she said.

"Daisy."

"No, Maurice! I'm a grown woman, and I can make my own decisions!"

I wasn't sure whether to laugh or scream. In the midst of life and death, I found myself wanting to slap her. The way she postured behind me was self-important, like she was standing up for her rights. Was it possible she was so intoxicated that she didn't know vampires were dying? Couldn't she see the flicker of flames?

There was no time. I grabbed her. She screamed and thrashed, kicking and punching me with every available limb.

"Daisy, goddammit ... !"

A flailing foot struck my groin. I don't care how old you are or how much blood you've sucked; getting hit in the nuts still brings a man to his knees.

I staggered, reeling, cupping my crotch while trying not to fall. My senses were overloaded, each amped up to fifteen, making concentration on any one thing impossible. I saw every detail of this room and the open space beyond; I heard not just the pop of shells but each whistling ricochet, each sub-audible *thunk!* as one struck flesh. I could smell not just blood and ash, but even the wood in the rounds, dry and crisp like a log sundered with an axe. I could even taste the unholy mixture on the back of my tongue — cellulose and iron, brick and sweat.

So it was no wonder I tripped, no wonder I fell backward

and accidentally slammed Daisy's head into the wall. She went limp and I looked back, but I couldn't tell whether the blood on her was from her scalp, from my Thrill-soaked clothes, or from some earlier blood orgy.

I stood, still with Daisy over my shoulder. She was inert: a sack of rags. I didn't think to wonder why. I just counted my blessings. She was a vampire; she'd be fine. Maybe all the Thrill in her system had finally blacked her out, or maybe a particularly stubborn bit of bone was working its way through her brain's motor centers after the crash, but the reason she'd gone limp didn't matter. What mattered was that we might have a shot after all. Without her screaming and slowing me down, I might be able to kill enough of them to get us out of here.

But in the front room, I noted a curious thing.

There were five shooters that I could see, but they hadn't bothered to block the exit. In fact, they'd moved away from it, as if meaning to let the ambitious escape. What's more, Frenzy's invaders were slow. They were black-clad from head to toe, including helmets and gloves like the police wore in extreme situations, or might if they wanted to protect their bodies from claws, their necks from fangs.

Humans?

Yes, they seemed to be. They weren't moving like vampires, and with my keyed-up senses, I could smell them.

All with guns. Firing more or less randomly, yet allowing the crowd to flee.

I circled left. Behind the bar. I kept low, bringing Daisy down to cradle so she wouldn't be a target high on my back. From there I needed to regroup, so I set her down gently, minding a forest of broken bottles. The little alcove reeked most strongly of liquor. Who knew? Thrill and booze: the ultimate party cocktail.

Peeking out, I took the time to get the full lay of the room. Vampires were escaping easily, but the shooters would shoot at anyone. I needed to vanish, to stay in the background and not draw their attention. The clock was ticking. A bottleneck at the stairwell was slowing the vampires down, and in their drunkenness, most were moving like mortals: slow, stupid, and panicked. They were too high to identify the threat behind them. What I saw was unfettered fear, without antecedent, reversing time to their human days.

They'd forgotten how to be vampires.

That was good for me and Daisy; it meant those who remained would give us cover. But it wouldn't last forever. Even at their glacial pace, they'd soon be gone, and so would my chance to vanish into them.

I scanned, waiting for my chance.

And as I scanned, I saw how much larger the problem was than I'd first seen.

Not five shooters.

At least *twenty*.

They'd ducked into the corners, so I hadn't seen them from the back. They were methodically clearing the space, now slipping back toward the room where Daisy and I had just been. It struck me as *organized* above all else. More organized than I'd have expected from anyone but trained soldiers.

Someone had sent a force to clear us out. *A military-grade force.*

Only, they weren't really *cleaning us out*, were they? The precision of their movements jarred against the way they'd left the only exit open, allowing their prey to escape. I could see a handful of burning corpses, and the killers kept firing their weapons ... but they weren't working like executioners. They didn't want to kill us all — just some of us. Why?

It didn't matter. I'd only been waiting for an opening; I

didn't plan to stay long. When a clot of Thrill-drenched club-goers passed the abandoned bandstand and knocked over a snare and a cymbal, enough heads turned that I was able to rush behind a group on the room's other end unseen.

I pushed toward the stairs, knowing they might turn and fire on us at any minute. And they did; a vampire not fifteen feet from us erupted after a volley of tommy gun shots finally found her heart. Three vampires around her lit with flame when she did, and new screams and new panic tinged the air.

I looked back, watching as a few of the black-clad killers watched us, wondering why they didn't keep right on firing. I caught the eye of one, Daisy's still-unconscious form held low in front of me. It made me feel guilty. I could dispatch a few of them; I was sure I could. They were frail humans, and the few vampires who'd been clear-headed enough to fight had, I'd seen earlier, brought one to the ground before another had ripped them open with bullets. But if I did that, what would I do with Daisy? I couldn't slump her in a corner while I fought. And what if they killed me? They could, easily, once I made myself a problem. And *then* what would become of Daisy?

So instead of fighting, I kept my head down. I focused on her — on getting her to safety. This was the only way she might survive, and it was my duty to see that she did.

When we finally found open air, I half expected a new squad of executioners to greet us. But they didn't; the streets were dark and clear. Most of my fellow vampires, remembering themselves once the worst of the panic was gone, had begun streaking away.

Daisy stirred. Her body lost its dishrag feeling, regaining enough attention, almost, to stand.

I carried her one last sprint, away from the bank, away from Frenzy, away from the slaughter within. Then we stopped, and I let her find her head, and I let her eyes find me.

"Maurice?" she said. It was very different in tone from the irritated way she'd greeted me before.

Soft, weak, and not petulant at all, she asked me, "Why are you here?"

"I'll always be here," I told her.

33

CHILDREN

I THOUGHT IT WAS OVER. It wasn't over.

We arrived back at our building to see fire in the windows. That same leather-wings flutter — the sound vampires would make if we stirred in a nest, I've often thought, like yellow jackets in a hive — came barely audible from within. Louder, I heard gunshots, screams, and shattering like doors and walls sundered.

Part of me could only stare in shock. Had we made a loop? Had we left the club, only to find it somehow relocated to our home?

The curious feeling lasted only a blink. What came on its heels was as white-hot as a fireplace poker gripped in a fist.

Celeste.

I flinched to sprint inside, but at first I couldn't go. I couldn't — *wouldn't* — drag Daisy inside. But if I left her here, would she be safe? Would she run back to Isaac — to another blood rave scene, in which to lose herself?

There was no choice. I moved to an alcove, set Daisy down, and told her to stay put. I wasn't sure if I believed her when she said she would, but in the end it didn't matter. I turned to find a vampire behind me, so close he could have staked me and I'd've never seen it coming.

But it was Malone.

He put his hand on my chest. "Don't," he said. "It's handled."

"*What's* handled?"

Instead of answering, he addressed my real concern. "Celeste is safe. *More* than safe. Shit, Maurice. Your wife is a cold-blooded badass."

"What happened here?" I demanded.

The front door of the building practically exploded. A knot of vampires emerged — but unlike the sheep at Frenzy, these were wide-eyed and sharp. Their minds weren't dulled. They were hard, ready to kill.

Sally, Madge, Celeste, and Rolf, looking like the Dirty One-Third Dozen.

"Police," Malone answered. "Riot squad. Shock troops. Army — I don't know."

I moved closer, glancing back, uncomfortable leaving Daisy even for a minute. Celeste saw but didn't run to me. I had to go to her. She doesn't fight much, but she's a thousand years old, with the strength and speed that go with it. Mass murder is like a casual slap to her.

Our minds connected. Instantly, she knew what I'd found and I knew what they'd been through here. It was the same: a group of black-clad troops stalking room to room in the all-vampire building, rubbing out some but not all. It didn't make sense. Not only had they struck one of the only fully armed vampire groups in the city, but they'd done so at night. It was beyond stupid. You didn't gas a wasp's nest in the height of a hot summer day. You waited until it was cool and quiet, then killed them in their sleep.

I knew, because Celeste's blood told me, that troops had come here same as they'd come to the club.

I knew that the CVA Crew, who seemed to have been an unpleasant surprise for the troops, had fought back hard.

Yet I knew the Crew hadn't managed to kill even one of the attackers. Somehow, protecting a building resident had taken precedence each time, or the killer had just managed to slip away.

I knew many inside were dead, their bodies burning. Even now I could see Dexter blurring in and out of the building at light speed, pulling buckets of water from somewhere unknown to keep the building from going up. I saw Inez inside Celeste's mind, dousing what she could with the building's only dry fire extinguisher. It was the ghetto, after all. Our neighbors were poor, and the builders hadn't put much thought into prevention.

Then I caught something else. But it was a partial thing — something Celeste was doing her best not to let me see.

"What are you hiding from me?" I asked.

She shook her head.

"Celeste?"

"Not now, Maurice. You've just been through your own thing. The important thing is that Daisy is safe. We're safe. Our friends are safe."

I looked for the hole in what she'd just said. *Daisy, us, our friends.* Who else was there?

Then I knew. Not for sure, but I could guess the truth from Celeste's face.

"No," I said.

I flinched to go inside, but she grabbed my arm.

"It's too late."

"Too late for what, Celeste?"

Now she looked like she might cry. I was making this too hard. "Maurice ..."

My returning anger didn't care. "Too late for *what?*"

"They shot at all of us. *All of us*, Maurice. But the bullets can only do so much because we're fast, because they have to hit us in the heart. Except for ..."

Except for those who aren't supernaturally fast. Except for those who can be mortally wounded without bullets needing to pierce the heart.

Except, I knew, for our human hosts.

Now she did cry. Too much stress, too much strength. We hadn't exactly bonded with the Flynn family, but they'd been our responsibility. They'd been ours, right or wrong.

"Are the killers still in the building?"

"Just one. The others ran off."

Meaning one black-clad soldier. *One* of fifteen or twenty who'd somehow run off while a building full of vampires stood helpless to see them, or catch them.

"If there's still one inside, why are you down here?"

Madge said, "The kids have him."

I opened my mouth to ask, but Celeste elaborated directly into my mind. One of the marauders had burst into their apartment, but had done so far too close to Sally, who'd been at the stove near the door. She'd taken his weapon with extreme prejudice, then been shot by his partner. The bullets had missed her heart, and she'd managed to drag herself away. She'd thought Madge had the kids and Madge had thought the opposite, and only after they'd regrouped had they realized Walter and Lucy were still upstairs. Even though Madge and Sally hadn't turned the kids, they shared the familial brand of blood ties that our kind grows out of closeness and love. They'd known right away that the children were fine, and that the soldier Sally had taken the weapon from still had no gun.

They had him now, cornered, in their shared bedroom. They hadn't taken him yet, but they also wouldn't let their adoptive parents enter. Walter had sent them one clear message: *This one is ours.* Transplanted payback, perhaps, for what a very different aggressor had done twenty years back, taking their first set of parents the way this human had tried to take their new ones.

I looked at Sally, whose face had gone slack. I knew something was happening; the children were likely ready to finish their would-be attacker. But then Madge lunged, as if to stop something unseen, and we all felt a jolt as a window high up exploded outward.

Walter and Lucy's bedroom on the 14th floor.

They'd driven him out. Through the glass. I looked up and could only watch in slow-motion as the body fell, impacting the concrete hard enough to crack it and throw chips into the air.

We all remained where we were. High above, two small heads peeked out the window: Walter and Lucy, pleased with their work. I inched closer, morosely curious. In all my years, I'd never seen a body strike concrete from 150 feet up. It seemed a glaring hole in my body of experience.

But then the body, which had exploded from burst seams like a water balloon filled with ooze, sat up.

Stood.

Looked at us.

And ran.

I could only blink.

"Hell," Malone said from behind me.

I turned. Met his eyes. And in them, I didn't see shock so much as anger and betrayal.

"They were vampires all along," he said, "trying to look human."

34

———

BODIES

WE DIDN'T NEED to cover the bodies. Vampires burn. What we needed was an ash bin.

All except for Henry, Irene, and Mort.

"Maurice," Celeste said. She was trying to hand me the corner of a sheet, but it wasn't the lack of a cover that had stopped me from dignifying the scene. I had a wadded-up bedsheet in my other hand; I just hadn't been able to lay it down yet. I wanted to look at them uncovered first — to cement the memory in my brain. I wanted to look at the people we'd taken from their lives, moved into a nest of demons, and gotten slaughtered. I wanted to take in the sight of the most recent lives I'd heaped atop my conscience.

When I still didn't move, Celeste took the sheet from my hand and covered them herself. I just let it happen. My limbs were frozen.

After she was done, she returned to my side and slipped an arm around my waist, leaning her head on my shoulder.

"We killed them," I said.

"The girls are still alive. We can atone by protecting them."

"They're safer away from us."

"They're orphans now, Maurice. *This?*" She indicated the sheet-covered bodies, already leaking spots of blood through white fabric. "This is done. What's happened here can't be fixed. We have to do what we can to fix what's left."

My lips pressed into a bloodless line. I didn't know what I felt. Whatever I felt, it was deep, deep down. I couldn't reach it, and didn't care to try.

Malone entered our apartment across the hall, then saw us in the Flynns' place and came to stand behind us. For ten seconds he was respectfully silent, papers rustling in his hands with the rise and fall of his chest.

I turned.

"I've called around. Talked to some brothers and sisters. It wasn't just the Frenzy club and here. Two other vampire clusters were hit. Same M.O. Soldiers in black, using wooden bullets. Once I started asking the right questions, I started getting the answers we thought we'd get."

"They were *all* vampires," I said. It was almost a question, but didn't sound like one because I knew the answer.

"Looks like it. They must have been wearing human musk, but a few folks said they smelled off, not like real humans. You can smell adrenaline in the sweat, right? Musk doesn't have that. Besides, a few of the vampires I talked to had deep enough blood ties to suspect they weren't human, because they could sense their assailants. And, of course, there's the fact that not one of the attackers were caught or killed."

I nodded. They'd been plenty fast enough to slip away, given the way their victims fought back expecting human vulnerability and speed.

But there was something else that bothered me. Something about how orderly the killers inside Frenzy had been. The working theory was that the vampire mafia had been behind the attacks for reasons unknown, but what I'd seen didn't look like mafia. It'd looked almost military.

"Why would they do this?" Celeste asked.

We had no idea.

"This building, I can almost understand," Malone said. "It's possible someone blabbed. Maybe someone leaked that the CVA lives here, and the vampire mafia wanted to get rid of a thorn in its side."

"But most of the building isn't even—"

"Doesn't matter," Malone said, cutting her off. "They wouldn't mind collateral damage. What bugs me is that if they were after *us*, they wouldn't have hit three other sites. And they for damn sure wouldn't have let us get away."

That's what'd been bugging me. You don't go in for an execution run, then fire randomly and make a hole so most of your targets can escape. In the case of our building, *all* the likeliest targets had escaped. They hadn't killed one of the Crew who'd been making problems for the distilleries. Not *one*.

We left it unsettled. There was simply nowhere to go.

When the silence returned, it stayed too long. Malone seemed to grow uncomfortable, as if he was intruding. And it was true; he *was* intruding on our moment with the Flynns. I welcomed him, but part of me wanted to mourn alone.

"I put a rotating guard on the doors," he said. "Day and night, inside the lobby. We should be safe."

I didn't reply. I was still staring at the bodies.

"I'll leave you to it," he said.

Celeste and I left the apartment when Malone was gone, then closed the door and crossed the hall. Dexter had said he'd remove the bodies — that out of respect for us, he'd even carry each of them out of the city and give them a decent burial, complete with a little wooden cross. Decades from now, their graves might be discovered and questions might be asked, but that was a problem for another day. For now, they'd sleep well in the eye of God.

We entered our own apartment, closed our own door. It would have been an overstatement to say we felt safe, but we didn't feel in danger, either. We were too tired to feel anything.

A quiet half-hour passed.

I was sitting beside Daisy's bed when Celeste came in. She stood in the doorway. It was daytime — the middle of vampire night. Neither of us should have been awake, but neither could sleep. Daisy, blessedly, hadn't woken since we'd led her here. She needed her rest. She was about to endure our protection, whether she wanted it or not.

"Maurice ..." Celeste said.

"I know."

That was all there was. It didn't take a mental connection to know what had passed between us. If we were human, the same would have been said and the same would be understood. I was through running. I was through hiding. For reasons not entirely known, the war had come to us. The vampire mafia had turned to eat its own customers, its own source of business. We already knew they were after me and Celeste: two foreign vampires who'd come to Chicago to make what should have been a peaceful home. I knew now that they'd never leave us alone. I knew now that until the Thrill trade ended, both mafias would have a stranglehold on this city.

We could have left the city, of course.

But no. I had a score to settle.

Celeste spoke inside my head: *Maurice, you have to join them. You have to fight the mob and help put an end to this.*

And to my wife's unspoken request, I'd said, *I know.*

35

CLIFFHANGER

ANNABEL BLINKED, as if coming out of another type of glamour, when Maurice turned to look at her for the first time in what felt like an hour. The awareness of suddenly-passed time made her consult her watch, which she'd bought for purely aesthetic reasons over her horrible husband's protests. It was after ten. She didn't know how long football games lasted, but perhaps if she stayed at the office until after her husband got back home, he'd question her far-too-long absence and think she was having an affair. That would be fantastic.

"How am I doing?" the vampire asked.

"How are you *doing*?" Annabel repeated.

"Well, I've never had therapy before."

"There's really no right or wrong. You talk, I listen."

"But do you think I'm crazy or neurotic or something?"

"I gave up 'crazy' when I started believing in vampires."

"Just neurotic, then."

She watched his eyes. He sounded like he was being sarcastic, but the eyes before her were serious and earnest — and, by the way, not glamoury at all. She knew he'd done something to her to make her believe, and that same something would keep her mouth shut about all he'd told her — something that, excepting the murders, she'd have done regardless out of professional courtesy. But right now, Maurice wasn't heaping on any extra persuasion. He wasn't trying to influence her thinking on the matter of his mental wellness. If he was a mess, he wanted to hear it.

But strangely, Maurice was striking Annabel as more and more balanced as the story rolled on. Few human patients were this forthcoming. Few patients of any type told a story with this many objective facets. When he was speaking, she felt like she was there, back in the Chicago of 1929 — not because he had mental force, but because the tale was such an immersive one.

"I'm still deciding," Annabel said. She hoped her answer came off the same as his: maybe sarcastic, maybe serious, and demonstrably neither.

"I need you to understand how ... *complicated* ... the situation with Daisy was. She wanted to fly right, I swear. She just—"

Annabel held up a hand to stop him. It was something she couldn't recall ever having done with a patient. The goal was always to let them speak, to let them tie their own harness or noose. But she wanted him to know that she understood it plenty, from ass to elbows.

"Daisy is clear to me, Maurice. I get it. Believe me."

He squinted. It wasn't quite a glamour, but it was as close as he could get without turning it on. She'd maybe said a little too much. Right now, he must be wondering how Annabel had been as a girl — if she'd acted out, same as Daisy. Because she really *did* get it. It was simple to step into that distant vampire girl's skin, crazy as the idea seemed.

But Maurice let it go, leaving her with her own secrets, both known and unknown.

"What do you think so far, then?" he asked.

"About what?"

"About me. I told you I was worried about my patterns. Celeste, Reginald, Daisy ..."

"I think it's too early for me to start venturing diagnoses," Annabel said.

"Anything at all," he said.

"All right. I will say this, at least: I think you're intuiting patterns from pretty dodgy evidence. You don't know what Reginald will be; you said you've only known him for a few weeks. Maybe your 'council' will take him away, or maybe they won't. And Celeste? Maurice, seriously. She's your *wife*. One you seem very happy with. It's hard for me to see turning her as a mistake no matter how I look at it."

"What about Daisy?"

"What *about* Daisy? You haven't finished the story."

Now Maurice looked at the clock on the wall. "It's getting late. Are you sure you want me to continue?"

Yes. *Yes*, she very much did. In fact, if he left her on the cliffhanger they'd reached, she'd have a very hard time sleeping. *He was just about to take on the vampire mafia!* It didn't matter how late they stayed. His AmEx was black — the card for big players, without a limit. He could pay, and she could stay. But it had become personal. She'd stay for free, just because she needed to know how the long tale ended.

"Of course," she said.

But Maurice, for his part, didn't seem sure. Maybe he thought she was just trying to be nice and (uncharacteristic for her patients) wanted to respect her time more than find resolution. Or maybe the somber note they'd paused on had him feeling low, same as Annabel's heart was sympathetically low. She was supposed to hold a distance between her patients' issues and herself, but this tale in particular had drawn her in.

She felt part of it, connected to it, tied to its center. Especially to Daisy, and her unknown fate.

Maurice waited, his manner too serious. She decided to lighten the mood.

"Oh, come on. If you don't keep talking, I won't learn enough about you to mind-rape my way into your blood."

Maurice took a second before saying, "What?"

"It's all part of my master plan," she told him.

They stared at each other for a long moment. Then Maurice laughed, and laughed hard. It was the first time he'd shown any real mirth, and his story had contained some funny moments. He was so *serious*. So *morose*. She wanted to tell him to lighten up. Life was so much easier if you let yourself enjoy the ride instead of gritting your teeth through it, no matter how long that life lasted.

Good point, Annabel thought. *Maybe you should take your own advice?* She hadn't smiled much, since her stupid marriage.

"All right," he said, shifting his weight, settling in to finish. "Where was I?"

36

———

WATCH

"WATCH," said Malone.

It's not easy for vampires to spy on other vampires. First of all, there's our kind's excellent vision to contend with — pretty easy to be spotted peeping if you don't hide just right. Second, there's always the chance the watcher shares blood ties with the watched, in which case the watched ends up sensing nerves from someone unseen, even if they never get any specific thoughts. To block it, you had to obfuscate: Malone's word for what I probably would have called clenching.

Building the obfuscation muscle, he'd told me, *means making yourself invisible from blood ties by using mental discipline. If you're not invisible when you try to peek in on them, we all die.*

To me, obfuscating felt like holding it when you really have to pee. I had to squeeze particularly hard, since I'm better at blood ties than most. Practicing was like doing full-body Kegels, only we didn't have the word "Kegels" back then. Just "obfuscating," apparently.

I clenched and Kegeled, trying to keep my thoughts to myself as we watched the vampires on the distant road. I had to close all the channels around me so that no intuition got in and none of my thoughts leaked out. It was hard as hell. I always ended up holding my breath, and that made me dizzy.

"Breathe, Maurice."

I did. Barely. This was our first live test of my ability, and if I breathed too readily and dropped my thought-clench, one or more of the vampires in the black cars below us might sense me and look up. We were fast and we were far, but even the least talented vampires can see detail on the horizon. Even if we got away, our jig would be up.

"You see that truck?" Rolf pointed.

I nodded.

"We've been following it for a while. It makes runs between Chicago and Alberta, Canada. Full of maple leaf whiskey and beer."

"Not Thrill?"

Rolf shook his head. "Not at this point in the route. These are human mafia trucks. The liquor trade works like the post office. All the mail from a bunch of post offices gets thrown together to head in approximately the same direction, then is broken out again by destination at the other end. Between, the shipping routes merge into these big, common arteries. Same for the two mafias, sending both of their cargos along the same roads in bulk. They'll often send Thrill and booze in the same trucks, certainly the same caravan. They split it out at the end and then settle. In this case, 'settling' means the vampire mafia gets paid and gives the regular mob their percentage. Money, at least, doesn't go the other way. Does that make sense?"

I nodded. There was no reason for the human mafia to pay the vampire mafia, since the humans were the ones providing the service. But there was still one thing that didn't make sense. For one, it was daytime, and even though we were deep in shade, I was boiling.

"If the trucks are human mafia ..." I started to ask.

"Just watch," Malone said.

The line of trucks and cars was approaching a large, multi-lane bridge. Once beneath it, the caravan stopped.

"Why did they stop?"

"They're waiting."

I felt like a kid on a road trip, trying not to force a rest stop. Or at least, I felt like I imagined such kids felt. During my childhood, we'd taken our road trips on horseback, and we hadn't gone far.

We watched the waiting caravan for what felt like forever. The concentration required to cut off accidental leaks through blood ties was exhausting me. We'd tested everyone in the Crew, and those who listened hard had been able to hear me most. Malone thought that was good; it meant that if I controlled myself, I might be a good mental spy. But on operations like this, it made my burden the heaviest if there were vampires in the trucks that we had to be up all day to watch. Which, it seemed, there weren't.

At the top of the hour — 4pm now, with our vampire skin sweating in what was essentially a waste culvert that offered shade but still got us sunburnt if we went too close to the end — a second line of trucks pulled under the bridge. This line was smaller and composed of shabbier vehicles. It was one of those wide bridge spans, with tons of room off the road, between it and a road running adjacent. The trucks had moved into this space and were now opening up. From the new line, only two figures emerged. Both were dressed as if for the arctic, complete with hoods and gloves.

"Vampires," Sally said.

We were barely outside of Chicago. It was probably the maximum a vampire could drive a truck with blacked-out windows in broad daylight, peering through a glorified periscope, heavily UV filtered, while wearing full-body cover and sunglasses.

"They're meeting with the vampires during the day?"

"I think we forced the change," Malone told me. "They're more worried about us than they'd admit."

I'd heard some of this when we'd sat around last night, bullshitting while trying to decide what came next. For now, we were still living in our old building. That would probably need to change. We figured the attacks on Frenzy and our building were random, and they hadn't been trying to hit the CVA. They'd just been trying to hit vampire populations, and found us instead.

But the thinking went: The vampire mafia was both a deeply powerful and deeply flawed organization. They were dangerous when in their power and under the cover of dark, but they weren't organized or connected enough yet to know who to trust. They were in a Devil's bargain with the human mob, and entire human structures existed, for that human mob, to counterbalance the handful of cops the vampires had been able to bribe or glamour on their own. According to Malone (and, in part, according to scribbled notes the CVA had found in their one big raid and several smaller ones), they were limited in who they could glamour or bribe anyway. The human mob didn't like it when police chiefs got glamoured; it meant those chiefs might obey the vampires instead of them if push came to shove. For the most part, the vampire mafia had to do as the humans said.

In Chicago, anyone running serious business either played ball with the mafia or became its enemy. So far, the vampires had played ball, and that meant they had no allies of their own. We were fairly sure that we'd benefitted from all their confusion, and that they believed the CVA was bigger and better-organized than it actually was.

"Can you hear them, Maurice?" Dexter asked.

I tried to listen using my superior ears, but I was already straining to keep thoughts from broadcasting through my blood. I caught words here and there, but had trouble concentrating on any of them.

But then I began to hear. I began to understand. And as I listened to the conversation happening hundreds of yards in the distance, my face must have changed. The others around me began to look very interested, curious what I was learning.

"What are they—?" Malone asked when I didn't respond.

I stopped him, holding up a hand. I kept it up until the trucks exchanged cargo and left, each caravan on its separate way.

When they were gone, I finally exhaled. I didn't realize how hard I'd been working to hold back until I let go. When I did, I almost fell over. I'd be sore tomorrow, boy howdy.

They were all looking at me. I hadn't lowered my pausing hand.

"Home first," I told them. "Explanations second."

37

FIFTY PERCENT

STILL I DIDN'T TELL them what I'd heard. I needed context first. I needed food, too. We'd snatched a few blood bags from a hospital as snacks in the event of an emergency, and as gross as cold blood is, the moment sure felt like an emergency to me. I felt like collapsing into bed and never getting up. I sucked down a pint of dead human juice like it was sex, licking my lips. When you're that beat, even shit satisfies.

Then, with the Crew following me around like an oracle due to pop, I took the books and notes the CVA had scavenged from the distillery raid and read through it all. They simply waited, but didn't have to wait long. I'm a fast reader, even for a vampire.

"Okay," Malone said. "Enough's enough. Tell us what you heard already, will you?"

I sat in a comfortable chair. Malone was standing. I looked up as I spoke, feeling like I was holding court.

"Neither of the vampires at the exchange we just saw was Santori," I said.

"Obviously," Malone replied.

"But one of them was his little errand boy."

"How could you tell?" They hadn't just been wearing hoods. They'd been wearing ski masks and goggles, too.

"His voice," I said. *"He talkth like thith."*

"All right," Malone said, sitting. Apparently my ears were worth something after all.

"I don't know who the other was. He just sounded like anyone else. But if Puffy was there ..."

"Then it means the vampire mafia isn't just controlling the Thrill trade," Lenore, Dexter's wife, said. "It means they're running it first-hand."

"Right," I said. "The reason I wanted to look through the papers and books you'd seized was to see if I could get a feel for what went into Thrill, or how hard it was to make. There's not much there. Not surprising; it's the sort of thing their chemists would keep in their heads. Remember what we found out from the university?"

A knowing mumble went through the group. We'd heard about vanishing chemists — two of them. If someone in the Thrill trade was turning chemists, they'd share blood as maker and progeny. It would mean they could share the formula mentally, without writing it down. For security, we assumed.

"But from what you've told me and what we've seen about the shipping schedule," I went on, "it's not quick to manufacture. They'd be shipping a lot more frequently if they could make it faster."

"But they have a bunch of distilleries," Madge said.

"Rumored distilleries," I replied. "I think there's a good chance that's just bullshit, or they've consolidated. We've seen two groups of trucks." I picked up a stack of photos the Crew had taken, and pointed out the trucks I meant. "Two groups, two regular schedules. That suggests two distilleries. You said they used to do the handoffs at night. Did the trucks look like they had two crews — the same vampires every time?"

Everyone looked at Sally, who nodded. "I guess," she said.

"Look. The guy I heard at the dropoff is Santori's errand boy. We know he pretty much does whatever any of their wiseguys need, but most often he's shining Santori's shoes or wiping his ass. The only reason I can think of to send him off to drive a truck during daytime is because there's just not enough personnel to go around. And, frankly, because that little ball-licker will eat anyone's shit and call it ice cream."

"But it's the vampire mafia," Madge said. "We can't just underestimate them."

"Nor should we overestimate them," I said. "Yes, they're vampire mafia — but right now, they're being squeezed by the human mafia. Capone's not an idiot. I'm sure he sees the potential of Thrill, and the potential of having vampires work for him ... *if* they behave like good dogs. Which they might not. Right now, Capone controls this city. I imagine he's doing all he can to make sure his fanged buddies don't try to pull a coup."

"Assuming they only have two distilleries and a skeleton crew is a big leap, Maurice," Malone said.

"Not as big as you might think. I heard enough of what they were saying at the handoff to get a good sense of how things are going. The answer is: *not that well* — not from the vampire perspective. I counted fifteen mobsters at that rendezvous, and only two vampires. And they kept circling the vampires for the entire handoff, as if meaning to pull their hoods off and shove them into the sun to show them who's boss. And did anyone see the point where it looked like they were arguing?"

Nods. We'd all spotted that. It seemed, from body language, like there might be a bloodbath. But vampires are more docile when the sun's out, even in the shade. There was no question the humans — today, at least — had held the upper hand.

"The argument was over Capone's men raising the Thrill kickback. One of the humans said, 'You're going to start giving us fifty percent, or you can find your own distributors.'"

"Fifty?"

I nodded meaningfully. Best we knew, the original percentage had been about twenty.

"Did the vampires agree?" Celeste, beside me, asked. Then she answered her own question. "They must have. They unloaded the barrels."

"Right. Because honestly, the vampires could just raise their prices to the end customer to compensate for the increased kickback, and use that strategy to keep their profits the same. If they did that, the only casualty would be vampire pride."

A few people in the room shrugged. "Vampire pride" wasn't something to be taken lightly. Murder had been done over it, without much forethought and zero regret.

"The bigger problem is something I heard the human leader tell the vampires before they all rolled out," I told them.

There must have been something in my voice, because that grabbed everyone's attention and held it hard. Celeste, who could see into my mind and knew the punchline already put her hand over her mouth.

"What?" Malone asked.

"He said, '... and if Logan doesn't like it, he can talk to the boss.'"

38

POWER AND CONTROL

LOGAN. As in the head of the American Vampire Council.

I needed my sleep. Badly. But I *couldn't* sleep, because I could sense Celeste awake beside me. Her thoughts were so loud, it was like someone was shouting into my brain.

I rolled over.

"Wine?" I said. "You know, since we're awake anyway?"

I thought she might protest or pretend to be asleep. For us, noon is the middle of the night.

But instead she threw her covers back and sat upright. "Oh, fuck. *Fine.*"

Celeste doesn't like to swear in English. She says it sounds too harsh, like a fingernail raking along your tongue. That single fuck, more than anything, got me out of bed.

I led. She didn't follow. I knew why, without ties or even intuition. It just seemed obvious. When I returned, she was up, with a nightgown on, sitting by Daisy's bedside, petting her hair as she slept. Daisy had been in and out, still recovering from her particularly brutal dose of Thrill now 36 hours in the past. Her body, at the time, had essentially been dead. It was a form of "dead" that took much longer to heal from than our usual injuries. What massive doses of Thrill do to ruin our bodies is so systemic, so completely thorough.

Instead of waiting for Celeste to join me in the kitchen, I returned to the bedroom with a bottle and two glasses. I handed her one of the glasses and poured. It was a lovely Cabernet, viscous as blood. The bouquet rose from the glasses in a mist of aromatic cherry and blackberry. Horrible, to make wine illegal.

For a while we didn't speak. Then:

"Did you know, before tonight?"

"I suspected," I told her. Then I explained how precise and orderly the killers at Frenzy had been, and how that precision had struck me as military. It was nothing but disciplined vampires pretending to be sloppy humans: Guards of the Vampire Council in cops' clothing.

She ran her hand over Daisy's hair again before speaking. I knew what she must be thinking, even without prying. It was a thought that began with, *What kind of a world do we live in, if ... ?* The kind thing any parent thinks when the world rips off its civil mask, revealing the hideous place it's capable of being.

"*Why*, Maurice? Why would the Council send Guard troops to kill vampire civilians?"

"To create fear," I answered. "What Logan wants to do to reshape American vampire society can't be done if we're not all very afraid. If we're not begging for the Council to pass new laws and restrictions — to control us in the name of protection."

"It's too bleak," Celeste said.

"But it's true. You saw them, Celeste. The vampires who killed the Flynns and so many of our neighbors were pretending to be human because the Council wants us to be afraid of what might happen if humans realize we exist. But they were letting vampires escape, because Logan's goal *isn't* to wipe us out like real humans would. The goal is to put as many terrified witnesses out into the world, so they'll tell the others how dangerous humans can be. The Council then hears their fears and responds to what's become the common will. They pass more restrictions, institute more 'quality control' standards for new vampires. Did you hear they're talking about requiring permits for all turnings from here on out?"

"That law will never pass," Celeste said.

"It will," I countered, "if enough vampires believe it'll make us stronger. If we think it'll keep us safe from the dangerous humans all around us."

Celeste sipped, uneasy and clearly not enjoying her wine. Between the two of us, she's the optimist. I don't think of myself as the pessimist. I'm just realistic.

"Do you really think Logan is behind Thrill?"

"You can see into my blood," I said. "Take a listen, if you don't believe me."

She wrapped her hands around her arms, hugging herself. She wouldn't focus on any one thing. Her thoughts moved from place to place, unable to rest.

Beside us, Daisy stirred. Her eyes opened slowly. She struck me as a fawn, waking to the world. There were, I'd always thought, *two* Daisys. The first was the one I'd first met and befriended — the one who was beside us now. That Daisy was sweet and quiet: the direct opposite of the second Daisy. The second one was more *thing* than girl — a vampire to the hilt, especially when she was on Thrill.

I wanted this first Daisy to stay. I wanted her to learn temperance, and restraint, and the wisdom that came with age. We'd all been young and wild once, but Daisy, so far, had lived enough killer youth to last an eternal lifetime.

I thought she'd ask why we were awake. I was afraid she'd feel the weight on our shoulders and rise. But it was a false awakening. Her eyes fluttered closed, and after a moment Celeste spoke again.

"*Why?*" she asked me. Meaning Thrill. Meaning the way our esteemed leader was behind the illegal trade, supporting the vampire mafia.

"Money. Power. Look what bootlegging has done for Capone."

"He has enough power."

"... said nobody ever, who seeks power."

"It's not good, Maurice. It means that if you tangle with Santori, you tangle with the Council."

I actually thought the exact opposite; I thought trouble in Santori's organization would drive the Council out of the trade for good. And even if I was wrong and the Council *did* get involved once we'd tussled, it's not like the Council hadn't already a hundred reasons to hate me. The French Council and I had certainly had our moments.

"I don't know, Celeste. Understanding the way things actually fit together makes things a lot simpler. Before we did that stakeout, Malone thought we were dealing with a big network of vampires all over the city — all over the *country*, really. Seeing how the mob has its thumb on them makes me think they're not all that large. Just two distilleries, and the same crew over and over."

"Backed by Council Guard."

"Cut off Thrill, and the Guard has nothing to protect. If the distilleries disappear, the trade stops. Then Logan has to back off. He'd leave Santori in the lurch. Without a reason to be in Chicago, Logan won't want to risk association with the Chicago mob."

"They'll hit back."

"Not if we hit first."

"I meant the Council, Maurice."

I laughed. Sometimes, my wife's sweet nature blinds her from the obvious. "Once there's no benefit to their association with Santori, the Council will stop doing the vampire mafia's dirty work. There's no such thing as loyalty for them, without a payday to back it up. They won't care about an eye for an eye. Public image matters a whole lot more to Logan than paying back someone else's grudge."

"Maurice. It's the vampire mafia. It doesn't matter if the humans are squeezing them or whether they've got the Council's support; they're going to want to push back. Do you really think they'll just keep taking it without doing something terrible? Do you really think what's happening now — with them, with us, with the city and the country — will last?"

No. I didn't, not for a second. I'd met Santori in Blue Eyes's memory; I'd seen him in person and sensed his menace; I'd heard his reputation more often than I could count. I could almost imagine him reacting to the errand boy's report. *Fifty percent?* He wouldn't just see the human mob's demand as a loss; he'd see it as a smack in the face. If I thought I could force another connection to Blue Eyes, I'd try just to see his rage.

No. Santori might keep things civil for a while, but Chicago's mob was closer than they realized to war. Our kind is smart — not like intellectuals; more like cunning predators. They wouldn't go quietly. They wouldn't lie down and let the world walk on their backs.

"We can beat them," I said. I didn't mean to say it. It came out for my own ears, mumbled before I could take it back. Not because I didn't mean it, but because I didn't like the agitation I immediately felt from Celeste.

"How?" she demanded, angry and worried in equal measure. "How the hell are you going to 'beat' a group of killers who you can't even find, that you don't even know the extent of?"

"We don't have to get rid of the baseball team," I said. "All we have to do, to make them stop playing, is to take away the ball."

She shook her head. To me, it felt hypocritical. She'd *asked* me to get involved. She'd insisted that I protect us, and I was already decided as to how I'd go about it.

"If we burn the distilleries and kill the chemists," I said, "this could all be over tomorrow."

39

BLANKET FORT

WHEN WE FOUND ISAAC, he was uncharacteristically sober, hiding inside some sort of weird blanket fort in his apartment. Instead of being actively high, he was merely waking from a day of *being* high. He was a mess, with clotted Thrill all over his front.

Malone pulled the blanket away and said, "Peekaboo."

Isaac flinched at the room light, stunned by brightness..

"Rise and shine, Isaac," I said.

He retreated more when his sluggish brain recognized me. I could tell he was having trouble focusing. Like Daisy the night I'd brought her home, Isaac's body was still half dead. Right now, he couldn't beat a ninety-year-old human in a foot race. But it'd be funny to watch him try.

He was about to reply when something beyond me drew his eye. He screamed. Then he stopped, because the only thing behind me were Elsie and Evelyn, identically dressed and holding hands.

Isaac seemed thoroughly confused.

"What are they doing here?" he asked, shifting his gaze between me and the human twins.

"I'm on babysitting duty. But mainly, I brought them so you'll know I don't plan to hurt you again. I wouldn't do anything bad in front of kids. Would I, girls?"

"Come and play with us, Isaac," they said in unison.

Isaac didn't reply, eyes still wide, fingertips white as they clenched the pulled-away blanket. The last time I'd seen him, I'd made a painful impression. In truth, the twins were with us for my benefit as much as for Isaac's. After finding Daisy in the state I had, I'd wanted to hurt Issac more, not less. I didn't have much patience these days, so maybe the presence of four innocent eyes would help keep me reasonable. And for this, it was best if I was reasonable.

Malone slapped Isaac's face to center. Isaac looked at Malone, then me. To me he said, "What's *he* doing here?"

"To take the girls out of the room if you don't play nice," Malone said.

"Are you going to break me backward and shove my head up my ass?" Isaac asked.

Man. I'd forgotten about that. I really wanted to try.

"No." Unfortunately. "Listen. Isaac. You said that your maker's maker is in the vampire mafia."

Isaac's brain wasn't *that* slow, it turned out. He looked between me and Malone, seemingly undecided as to whom he was addressing.

"It was a bluff, nothing more!" Isaac blurted, defensive. "We don't talk. He hates me! His maker, in the mafia, hates *him*. We're all estranged.. My maker broke his bond with both of us. I was just looking for something to say when you were holding me up like that, but don't worry! I can't actually get in touch with him to have you—!"

Malone cut him off. "Relax, asshole. We know that. Think we'd have let you anywhere near the CVA if you'd still had active ties to the group we're fighting?"

"Let's run through the hedge maze, Isaac," Elsie and Evelyn said in unison from behind us.

"*Girls!* Go find your mother."

Poor choice of words. Their mother was dead. But as glamoured as they were, they seemed to realize I'd meant Celeste. They turned without unlinking hands and walked away in slow lockstep.

I raised the wet object I'd been holding. I wanted to put it over my nose so I could breathe through it. Isaac stunk from both body odor and the rotting blood he'd caked himself with. I felt like puking.

Isaac's eyes found it.

"What's that?" he asked, flinching again.

"It's a *washcloth*, Isaac. *Jesus.*" Malone shook his head. Thrill had turned Isaac into a toddler. A *stupid* toddler.

Malone gripped Isaac's head in both of his hands. I reached the washcloth toward Isaac's filthy neck. Then I watched it, knowing what came next and why I was doing it, more disgusted than ever.

"I hate you for having this idea," I told Malone.

40

—

PIG

BY THE TIME NIGHTFALL CAME, I still hadn't gotten the taste of Isaac's blood out of my mouth. It was like something dead, like I'd sucked three-day-old roadkill. I kept wanting to spit. Malone made fun of me for it a while, but then he seemed to feel sorry. This wasn't something I'd be telling Celeste about. Swapping blood between vampires was decidedly intimate, and I'd basically just cheated on her with the biggest asshole in the world.

Malone whispered to the members of the Crew to stay put, then pulled me farther down the alleyway.

"Are you okay?" he asked.

I spat again. "It's like I fucked a pig."

"I promise you, it was worth it. I don't know how you did that, my friend. I didn't know it was possible to see through a broken maker bond, let alone two of them."

"Yeah." *Spit.* "Well, it's a gift I wish I didn't have right about now. I don't like traveling blood even when it *doesn't* involve actual liquid blood in my mouth. Maybe this is too much information, but Celeste keeps her blood a whole lot less rancid than Isaac does these days."

"That *is* too much information."

"Tough shit," I said.

Malone nodded toward the alleyway's other end, to where the Crew stood ready. We had a few guns and had found a place that carried costume chain mail — for Halloween, maybe — that we were all wearing. Still, this plan relied on two things: the element of surprise, and the hope that Isaac's maker's maker hadn't seen me when I'd peeked down their bloodline. I didn't think he had, but with the blood gone from my system I could no longer check to be sure. It's not like I could push my way back into Blue Eyes by pure will to see if there was any new mob activity, either. If I could have, I'd have done *that* to sniff out the distilleries' locations. Anything was better than putting lips on Isaac.

"You still feel good about this building?" Malone asked.

"Define 'feeling good.'" I spat again. The taste was stubborn, sticking to my gums like oil. What was Isaac pumping? Dog shit?

"You know what I mean."

My patience slipped. After what I'd done, I didn't particularly want to be doubted. I'd already told them all twice: I was as sure of both distillery locations as I was of my own apartment. For a disgusting few minutes, I'd practically worn that gangster like a glove.

"This is it, Malone. Now let's get it over with."

He hesitated. My patience slipped again. The terrible thing about blood ties is that the more you use them, the easier they become. For a vampire like me, who hates being in blood, it felt like a stink that wouldn't dissipate. I must have had some distant connection to Malone, because after Isaac I'd found myself catching the gist of a lot of Malone's thoughts. And was annoyed by the hesitation in them.

"This is the only way. You said you wanted to stop the Thrill trade," I said.

"But there are two distilleries. We're only stopping this one."

"They don't know that we know where the other one is, too. We hit one tonight, the next tomorrow. We don't have enough people to hit both at once. Do you see?"

Malone seemed to want to say more — and if I just pushed, I could probably suss out what it was — but he just nodded.

We returned to the group. They huddled around, all looking to me. For some type of pep talk, it seemed.

"The last time you hit a distillery," I told them, "it was an accident. You didn't know what you'd find, and you didn't know whose business you were sticking your hands into. This time, you know. It changes nothing. You took one of these places before, and you'll take another today. And because of it, tomorrow, the streets will be that much safer."

It wasn't much of a pep talk. But then again, I'm not much of a leader.

Sally and Madge were holding a heavy piece of railroad iron, ripped from a derelict track. Madge had welded handles onto it, and now they raised it to slam against the distillery's back door.

I took a deep breath. Maybe, after that little speech, they thought I wasn't scared. They were wrong.

"Do it," I told them.

41

———

RAID

I COULD HEAR and smell my own breath, as if my head were trapped inside a modern-day helmet. We were in the wide open of the nighttime city, but I felt claustrophobic, like the sky was closing in. Nobody is so brave as to be fearless. We do bold things despite the fear, or we do bold things because we're stupid. In that moment, striking the second of the three Chicago distilleries felt stupid as hell. It didn't matter that we'd planned as best we could; it didn't matter that Isaac's maker's maker had visited all the distilleries and given me perfect intel: layout, staffing, positions of power. In the moment it took for Madge and Sally to swing the makeshift battering ram, time seemed to stop. I saw every mote of dust in the streetlight at the corner; I felt the subtle wick of wind as the big iron bar swung. In that speck of time, I wanted to tell them to stop. Not to do this. It was a suicide run, and our adversaries were just on the door's other side, waiting for us to break in.

I actually opened my mouth, but then metal struck metal and the back doors to what was supposed to be an abandoned machine shop banged open and the Crew was rushing in around me, adrenaline on all their exhales. With my heightened vampire senses, I could hear every rapid heartbeat, every borderline-hyperventilated breath, the throb of half a dozen carotid arteries.

It was all slow motion. A moment that lasted a day.

But then time seemed to return to normal and we were inside, and Madge and Sally and Rolf and Dexter and Malone and Lenore all had guns up, then stowing guns when a tech decided to test them, chasing the tech down, ripping him open with bare teeth and claws.

When a sturdy man in overalls who I believed to be the foreman reached for something under the deck, Malone opened fire: a curious hybrid shotgun that fired heavy metal shot covered in wood. He caught the foreman in the chest. The man detonated in gore and caught fire all at once. His blood rained across ranks of glass-fronted chambers filled with desiccated humans as he began to burn.

Screams.

Running, at both vampire speeds and confused human shambles.

Panic fire.

Two of the distillery workers came at Rolf as he advanced, leaping high and taking him in a flying tackle before he could aim his weapon. They were at his throat, which he — and the rest of us — had wrapped in heavy swatches of leather, and Rolf kicked them away and fired, missing.

A bang came from higher up, from a crow's nest office I'd warned them all might be a problem. A man in a pinstripe suit and fedora emerged, tommy gun in hand, shaking with the thrum of its fire. He struck Lenore, who fell back. She seemed unhurt; the chain mail had protected her from the wooden round. But then she inspected her chest, where the slugs had hit, and shouted something to Malone that I couldn't make out.

I ran, sensing unexpected danger from Lenore's cries, and sprinted up the steps to take down the man with the gun. But somehow he trained its muzzle on me, too, and its punch stopped me in my tracks. I didn't fall right away; I took a volley in the chest and a few that went high, ripping my eye out of my head. Another must have hit my brain; I lost clarity for an unknown time and woke up healed but bloody. Something was wrong with my chest. I looked down, saw that my chain mail was a shattered joke. As I watched, my chest healed the rest of the way, expelling a small metal ball: a conventional slug, interspersed with the wooden rounds. They'd thought of chain mail, somehow. The tommy gun was spitting both types: lead and birch. The metal broke the armor; the wood dove deep for the kill.

I'd gotten lucky.

But as I rose, unsure how much time had passed (seconds? Minutes?), I saw that the Crew had also gotten lucky. There'd just been the one man with the tommy gun, and by the time my eyes found him he was little more than ash on the catwalk. Dexter stood over his remains, breathing hard.

I counted. There were still seven of us. I wasn't the only one pulling off my chain mail, finding it shattered and useless but silently thanking it for the little protection it gave. We'd never get more; six vests was all they'd had, and Malone hadn't worn any. But by stopping a wooden, heart-bound slug or two before shattering, I was willing to bet it had saved at least one of us.

"*Clear?*" Malone barked to the others.

Peeking around corners and beneath equipment, the others answered in turn:

"*Clear!*"

"*Clear!*"

"*Clear!*"

Sally nodded at Madge, then answered for both of them. "*Clear!*"

I didn't answer, but after a quick peek around me, I gave Malone a nod.

Just like that, it was over. We'd cleared the distillery and taken it intact. For the time being, at least.

Malone seemed satisfied, but then his face went curious and he looked behind him. My heart spiked again; I'd dropped my weapon but was ready to run at whatever needed attacking. Malone crouched, mumbling. He seemed to grope for something beneath one of the vats, then emerged holding the collar of a vampire so bland-looking, he'd vanish into the background in a beige-painted room.

"Well now," Malone said, holding the man up so everyone could see as the room otherwise finally fell silent. "What do we have here?"

42

BOSS

BACK AT HOME, we used silver chains to bind the bland man in the basement of our all-vampire building, Malone wringing his hands and making plans to extract information from our captured asset. The way Malone saw it, the vampire we'd taken was a gift from God, who Malone and Inez firmly believed in despite our kind's reputation as the damned. Nobody would know the prisoner hadn't been killed when we'd raided the distillery. Vampires burn when we die, and you can't do that dental records thing for vampires — because through a mechanism I've never understood, our teeth burn, too.

We'd known from the start that we couldn't hit both distilleries in the same night. Assuming any of us survived the first raid — and somehow, we all had — we couldn't regroup fast enough to do it sooner. We were still mostly ordinary folks who couldn't make two commando runs without at least a little bit of rest. But the rest was a catch-22, because even one night's delay would let Santori in on what we'd done. The second distillery would be much, much harder. If it was still possible to take it at all ... or even in the same location by tomorrow.

Malone figured that with the vampire tied in our basement, we'd just gained all the advantage we needed. He looked at me when he said it, because he meant for me to be the one to salvage the information.

"No," I said.

"Yes," Malone echoed.

But it wasn't that simple. What I'd done, in drinking Isaac's blood and pushing myself through two sets of severed maker ties to get a glimpse into his vampire mafia cousin, was an act of deep violence. Not the teeth kind — the brain and heart kind. I'd owed Isaac one for what he'd gotten Daisy into, but to tell the truth I didn't think I could do anything that sinister to anyone again. *Literally*, perhaps. Not everyone is as accessible as Isaac had been, and not everyone is observant enough for what they'd seen to be of any use. And besides, finding that final distillery was nowhere near necessary enough for me to give myself another set of shameful memories. We knew where it was already. If it moved, our captive wouldn't know where. I'd already tested him, just a little. He was almost mute in terms of blood ties, like so many of our modern kind.

"You play too nice, Maurice," Malone told me.

That pissed me off. I couldn't even say why, beyond the obvious. Something had crawled under my skin. I was nervous, agitated, angry, and fighting-mean. Everyone else was acting like we'd scored a great victory, but the way I saw things, we were worse off than ever. If we were able to take down the second distillery, great — *then* we'd have our victory. But for now, Thrill was still flowing. Santori still ruled the vampire underground. The vampire mafia wouldn't like what we'd done; if they found out who'd done it we'd be in some serious hot water. They'd already hit the very building we stupidly still inhabited. Until it was all over, I felt like we were wearing a massive target and asking for the same thing to happen again.

Malone said that first attack on our building had been coincidence; they'd hit one of the city's few all-vampire buildings to stir things up last time, not because they'd known the Crew lived there. In his mind, that meant the already-raided building was the safest spot, not the most dangerous. Lightning, he said, wouldn't strike twice.

I wanted to punch him. I should have felt happy, but instead I felt like murder.

I told Malone to set a guard. To watch more closely than usual. After that, after dodging him for a few hours while he tried to get me to mind-rape our captive, I decided I had to get out. Just to clear my head. I'd accepted a lot, but I couldn't take it anymore.

So I took a walk. I had no destination in mind.

Without intending to, I found myself walking past The Bomber.

The doors were boarded, taped up and nailed with signs. The air for two blocks, to my sensitive nose, smelled like liquor and brimstone. And, beneath it all, I caught the insidious scent of Thrill. It was like blood, times a thousand.

I stood on a porch opposite The Bomber — of a sundries store called Nat's — with my hands on the railing.

It had been a month, perhaps, since I'd worked behind the bar in Timothy's old speakeasy. A month since Timothy had last been alive. A month since Daisy's turning, since Celeste's new and blighted sense of potential for our social standing, since the arrival of the Crew and the mafia into our lives. A month, it seemed to me, since the days of contentment had buttonhooked on us, becoming something broken and twisted.

Now, standing before the place where everything had changed, the very air seemed heavy. I hadn't wanted this. I'd *never* wanted this. What I wouldn't have done to turn back the clock.

A voice, from the far side of the porch.

"Maurice, isn't it?"

I turned my head to see a slim vampire in a white suit and fedora emerging from the shadows. To my eyes, he was unfamiliar. But in my blood, I'd seen him before. I surprised myself by not reacting. I think I was simply too tired to be afraid.

He extended a hand.

"My name is Vincenzo Santori."

I didn't shake it. "I know who you are."

He dropped the hand, unoffended.

"May I join you?"

It struck me as a strange thing to say. He knew who I was, so he probably knew a lot more — that I'd raided and then destroyed one of his distilleries last night, perhaps. But his manner was civil. Polite.

I shrugged. He took up station just two feet away, both of us leaning on the railing of metal pipe, looking across at the home of my former life.

"Look over there," he said. He tipped his head toward the porch's other end. There was a huge man there I hadn't seen before, holding a tommy gun.

"Not to threaten you," Santori explained. "He's there, more than anything, to protect our conversation. From what I've heard, I respect you, Maurice. May I call you Maurice?" He didn't wait for an answer. "I know how old you are, and I know how fast and strong you are. If you decide you want to end our chat, I think it will end. Bobby is here to make sure you think twice. I'd like you to stay rather than making me do something I'd rather not. Will you stay, Maurice, and talk to me man to man?"

I shrugged.

Santori reached beneath his jacket. It made sense he'd be going for a wood-filled gun, and it was telling that I found I wouldn't mind. But instead of a weapon, Santori's hand emerged holding a flask. He offered it to me.

"I don't drink your poison," I told him.

"It's not the same formulation. It's more like whiskey for humans. And thanks to your little stunt last night, it's now a *very* limited vintage."

Without looking over, I laughed a little.

"You thought I might not know?" he asked.

I sighed and straightened. My eyes wandered, more from nostalgia than reconnaissance. In that quick glance, I saw Big Bobby With a Gun had a counterpart on the porch's other end. This one was smaller and more subtle, but also holding a tommy. And Santori, I saw, was wearing a chain mail vest. They'd be able to fill the porch with rounds and never fear hitting the boss.

"I knew you'd know."

Santori took a sip on his flask, breathed with gentlemanly contentment, and then put it away. He hadn't even stained his lips.

"And yet you did it anyway," he said. "It takes balls to cross me." He didn't project anger. This was something different.

"Someone has to."

"Do they? I'm not so sure. All I'm doing is providing a service that the people want, just like my friends in *La Cosa Nostra*. Nobody minds liquor. Only the government. The same is true of Thrilloglobin."

"Except that even the government doesn't mind Thrill. Right?"

That surprised him. But he laughed.

Then he said, "You have something I need. Or perhaps some*one*."

"I don't know what you're talking about."

"Of course you do." He gently struck the railing with his

fist, one-two-three. "I'm missing a chemist. I know he's still alive because I have other chemists. They work through blood ties, as a collective, and they can still feel him. But before you start thinking that gives you an advantage, it doesn't. You're not going to break into his brain unless you care to spend years talking to him, getting all the quirks of his personality and making a mental key. He's not wired like you and me. That's why we chose him. But I need him, Maurice. My operation is handicapped without him, and despite what you're no doubt planning, probably for dusk of the coming night, you will not be able to shut us down."

I ran through what he'd told me, looking for truth. It all felt real, right down to not being able to access the chemist the way I'd accessed Isaac's cousin. He felt, even at first touch, like someone with different wiring, perhaps on an alternate spectrum.

I looked at the gunmen. I shouldn't have to say it, and Santori wouldn't make me. Because the truth was, it didn't matter if I died. My dying earned Santori nothing. It certainly didn't get him his man back. The way I'd felt lately, dying would be a relief.

"You can't use him, can you?" I asked. "You can't see through his eyes, to find where we've got him."

"The other chemists are ... *difficult*," Santori admitted.

Nat's, in addition to being a store, was also a place where old men hung out to play checkers. So I sat into a rocker, enjoying the stalemate.

Santori sat opposite. He took a beat and said, "I'd like you to give him back."

"Why would I do that?"

"Because if you do, I'll consider everything forgiven."

"I don't particularly care if you forgive me."

"Are you sure?"

I nodded. "Even when we were still behaving, you slaughtered dozens of vampires who were just going about their business. *Families.*"

"That was the Council, not me."

"But they did those raids *for* you."

"The Council does nothing that is not for the Council," Santori said. "They are not my friends any more than they are yours." He sat forward, and for a bizarre moment I thought he might take my hands. "I've asked a lot of people about you. I know you tried to disappear when you came to town, but a vampire such as yourself stands out. I know your reputation. I know how, in Europe, you pushed back against the Council. I know you're a rebel. I'm a rebel too. Don't be so quick to dismiss me, Maurice. We're more alike than you know."

"I don't kill innocents."

"Maybe not with your own hands, but how many innocents have died *because* of you?"

"That's a ridiculous argument."

"And how many more innocents will die if you focus on me as your enemy, instead of the Council?" He pointed directly at me, voice becoming earnest. "See, that's what I don't think you're getting. Whether or not Thrill succeeds, the Council wins. They already have what they need from all of this. You aren't making *them* unhappy the way you're making me unhappy, my friend. All they want is violence and fear. Think about it. Are your actions creating less violence and fear in Chicago, or more?"

I looked away.

"Listen to me, Maurice," Santori said. "I am not your enemy. My organization is the only check this town has on the power of the Vampire Council. The police cannot help us. If we don't stand up for ourselves, who will?"

"And at the same time, why not make a lot of money?" I asked him.

"If we don't have resources, we have no way of fighting."

"Please. You're not freedom fighters. You're arm-in-arm with the mob."

"We need allies. We need friends, on the human side."

"Friends who rip you off to the tune of fifty percent of all you earn?"

That made Santori blink. Apparently he didn't know everything about me after all.

"It's being negotiated," he said.

"If I were in your shoes," I told him, "that kind of thing would strike me as extortion. If I were you, Capone's demand — fully *half* of something *I'd* built and manufactured and sold without any human help — would really piss me off."

He shifted in his chair. He hadn't known I knew. He hadn't seen this coming, and was having a hard time holding a straight face.

"What happens," I asked, "when you decide you've had enough of the mob's bullshit?"

"It's just the price of doing business in Chicago," he mumbled.

"So says Capone. But I hear the rumblings. I can feel it in my blood. How long before you flip on them? Or are you already cheating them, skimming profits off the top?"

He said nothing. His jaw moved side to side.

"What happens," I asked, "when you throw your little tantrum and Capone hits back? Are you really so deluded that you believe you'll survive? Am I really supposed to believe that my people will be *safer* in Chicago after you have your way?"

"Give me my chemist," he said, "so I can fix what you've broken, and together we can find out."

I stood. I shook my head. "Come and take him."

Santori stood to match me. He was having an impossible time, now, holding a civil expression. I knew the type. My very own *brother* was Santori's type. I couldn't back down. In this moment, the worst thing I could do would be to show weakness — or God forbid, make a deal. When an alpha hits you, you'd damn well hit back.

So I went on:

"You can't find him. Go ahead and kill me, if it makes you feel better. But I won't give him to you, and if you try to follow me to him, I'll know."

He watched me for a very long time. We were at stalemate. Then he said, "How's Celeste?"

"You won't find my wife either." It was bullshit. I prayed he couldn't hear my racing thoughts, because if he could, he'd know how terrified I actually was. Celeste and the chemist weren't in some sort of super-secret bunker; they were in a building downtown that the mob (or at least the Council) had already proven it could easily hit. I was counting on the city's size to cloak us, but it was already stupidly clear that we couldn't stay where we were.

I held my poker face.

Santori said, "And how's Daisy?"

I didn't bother to repeat myself. Daisy was in the same place, but I could tell he still felt he had an ace up his sleeve.

"Oh," he said, faux-casually picking a speck of dark lint off his pristine white suit sleeve, "I'm sure Daisy is with you. In this impenetrable, super-secret bunker of yours. I'm sure she's quite untouchable, along with the rest of your friends."

I kept my jaw still. Any movement might betray me.

"But she was human recently, wasn't she? I believe my associates and I already met her mother and brother."

My fingers gripped the metal bar. Breathing came deliberately slow. My heart beat faster, anticipating something yet-unknown — something Santori, at least, felt gave him leverage.

"Girl like that," he said, "must have other family *somewhere.*"

And then I realized: He had to mean her father, who'd gone missing. Or an aunt or a cousin or anyone else. All those people shared blood with Daisy. Seeing through human blood ties is harder than seeing through broken maker bonds, but what if Santori's people found one of her relatives and turned them? Blood is blood. If they didn't mind pushing, they'd be able to see right through her eyes.

When I didn't reply again, Santori put a hand on my shoulder.

"Think about it," he said, turning to go. "And maybe, if you're smart, you'll decide to meet me here tomorrow — same time, same place."

43

———

STUPID

I'VE NEVER RUN SO FAST.

I kept my blood sense perked, constantly looking over my shoulder. I knew I wasn't being watched; I'd have felt them if I was. Still I circled the city, in and out of buildings, up and down stairwells, taking long leaps from rooftop to rooftop, doing all I could to lose anyone who might be on my tail.

I broke into the apartment like a battering ram and told them all to throw their shit together. To pack a bag meant for never looking back.

Malone found me when my arm was wrist-deep in a duffel bag.

"You can't run."

"Watch me."

"They'll follow you."

"Let them try."

I'd already told Malone the whole story. The entire CVA had heard it. I'd briefed them out of duty, not preparation. I'd told *them* to run, too — or at the very least, to find a more secure location. Celeste had already run the Flynn twins to a suburban home far from our epicenter and glamoured the family there into believing Elsie and Evelyn were their own. She'd probably turned everyone crazy in the process, but it was better than staying here. I had no idea what the vampires would do, but it didn't matter. I'd done my duty. If they wanted to go down with the sinking ship, that was their business.

"Is it true? What they said about Daisy? Could they really find one of her relatives and—?"

"Yes. That's why on our way out of town, we're going to round them up."

"What about her father?"

"We'll find him."

"What about—?"

"We'll find them all, Malone."

"What if there's something she hasn't told you? Or that she's forgotten?"

"You worry about you. I'll worry about me."

Malone sat in the ancient red-leather chair in our room's corner. Its rusty springs creaked.

"You're a fucking fool," he said.

"Running doesn't make me a fool."

"You're wrong," he said with that accent of his. "It makes you a coward because you're running from what you know is right, and it makes you a son of a bitch because we said we were all in this together. It makes you a hypocrite because just yesterday, you were the one who declared we needed to hit the distilleries. It was *your* plan, Maurice. 'Stop the Thrill, stop the threat.' But—"

"We were too slow. We'll never be able to—"

But Malone wasn't done. "But above all those things, you're a *fool.* You're a moron, an idiot, a dumb fucking bunny. If you just meant to run because you were too chicken-shit to stay, I'd halfway understand. I wouldn't *respect* you more than the gum on my shoe, but I'd *understand*. But that's not why you're running, is it? No. Because when we get right down to it, you're actually *not* a coward. You're *not* a son of a bitch. You're *not* a hypocrite. I've known you long enough by now to know that you'll fight for what's right, even if it feels wrong. Even if you have to be dragged kicking and screaming. If only that were the problem now, I could let you go and be content. But it's not, now, is it?"

His soliloquy stopped me. I was holding the duffel by the handles, but had added nothing more to it.

"It's not?"

"No. The problem is that you're stupid."

"How am I stupid?"

"In every way that counts." He resettled himself, leaning forward with elbows on knees. There was a slight smirk on his face, as if we were both in on this absurd joke of my idiocy. "You think," he said, "that running makes you safest."

"I told you. We'll find her relatives and—"

"But what you're too dumb to realize, even though you know better, is that the best way to deal with a bully is to be a bully right back. You don't turn and scamper off when some big ass demands your lunch money, or says he'll beat you up after school. No. You turn right around and you punch him in the eye."

"We punched him when we took the distillery and caught the chemist. The problem is, rather than backing off, he's about to gather his friends and hit back."

Malone laughed. "This isn't *gay Pair-ee*," he said, practically flapping a hand with his over-the-top pronunciation of Paris. "This is *Chicago*. You don't just knock the bully down here. If you simply knock him down, he's gonna get right back up. No. You knock him to the dirt, and then you sit on his chest and you punch him some more. When your fists get sore, you stand up and you kick him. You pull a pipe from the fence; you rip a board from the shed, making sure there's still a good sharp nail in it. You can't walk away from Santori *now*, Maurice. The job's not done. You want him dealt with? Then *deal with him.* That's the Chicago way."

Finally, I found breath enough to respond.

"He'd know we were coming. He's got one distillery left, and he'll protect it."

Malone shook his head. "Lucky for us, he thinks you're as stupid as you are. I'm sure it won't be a cakewalk, but I'm willing to bet he expects you to show up at Nat's tomorrow to hand over his chemist, not stick your hand the rest of the way into the wasp's nest. He's got Thrill to make, and a distillery is hard to move. Moving it would mean days of disrupted production, maybe more, and thanks to us he's just got this one left." Malone shook his head. "No, you can bet it'll still be there tonight. Sure as sugar."

"If we're talking about stupid, it seems pretty stupid to stick your fist into a wasp's nest," I said.

"It's a sliding scale," Malone replied.

I considered. He was right. I wasn't a coward. I was just practical. And unfortunately, the most practical solution was the one nobody wanted to make. Going after that final factory felt like suicide — but if it worked, the war would end.

The building was chaotic all around us. The apartments below, above, and to both sides were filled with soldiers from Malone's crew. They'd already chosen a new HQ, in a meat-packing plant in the outskirts. If I came with, we could make the move unseen. I listened to the sounds of moving, wondering if the best idea, perhaps, was to go with them — to push through rather than turning away.

It was safe. We could keep the vampire mafia from finding us through one of Daisy's relatives by sedating her until it was all over, but it'd need to be through a hospital IV to keep up with her vampire metabolism, All those we cared about could lay low until we'd made that final, suicidal raid on the final distillery — for better or for worse.

"Okay," I said, setting down the duffel. "Let's do it."

44

CATWALK

MADGE AND SALLY swung the battering ram. The door blew open.

They were waiting for us.

Not with guns drawn. Not with slugs ready to fire, teeth ready to bite. But by the door were half a dozen extra guards, not there to work the factory but to protect it. Men dressed to the nines: pinstripe suits of the finest cuts, fedoras, shoes so shiny they caught the light.

We surprised them. Then they surprised us.

I didn't think. Sally and Dexter were closest, so I tackled both and fireman-carried them to the opposite side of the room. There wasn't as much to hide behind as before; we must have hit the bigger distillery the other night and saved the smaller, final one for our last stand. There were fewer casks, fewer chemistry sets. Lots of unthreaded pipes and cleared spots, as if equipment had been shifted as we'd become a thorn in the Thrill trade's side.

But the techs had guns, too.

And more importantly, they had teeth.

Unlike at the last raid, they didn't hesitate. I watched two leap at Rolf, pinning him down. Lenore wasn't far, she tackled back, rolled with one, and then Rolf freed his weapon and turned one to cinders. Lenore ripped out the second tech's throat, spraying the scaffolding with blood. The vampire thrashed and Lenore pounced away, but by the time his throat began to knit and he threatened to rise, Lenore was above him with one of the stakes she'd had on a bandolier over her shoulder. This one must have been older; his death came with an explosive *foomp!* and a spray of sparks amidst the ash.

One clambered up my back. I dropped, rolling over him, forgetting I still had Sally and Dexter in my grip. I banged Dexter's head and cut Sally's arm on a splintered wooden cask, then reached past her to rip away the large wooden splinter, like a stake, and jammed it into the vampire I'd tossed away. He, like more of the techs than I'd expected, was armed — this one with a pistol, aimed at my heart, the bullet striking me in the shoulder as I dodged away. The dodge sent my aim off target and I hit him too far right with my makeshift stake, collapsing a lung. The vampire gasped and a sucking sound came from the wound. It was enough distraction to knock him away, and then Sally kicked him, sending him through the wall of a cask, which turned out to be empty, and then she was in after him with her pistol drawn. I heard two pops and an explosive decompression, and then cinders filled the air.

I lost track of what was happening around me. I only knew, soon enough, that something was wrong. It was something in the air, something that hadn't been there before.

I caught Malone's eye, to my left. Then I saw hands grab him and pull him back, out of sight. I waited for a flash of fire and ash, but none came. Activity across the room drew my attention away: Lenore and Madge and Rolf, surrounded by a ring of gangsters, in a standoff like something from a kung-fu movie.

I scampered high, climbing the walls, making my way across a catwalk. The room was quieter than it should be. The fighting was too slow — perhaps too careful, too predictable, too well-organized. It gave me a chill, but at first I didn't see why.

Only when I was directly above the circle did I realize the problem.

I couldn't see Malone. He'd vanished, but I was reasonably sure I hadn't heard or seen or smelled him die. Beneath me, Lenore, Madge, and Rolf were surrounded, their weapons seemingly stripped ... but the vampires ringing them weren't opening fire. Most — even the techs, and that was strange — were strapped with pistols at least, tommy guns at worst. None were raised. They were in a traditional vampire standoff: fangs out, hands in claws, legs tensed, waiting to spring.

But waiting for what?

That's when I realized that I'd been watching them not through a random warehouse obstruction, but a net.

A net made of fine silver thread.

It fell. Instantly weakened, my friends dropped to the floor.

I realized the entire building had gone still. The fighting had stopped.

"*Mauriiiiiice,*" a voice called, insultingly sing-song. "Come out, come out, wherever you are!"

Below, I watched as the others were paraded out in silver bindings: Malone, Dexter, and Sally.

All six of them, alive. All six, in silver bondage.

With them was Santori, who apparently had known just how stupid I was or wasn't, depending on Malone's definition.

He'd known this would happen. He'd set a trap.

And then I realized. *Of course.* He needed them alive because he wanted his chemist back and didn't know where to find him ... so he intended to blood-fuck us all to find out.

But the joke was on him. Of the seven of us, only I knew where the chemist was. We'd always known this might happen, and only I was strong enough to resist. We'd sent the chemist off with an escort, who'd take him to places unknown, so that if everything else failed, the mission would endure. We needed him out of Santori's grasp, but ideally wanted to suck out the information he held. Fortunately, both could be served by the precaution we'd taken. The chemist's unusual mind required a particularly blunt-edged glamour to extract Thrill's secrets, and I just happened to know the bluntest glamourer who'd ever lived.

Even now, my blood could feel Celeste breaking into the chemist's brain.

"Maurice! I have your friends!" Santori called.

I watched him pace below. He looked up as his eyes scanned the room, but I was mostly concealed; he wouldn't see me unless he already knew I was up here. Malone, who must have seen me climb, did look up when nobody was looking — did catch my eye.

And that eye said, *Don't you come down, Maurice. Don't you motherfucking dare.*

"No?" Santori asked. "Well then ... how about a snack?"

He grabbed Dexter by the arm and pulled him forward. Lenore yelled and somehow, finding strength, pulled herself from beneath the silver net. She was too slow; Santori sunk his fangs into Dexter's neck and began to suck. The movement was animal. Dexter flexed and strained against him, weakened by the cuffs, but Santori's mouth stayed in place, my precise vision seeing every movement of his throat as he swallowed.

One of the gangsters grabbed Lenore and, without hesitating, staked her from behind. She was screaming as she burned, and Dexter screamed, and Santori's eyes lit with fury. He tossed Dexter aside. His mouth wore a goatee of blood, his white suit stained down its entire front from carotid flow. When Dexter came anyway, weakened by both blood loss and silver, Santori took his bleeding neck in his fist.

"Don't kill them! Not until I see!"

The gangster who'd staked Lenore raised his hands and backed away, but Santori grabbed his lapel with his free hand. The man blabbered, apologizing, but seconds after Santori had let go of his man, he'd thrust his fist through the gangster's chest. The vampire began to burn, as if staked. Santori's ring must have been made of wood.

Dexter staggered. Santori concentrated. Then, when he apparently learned nothing by sending his mind through Dexter's blood, he swore, turned, and ripped his gun from its shoulder holster to put it against Dexter's chest. Dexter's flesh muffled the shot. I heard only a slight pop before Dexter's back exploded, spraying blood all over the oak cask behind him. Then he began to burn, just like Lenore had.

The remaining four — Sally, Madge, Malone, and Rolf — struggled to no avail. They chattered, shouted; I could make out none of the words. But still Malone found my eye.

This was the contingency. This is what we promised. Every single one of us.

None of them knew the information Santori was trying to learn: the location of his missing chemist. None but me. I was a safe bet. Vampires as young as Santori and his people would never break through my defenses.

But Santori meant to try again anyway, to see what the others knew. He bit into Sally like a ripe peach. He seemed to sniff the air — to search her blood memory for the whereabouts of his chemist. He spit out her blood, raged, and ended her as he'd ended Dexter.

And then Madge.

And then Rolf.

When Santori reached Malone, he put a finger to his chest. Even from above, I could imagine how Santori must look up close. His face was painted with the blood of four vampires, his teeth red with our dark blood.

"*You*," he said. "I think that *your* blood knows what I'd like to know."

Malone's eyes flicked up. He must have known how I felt watching this and how much I wanted to drop like an avenging angel to save him. It would be easy.

Unless it wouldn't be.

Unless, against all odds, they captured me.

And unless, against *greater* odds, they managed to see through my blood.

It's not worth it, Malone had told me before we'd come. *If it all goes south, you need to take the chemist and leave. Let us go. As long as you don't try to be a hero in the moment, you can burn it all down later.*

If it comes down to you, Malone had said, *I'll let you die so I can fight them another day. If you have any respect in you, you'll do the same.*

But this time, Malone wasn't quick enough. Santori saw the gaze and looked up. I hid in time, but his pause, after he looked where I'd been, was suspicious.

"Maurice, my friend," he said, projecting his voice, "you are outnumbered. You will not escape." I chanced a peek and saw the way he twirled a finger in the air, indicating the walls, pointing for his soldiers to move to all corners and begin making their way skyward. "Come on down, and I will spare you and your friend's life."

I saw them coming, crawling up the walls to find me. I peeked toward the ceiling, and saw a propped-open vent just large enough for a small man like me to squeeze through.

I began making my way, a weight in my chest.

You can't run.

But what was I supposed to do?

If it goes bad, Malone had said, *that is the time you MUST run.*

The remains of the distillery's door banged open. I looked back, saw Santori's bloodied head turn.

A gangster approached below me, then spoke to Santori. The echoes were strange; I couldn't hear what was said. But whatever it was, it made Santori smile.

"Well then, Maurice," Santori said. "Let us see if *this* changes your mind."

A new gangster entered.

With Celeste, bound in silver, by his side.

45

OUTSIDE

SILVER WEAKENS ALL our vampire powers. The telepathy of blood is no exception. I could feel enough into Celeste to let her know I was close, and I could feel enough from her to know what must have happened. But beyond that, as far as details, she was too weak to send me anything.

It didn't matter. I knew enough.

I'd told her to stay behind. To stay out of the line of fire, because we'd all known there was a fair chance exactly what had happened might happen. It was okay; despite my deal with Malone (the one that said I'd keep the chemist's location secret, and run off with him if all went sour), I'd planned to fight to my death whether Santori had increased distillery security or not. I'd given myself a fifty-fifty chance of going home alive tonight ... but that was all okay, so long as Celeste stayed alive, and kept the chemist from their clutches.

But even now, I could feel the burning sense of impending loss within her. She'd known I might not return; of course I hadn't been able to keep that from her. So she'd followed. She'd come after us and stayed hidden — or so she'd thought. Fat load of good it had done us.

Now we'd both die, and Santori would win.

My eyes once again found the ceiling hatch, but I was already turning away. I couldn't run anymore, no matter what Malone wanted.

"Maurice?" Santori called.

"I'm coming," I said.

I watched Malone's head jerk toward the ground, swearing my name.

The vampires backed off. They gave me room below as I hung from the rafters and dropped. It was a long fall, enough to send intense pain up my legs. But then the pain was gone and it was just me in the warehouse's middle, waiting to see what happened next.

"I thought we had a deal," Santori said.

"You thought."

"Where is my chemist?"

"I don't know."

Santori went to Celeste. He pulled on a pair of thick leather gloves, then grabbed the silver chain around her neck. He twisted it like a noose, tightening until it bit into her flesh.

Celeste screamed.

"Where is he?" Santori repeated.

"Dead."

"Bullshit. The other chemists can feel him."

"When did they tell you that? Was it before or after I decided to take down your final distillery instead of delivering your boy with a big red bow? Think about it for a second: if I couldn't learn anything from your chemist but could weaken the trade by killing him, why *would* he still be alive?"

Santori's features twitched. I was bluffing, but what I'd said was plausible. *More* than plausible, actually. I knew he couldn't check with his other chemists now, and had to consider the possibility that I was telling the truth: that his man was dead — and one-third of Thrill's brainpower gone with him.

Instead of loosening, Santori tightened the chain on Celeste's neck. "If he's dead, there's no reason to spare any of you."

I reached into Celeste. I tried to see something it seemed her eyes were trying desperately to tell me. I could almost feel the silver on her throat as if it were on mine, but still I could sense weak thoughts trying to find me. Blood to blood, heart to heart.

Outside, she seemed to say. *Coming.*

I tried to say back, *What's outside? What's coming?*

But her eyes were glassy. Her muscles were sagging. It's nearly impossible to kill a vampire with silver, but if we're bound tight enough for long enough, it sure feels like it.

Santori's gun was out again. He held both ends of the silver lanyard in one gloved hand, but the wood-filled weapon kept drifting toward my wife's chest.

Santori turned to his lackey. The little one, with the lisp.

"Find out if it's true," Santori said. "Ask the chemists if Harris is dead."

Then he turned to me, holding Celeste's chain with a death grip. It was taking everything in me not to pounce, but Santori knew who he was dealing with. He'd kept just enough distance between us, and half of his gunmen had me in their sights. Their rounds were probably half lead, half birch, but it didn't matter. We'd used all our chain mail. We were just soft flesh, waiting for the kiss of wood.

My fists clenched. My blood boiled. I met Celeste's desperate eyes. She seemed to apologize. She seemed to be trying to tell me of something coming — a larger danger, perhaps, that was about to make our impossible situation a whole lot worse. I glanced at Malone, but there was no help there. He was as bound and fixed as she was, and the rest of our friends were dead.

Three vampires against them all. Against all those guns, all those fast hands. I might be able to get away alone, but I wouldn't leave them. Certainly not Celeste. But not Malone, either. Fuck our deal. After all that had happened, I wouldn't let them win. I wouldn't leave any of my friends behind.

I felt it from Celeste again: *Outside. Coming.*

And could only wait for all of us to die.

The little man had gone. He'd exited the distillery, presumably to find someone to talk to the chemists still within their circle. What would they do when they found out he was still alive? Would they torture Celeste before me, going until I gave us all up?

There was a pop outside the door, like something breaking.

We waited.

Then a knock came.

When Santori turned to look, he slackened Celeste's chain just enough. She mustered her strength and pushed to me all that I'd been missing. All she'd seen, and discovered, and done before the gangsters had caught her.

And I knew.

When the doors opened, I knew to hit the ground. I knew to scramble for Celeste, and Malone, and drag them under one of the big vats using the only thing I could reach: the silver ropes, which Santori had dropped when the visitors arrived.

The sun rose inside the distillery. I pulled on the silver, using every bit of diminishing strength I could muster.

Not long after, the whole place began to burn.

46

―――――

DAYLIGHT

FLUORESCENT LIGHTING HAS COME A VERY long way, but it's existed for longer than you'd think.

In 1929, the lights were big and bulky and fragile, and in order to get anything out of them, the newcomers who broke down the distillery doors with guns blazing had needed to create something both clunky and terrible.

They'd rigged a massive wagon, like something pulled behind a tractor. On its back were huge banks of fluorescent rigs, the bulbs peeking between bundles of wires. The wires themselves trailed behind the thing like a black and twining umbilicus — a dark hand reaching into the Chicago night for places unknown. I can only assume they'd used city connections to break into the power grid. I can only assume they'd raided a lab, snatching all the plant-growing and sterilizing lamps they could find to wire together.

I only saw bits of it, as I shoved my two charges beneath the cask of Thrill. As old as I am, I tolerate sunlight — real or false — far worse than young vampires. I looked away; I kept my shirt tucked to prevent my back's exposure to the world's worst sunburn. But from the rumbling of the cart and the screams and flames of our vampire antagonists, I could surmise what was going on: The newcomers were pushing their enormous artificial sun into the middle of the distillery, using tommy guns to drop anyone who tried to run.

I pushed us deeper. There wasn't much room, not far to go. The floor beneath us was cool stone, but the warehouse behind me, flooded with ultraviolet, felt like a sauna.

With effort, I managed to get the silver lanyard off of Celeste. Malone had freed himself of all but the handcuffs, which we'd need a key to handle.

"The fools," Malone said. "They'll kill themselves, same as us."

But now I could see the rest in Celeste's mind. And I said, "It's not the vampire mafia. Those are Capone's men."

Something rammed the cask. I looked back, unable to see what it was. The cask cracked, and blood began to drip into our hidey hole.

Gunshots. I squinted, trying to see into the room. It was painful. The entire room was bright light, not a shadow in sight.

Then the lights turned, showing me that there were men in hats behind them, shining the UV this way and that. I saw them as silhouettes, their outlines burned into my retinas.

I saw a human shredded by a blur, turned to hot meat that smacked the dust beyond our leaking cask. It was impossible to tell who was who — vampire? Human? The walls were covered in blood and ash and deadly light and gore.

Celeste was scrambling toward the light. I tried to pull her back, but I was too slow.

She hissed to someone. Someone in a suit, too far out where I couldn't see. I grabbed her leg but she kicked me away. I got a mental shout, which made me recoil and wait.

Celeste looked back. The light shifted, away from us. I

heard more vampires scream, smelled more burn. I was too warm. The air was thick, even the ambient UV making me sweat.

"Now," she said.

"What? Where?"

"*NOW!*"

She didn't wait. She rushed out. I was sure she'd be gunned down or washed in light and burn, but she did nothing of the kind. She squatted, impatient, gesturing for both Malone and me to come from within her narrow cone of relative darkness.

When I still didn't move, she sent me a garbled mental message, almost too fast to understand.

*I-MADE-A-DEAL-THEY-WILL-LET-US-GO-BUT-ONLY-IF-WE-**HURRY!***

She rolled her eyes, grabbing me and Malone by the scruffs. Then she dragged us around a vat, toward a hole someone had literally ripped in the distillery's outer wall. It was stone and metal, all sharp edges.

"*Come on!*"

There was a man beside it, guarding it, holding a gun. It was centered on my chest — on all of our chests — before I thought to move.

But the man didn't pull the trigger. Instead, he gestured impatiently toward the hole.

We went toward it, staying low.

There was the bark of a firearm. The man's head exploded and he fell to the ground. *Human.*

We looked back, and saw the vampire who'd fired the shot.

It was Blue Eyes, who'd found our shelter of shadow.

He shifted the gun past me, to center on Celeste. She was still too far from the door. She might make it before he shot her, but the odds weren't better than 50/50.

"Where do you think *you're* going?" he said.

Malone moved in front of me. His hands were still in silver handcuffs. He held them up and said, "We'll come quietly."

But of course this was my cue to run. Of course this was just Malone, one more time, trying to open a door for the bigger mission.

We *couldn't* go quietly. If we did that, it'd all be over. We had no cards left to play. I knew Malone was planning a diversion, just trying to draw Blue Eye's attention so we'd have time to escape.

"Malone," I said.

It was the last thing I ever said to him. Just as I was planning to duck past to gut Blue Eyes from behind, he pulled the trigger. The shot was exact. The wooden bullet pierced Malone's heart, and within seconds he'd begun to burn.

"*No!*" Celeste screamed, rushing forward.

I tried to dodge in front of her. I wasn't fast enough; Blue Eyes fired a volley of slugs through her right side. She hit the deck howling in pain, but already I could see her starting to heal.

She was on hands and knees when Blue Eyes put the muzzle of his weapon against her head — and then, when she raised her hands, against her heart.

I couldn't stop him. He was a vampire, same as me. I was fast, but not fast enough to stop a point-blank bullet.

"It's fine," I said. "You don't need to hurt her."

He pushed her back. His eyes were on me. He knew exactly who I was, and had to be remembering the blood of the last time we'd met.

His lips parted, showing a grin.

"I don't *need* to," he said. "But I *want* to."

Forearm muscles tightening, squeezing the trigger, and—

Something punched through his throat like a runner through a macabre finish line. Blood and sinew sprayed my face. Something long and wet struck my arm before dropping away: a tendon, perhaps. Blue Eyes lost motor control, his gun arm dropping, my fast hands snatching Celeste back to my side. He dropped to his knees but was already stirring, eyes already focusing, as the wound began to heel.

Blue Eyes blinked, skin knitting, and rose to find Little Sammy with a wood-spitting weapon against his chest.

"This is *our* town," Sammy said.

And Blue Eyes, when the bullet entered his chest, practically exploded.

I couldn't move. Sammy stood across from me and Celeste. Malone was gone; he was the pile of ash beside us. Blue Eyes's evidence covered our clothes, and beyond Sammy, the fake daylight continued to flash. The front door was open, and judging from the slowing melee, I had to assume what had happened was almost over. The walls were burning. The casks, full of their illicit Thrill, were leaking and curdling in the heat.

I waited for Sammy to raise his weapon.

But instead, he gave me and Celeste a barely perceptible nod and turned away.

47

ENEMY OF MY ENEMY

MY BLOOD SENSE was alive and burning. I didn't want to rush home, for fear someone might follow. I don't know, even now, if what I felt was blood ties or plain old intuition. All I knew was that the city was unrestful tonight.

Nobody was out. Even in the human quarters. Even at the old speakeasies, the old mob haunts. At all the usual spots, only a skeleton crew remained. It was as if the world itself knew everything had just turned upside down.

We ended up climbing a hill to wait it out. From there, we watched the distillery fire grow. The burn of dying vampires had started it, but the mob must have doused the place in accelerant to keep it going.

"You went to Sammy," I said as I sat beside Celeste.

"They were planning an ambush. It was the only way."

"But ... *the mafia,* Celeste."

"I told them what you told me. Then I showed them the books you confiscated the other night, from the second-to-last distillery. You were right, Maurice. The vampires were skimming. They were planning a move against the mob. I figured the enemy of our enemy might want to be our friend."

I sat with that. It was so predictable. My kind, they're infected with greed — with a need to never be subjugated, to always feel on top. Well. That wasn't such a great idea in Alphonse Capone's Chicago.

Not long ago, we'd seen something large and unwieldy leaving the burning distillery building. If I listened very carefully, I could hear its wheels squeaking. They'd left their fluorescent sun on until the fire had become too much to handle. None would remain in the shadows tonight.

"Is this the end?" Celeste asked me.

"The distilleries are gone. The stores of Thrill are either gone ... or, if they have a stash, on their way to *being* gone. They've made enemies of the mob, who control the speakeasies, both vampire and human, plus the distribution. So yes. I'd say they are out of business."

"They have their chemists."

I'd already decided to kill the one we had in custody.

"For now," I said.

And that would be enough. The vampire mafia would lose council support same as they lost mob support. Maybe we could pursue change, now that the worst was over. There had to be good vampires left who'd stand up — who'd make sure Thrill never returned, in a city where it had made so many enemies.

"At least Santori is dead," she said.

But I wasn't so sure. He'd been right by the door when the false sun had been carted in, and he'd surely been top of the mob's hit list. But for some reason, I was less than certain. But that, too, was okay. For now. Until the time came to shake down another day.

Celeste hugged up against me. We needed to go and we wanted to go.

But for the moment, I just wanted to watch it all happen.

We sat and held hands, to watch Santori and Logan's enterprise burn.

48

———

WALK

WE DIDN'T TAKE any chances. I did my mental-kegels thing, holding in all the thoughts that might leak and reveal us to a particularly gifted glamourer — someone I didn't expect to find, but safe felt better than sorry. Celeste took a simpler path to mental silence; she draped herself in the silver chain Santori had first bound her with. It made her slow and caused her pain, but Celeste didn't care. Slow was good because it made for safety, and pain didn't matter because despite our heavy losses, at least we could finally let it go.

She was huffing and puffing as we walked through the outskirts like humans, making for the packing plant. I wanted to loosen her silver, but she seemed to be wearing it like penance. In truth, her deal with the human mafia had saved our lives. But inside, I was sure that the second she removed her silver, she'd feel the guilt that came with it. She felt responsible for all our friends' deaths — but especially for Malone, who'd died trying to protect us.

Murdered like an animal, even as he'd gone to surrender.

I wrapped my arm around Celeste, fighting the urge to pull away from the silver that draped her. It made me feel heavy —

but then again, the deaths of the Crew were on my conscience, too. I could bear a yoke if she could.

"You're going to kill him, aren't you? The chemist?"

I was immediately defensive. "It's not an eye for an eye, Celeste. His mind is one-third responsible for holding the Thrill recipe. If he lives or if I let him go, they'll just start new distilleries and start it up all over again. Taking him out of the equation will at least slow them down. Give the mafia time to clean up a bit more, or drive them out of town."

"No, no ..." She held my hand. "I wasn't saying you shouldn't. I just ..."

That thought seemed to go nowhere.

Then: "Are you happy, Maurice?"

"Why?"

"You said that it didn't matter who had to make a sacrifice, so long as the Thrill trade ended. I know it can start back up, but—"

I cut her off. "I'm happy about that."

"And the rest?"

"Do you mean all the death? Am I happy about that?"

She sighed. I could tell she was trying to find an impossible silver lining on a pitch-black cloud.

I beat her to the next words, understanding her meaning.

"I'm grateful that our family survived. I'm grateful we put an end to it. But ... Jesus, Celeste. *Malone. Sally. Madge. Dexter and Lenore. Rolf.* Not to mention the Flynns and Timothy and all those vampires in the club, and in our old building."

I thought she might say more, but she didn't.

We walked. I tried to feel satisfied. I tried to see the victory. The happy ending. I realized there wasn't one, but that was how life worked. Life was shit and shine, and all you could hope for was the latter outweighing the former.

At least we had our family.

At least we'd slowed them down.

At least we had, in our own little way, made the vampire world that much safer.

And — this one was a biggie — we'd cut Logan and his Vampire Council right off at the balls. Good luck raking in more illicit Thrill profits, with which to buy lawmakers and bribe their way to power. And good luck playing the fear card to push unfair laws, now that we'd be able to tell the world the story of how the bad guys had finally gotten their due. We might even be able to drop some hints about Logan's involvement. Ruffle some feathers. What the hell; I was good at that.

And perhaps most importantly, I'd get to drop my mantle. To stop being a crusader. To go back into my little isolated capsule again, and stop being so fucking *vampire* all the time.

I tried very hard to put the twinge of a smile on my face.

Little by little, as our new home came into view, that smile found its place for both of us.

49

DARKER

ANNABEL WAITED FOR MORE, but the vampire was silent.

"So you won," she finally said. "You beat them."

Maurice didn't answer. He was solemn, staring off into the distance.

Something was still on his mind. Something that made the dark office feel a thousand times darker. Something that hung like a pall above them, waiting to make its presence known.

"Maurice?" Annabel said.

"*Maurice ... ?*"

50

———

SILVER

IT'S ALMOST impossible for silver to kill a vampire.

Unless, of course, you make a silver nitrate solution, then hook it directly into a vein.

It's a really impractical solution. We're very hard to catch, and the idea of catching us and *then* pinning us down for the IV treatment blurs into absurdity. That's why humans kill us by opening our homes to the sun or staking us in our sleep. It's why other vampires kill us with claws or beheadings — or, thanks to a certain innovative faction, using wooden bullets. We're hard to take alive, and there's no reason to do so unless you're a sadistic son of a bitch who wants to make a point.

The piles of ash that had once been the packing plant's guards had not been worthy of making that point.

The fire still burning in the plant's office — which I think might have been Malone's wife Inez, judging by the purse nearby — had not been worthy of that point.

Even the three strapping vampires we'd stationed in the chemist's room hadn't been worth the effort of a silver nitrate drip. Near as Celeste and I could tell, they'd been staked with legs off of a chair, the remains of which was canted broken in a corner.

The chemist had been freed from his captors — surely back with his chemist fellows by now — and that must have been enough, as far as dispatching those who'd been holding him was concerned.

But there *was* a point worth making, in the raided meat-packing plant that night.

We found it amidst the charred bodies of the rest of our friends, who'd been exterminated while we'd been away.

The thing on Daisy's mattress didn't look like Daisy anymore. Her skin was dark marble: black interwoven with dazzling lines of silver. Her eyes, barely open, were like mirrors. Her fingers seemed brittle and about to break off. Even from the doorway I could smell the tang of metal coming off her like sweat. The lights were dim but pointedly on, shining at the center. She'd been spot-lighted. Whoever had done this had wanted to make sure we saw.

Celeste's face broke and she bolted to the bed, legs failing before she reached Daisy's side. She must have seen what had happened because she yanked the IV line from the back of Daisy's hand, but it was clear to me, as I found myself frozen in the doorway, that the damage had already been done. The vial at the IV's top was empty, its deadly solution already circu-lating Daisy's veins.

"Daisy! Wake up!"

Celeste was slapping her face lightly, cradling her drooping hand. She wasn't dead. Yet. But with a full vial of silver nitrate inside her, it wouldn't be long. She couldn't expel it the way she could expel a lead bullet. Silver in the blood is like cancer. It doesn't just kill us; it kills our ability to rid ourselves of it. She was a soldier bleeding out in battle, a terminal patient well into her final hour.

Daisy tried to roll and threw up. Tried to shift and pissed herself. It broke something so profound inside me, I was unable to think.

"Daisy! Wake up! It's Mommy!"

Weak knees. I think I was crying. Celeste certainly was. I couldn't process anything else. All I heard was Celeste using that word. She'd never used it before, but now it came spilling out, desperate like a prayer.

Mommy.

Daisy, it's Mommy.

"Mommy?" Daisy croaked.

Celeste tried a brave smile. It was too wide, too falsely manic. She gripped Daisy's hand, and I heard Daisy's skin crackle as if her skin were dry bark.

"Celeste," I began. Too quiet to be heard.

"Who did this to you?" Celeste barked. Now petting her hair, now running a hand down her back, sobbing without control. "Who did this?"

"Men."

I'd grabbed the doorway when we'd entered. The frame broke off in my hand, crushed to powder.

What *else* had they done? What the hell had they done to our baby, to make their motherfucking point?

"You'll be okay. I took the needle out, Baby."

But she was lying. To Daisy and to herself. Daisy had minutes left. Seconds.

I went to her. Knelt beside Celeste, whose face was a wet mess.

She saw me. Stretched out a hand.

"I tried to fight them," she told me, reaching to touch my fingers. She missed, so I took hers instead. Her skin was like sandpaper. It wouldn't stand the weight of me clasping. I could feel it wanting to slough off like a one-finger glove. "I tried to be like you taught me."

I wiped my face. Once. Twice. There were things I wanted to say, but I wouldn't. Not until she was finally gone.

She couldn't fight them because we'd sedated her — to keep her mind quiet, to keep them from tunneling through the blood of unknown relatives to find Daisy, then find us. But when they'd found her anyway, all our precautions had done was make it easy for them. Sleeping draught had turned her into a sitting duck. It was dark out, and she'd miles of open land through which to escape. But she hadn't been able. Because of us, she'd only been able to lay here while they'd switched her sedative for liquid death.

"It's okay," was all I could say.

Celeste, petting her hair. Both of us ignoring that as she petted, her scalp failed and all that pretty brown hair came out by the roots.

"*Daisy,*" Celeste said.

But her breathing had stopped. Her face went from marble to grey, like a statue cast in fragile ash. Fingers crumbled in our fingers, and all I could do was watch the grains fall to the ground.

Each was like a tiny bomb.

They hadn't gotten to Daisy through Daisy. The sedative prevented it.

An ash, hitting the floor beneath our dead daughter.

They hadn't gotten to Daisy through us. We would have felt it.

We hadn't been followed.

Or snooped.

And that told me that somehow, some way, we'd been given up by someone inside.

I let go of what had, until so recently, been Daisy's hand.

I stood.

Celeste looked up at me. In her eyes, I saw fear. At the same time, something in the other room tottered and dropped. It was a sound like someone else coming. Someone standing by and waiting for us to make our macabre discovery before rushing in to finish us off.

"We have to go," she said. "Before they come for us, too."

But no. That was something the old Maurice might have believed.

I barely heard my own answer.

To Celeste, I said, "That's the last thing we should do."

51
_____

FISTS

"OH, GREAT," Isaac said. "Not *you* fuc—"

He might have been about to swear at me, but I never found out. I thrust my fist into his abdomen, grabbed his small intestine, then spun him around and used it to tie off his windpipe. Across the room, Charles flexed to stand, but I stared him down. "Move toward me," I said, "and you'll never move again."

He seemed to consider, then wisely sat, body insultingly at the ready.

Isaac was gagging. My hands were running with blood and guts and leaking shit. It smelled like hell.

He couldn't speak. It didn't matter. I used my teeth to rip off half of his face, then licked the wound to meet his blood. Last time, I'd had to push. This time, I tapped something new and something I've never tapped since. The force of my blood intrusion was like a bus through a pane of glass. If Isaac hadn't already been asphyxiating, the force would have stopped his breath.

Through one maker. Through another. Into Isaac's kin, who I felt collapse when my fist entered his brain.

I dropped Isaac, his own intestine still around his throat.

He gasped, healing around it, pushing the gore aside.

"He felt that," Isaac said, just petulant enough for bravado, not quite petulant to make me hurt him again. "My cousin? You just knocked him over, and he knows you were there."

I thought of the vampire I'd just seen into, through Isaac's blood. Yes, he'd felt me. But he'd feared me, too.

I wanted to break Isaac in half. But my fury was misplaced, and I knew it.

"You didn't give us away," I said.

"Give you away for what?"

"Your stupid, lazy fucking ass didn't even *know* about the raids. *We're all dead,* and you were just sitting up here, high on Thrill."

"You don't look dead to me," Isaac said.

I hit him so hard, his neck broke.

Then, knowing a tantrum when I see one (but not exactly minding Isaac's pain to get there), I stood. My fists wouldn't unclench. I couldn't stop seeing red, and not just from Isaac's abundant blood.

"Where is it? Where do they meet?" I demanded.

"Who?"

I made to strike, and Isaac held up his hands.

"I don't know what you're talking about! I'm *serious*, Maurice, shit!"

Then I said what I had, of course, already realized.

"You don't know *that*, either." But of course he didn't. It was his vampire mafia cousin who knew. And if I focused just right ...

I stepped away from Isaac and Charles. It was night, so I looked out the window. I trained my focus on the blood in my gut. On Isaac's blood, with all its ties ... before it slipped away.

A scene began to unfold inside my mind.

A room of gangsters, nowhere near their dapper selves. They wear tatters, fine suits burnt, skin exposed, caked with blood from wounds long since healed. There is dirt and mud on the plush carpet underfoot, dragged in from shoes that have walked here through culverts and sewers, half alive and half dead, crippled more by the UV light than by silver or stakes. The air smells rank, like meat gone bad.

Someone's eyes, my eyes, see hands, my hands, as they try to adjust a suit that's been nearly halved, and this vampire (me) crosses in front of the big table, and there is the boss, not far from him (me), playing poker and losing, all his emotion in what's just gone so wrong.

A small man approaches and says, "The chemitht hath rejoined the collective without problem, sir."

And the boss, Santori, says, "I want us out of here tonight."

I let my attention slip from the blood. Returning to Maurice, to my own body. I was no longer inside the mobster's mind, but something in me remained alive and furiously hungry. I let it go. I let my blood take Isaac's blood through places I've always been able. Places a decent vampire should know better than to go.

Into others — those barely related. It's another thing, like flying, that only adrenaline can bring out of me.

I realized: *They're leaving town.*

The vampire mafia was planning to find a new place, away from Capone, away from the rest of their new and old enemies.

With that, I had two thoughts.

The first was: *We've done it after all. We drove the vampire mafia and the Thrill trade out of Chicago.*

My fists clenched hard enough to drive fingernails through the meat of my palm.

My second thought was, *But that's not nearly good enough.*

52

FUGUE

I SEE myself in a series of moving images. I am not *in* them so much as *of* them. I am both observer and observed. I do not remember control. All I remember is that this is what happened:

Approaching the club, the bouncer asks me for the password. He's wearing a pistol and his hand never leaves its butt. For some reason, this infuriates me. I suddenly wonder what's become of us. I've never liked being a vampire, but maybe that's because I've actually liked it *far too much*. The others? Especially today and then, in America? *They* are the ones who don't want to be vampires. Every year they refine their standards of physical beauty and ability. Every year, they become more like a clique the rest of us aren't good enough to join. And in 1929, they all wear guns. Like humans.

A real vampire fights with tooth and claw and speed and strength.

Like I do, when he makes the mistake of grabbing his stupid little pop gun.

I rip his throat from his neck. I zip around him while he staggers, letting him think he can touch me. I sever limbs, just to show him what a true monster can do.

When I get serious, he doesn't last long.

Nor do the two men inside.

Nor the three who come at me in the red-lined hallway.

I walk on without worry and ...

Into the room they call the Parlor. I know this because the vampire I invaded earlier knows this — plus the two from Hall Patrol who I similarly invaded, drinking their blood while the last sputtered and tried to breathe. I know the club's entire blueprint before long, and if I listen carefully, I find I can hear their every step. Their every rustle, as they turn with clothes sliding across their skin. It feels easy. I simply let myself be. It's not *trying to do* so much as a *trying not to resist*. Because this is what vampires have always done, before we forgot.

Back through my own bloodline.

Borrowing the anger of a great-great grandmother, the insanity of a cousin two generations farther back.

Not long ago, we were creatures in the shadows.

As I am now all over again, entering the club's bedrooms where gangsters screw their whores, where I paint the walls red before turning them to ash, shooing the whores away, naked and screaming.

As I am when I enter the offices and read all there is to learn about what Santori has built. Where I light the drapes and the desks and the paperwork on fire. As I am when I enter the shed beyond and find two gas cans, with which I rush back and forth using supernatural speed, filling the rooms with amber joy. When they see me, I deal with them. But so many are sleeping, and vampires sleep like the dead. Because we *are* the dead. And the sun is already rising.

Half the house is on fire before the other half even knows I'm there.

And then I enter the room they call the Armory, where ...

Big fat gangsters, mostly men and some women, counting their money, one of them on the phone with someone he keeps calling Logan, surely *the* Logan, and I make sure to keep the connection live even after I've bent iron newel posts around all the gangsters except the one I mean to take apart piece by piece. Logan's voice, confused by the screams, demands, *"Who is this?"* I don't know why I pick up the receiver, but I do. And into it, I say, "You're done in Chicago. You're *done*, unless you want to end up like the things that used to be your friends." Then I hang up. I never actually answer Logan's question.

Because this is the Armory, a few of them are able to get to weapons before I start disassembling bodies. But the silly fools are armed against humans, not vampires. Why would a *vampire* turn on them? Who would have the nerve?

They fill me so full of lead, I feel a ball form in my belly. One of them blows half my brain out of my head, but somehow my body remembers while my mind is out of order. When I blink awake with my skull whole again, there are no guns and nobody left to use them. Just what has burned around me.

And then, through some passage or primitive phone or dumbwaiter, I heard someone shout ...

... for me to get out *now*, while I still fucking can, while my balls are still intact and attached to my body, if I fucking know what's good for me.

But in that voice, I can hear terror. Besides, I know something the voice does not: I don't care if I die. I've made my peace. I would fear for Celeste, but I know none of them are near her or will ever reach her. I have beads on all of them. They won't get close while I'm headed upstairs, and even if they do, I very much hope they'll try because I have a sneaking suspicion I'm on some sort of berserker run, out of my mother-fucking mind with two fists made of fire. I could fly, right now. I could practically travel through time, the way I feel. Because bring it on, while I'm still crazy enough to ...

Up to the second floor, this space done up like the red lounge below with its giant golden relief of the lion's face, with the elegant scrollwork, with the smell of burning so close behind me, I think my skin might blister. The vampire mafia's club is larger than I expect. It's burning slower. But that's okay. *The better to slowly torture you with, my pretty.* Until I run into ...

Three tall, strong guards, two female and one male. All highly trained. I'm sure, as they face me with swords and smaller blades, each lined and tipped with wood, that they were once Council Guard. They strike me as the elitist of the elite. The best of the best. And why not? Santori wanted the best around him, so he bribed them away from Logan and took them for himself. One more bit of proof that as far as vampires go, there's no honor among thieves.

One thrusts at me. I dodge, spin around, and break wrists to drive the assailant's sword into his own back. The other two come at me, opposite-charges style, so I leap and cling to a chandelier while they collide beneath me. I fall atop one, then use her like a shield when the other comes driving. He misses, shanks her in the shoulder, so I pick my wounded shield up and throw her at him. I'm on them in seconds, ripping off the head of the first and then piling furniture atop the other to pin his neck until the sheer force of it breaks his cervical vertebrae and severs his spinal column and he begins to burn, too.

Through the door, to ...

Santori. Not even holding a weapon. Hands up. Like a coward. Like a coward with a fake smile, as if he's still in control here, as if he has something to offer that I'd actually care to hear.

"Maurice. Thank God. You just showed me how bad my security is. Well done."

Silence from me.

"I had an idea." He tries to reach into a pocket, still shredded from his fight with the real mafia. He fumbles, tries the other pocket, comes up empty. "I had an idea, Maurice. You're smart. You're ambitious. We could really be assets to each other."

I walk toward him. Without hurry.

"You can run the trade," he says. "I'll give you half. Run it however you want."

"There's no supply," I hear myself saying. "We burned you down."

"But I have my chemists. You can't get them, Maurice! We sent them to ..."

Myself, before coming here, having seen the chemists in another's blood, finding where they're kept, all foolishly together. Popping their tops one by one. They make black totems when they burn, once I am done with them.

. . .

"They're dead," I tell Santori now. "All three of them."

"Well ... then we can find others! We can ..."

"I'm not interested."

"I'm the only one who knows where the money is!" Santori shouts, desperate for an ace. " I'm the only one who knows ... !"

Myself, earlier, finding Isaac's cousin after he left the club but before I came here, after he'd gone home. Using the cousin to find the bookkeeper, the bookkeeper to find the books, the books to find the money. That, I burned, too.

And back to Santori, more and more nervous. Backstepping. Tripping as I walk toward him.

He decides to be brave.

Grabbing the most ludicrous thing — a wooden letter-opener from his desk — he faces me like a street thug with a dagger.

"*Fuck you, then! Fuck you and your mother, Maurice!* You think you can cross me in my town? You don't know who the fuck you're dealing with!"

I blur to him without effort. These stupid kids today, they don't realize how much power a vampire gains after two thousand years of life. I'm able to return the letter opener to his desk, back to its little holder, before pinning him against the wall.

And he transforms again.

Crying now.

Like a pussy.

"*I'm sorry, okay!* I'm sorry I tracked down Daisy's—!"

I remove his lungs. He gasps in front of me.

"You're forgiven," I tell him.

Then I separate head from neck using my teeth.

It went on. And on. Looking back, it's impossible to know the forward march of time. I'm pretty sure I burned the mob's cash and killed the chemists before visiting the club, but the order of the rest is a guess at best. I don't even remember how I found each link in the chain, or what I did to each. It's all a fugue.

I know only that I left scorched earth behind me.

By the time Santori's body was burning beneath my grip, the sun was already rising. I didn't care. I could see no possibility other than the most dangerous one. So I left through the door that faced away from the sun, then ran from shadow to shadow. As I moved around that morning, I had to make a few sprints in the daylight, but the sun was low, and I huddled beneath a coat to stop the worst of it. More than once I caught fire. Each time I shook it off. The pain felt tolerable — good, even. It's dumb luck, in retrospect, that I survived. I only knew that nothing could remain when I was done — and if that meant dying by exposure, so it would have to be.

I burned all three emptied-out distilleries, just in case. The one that was already burned, I burned again.

So it was for Isaac's cousin's house.

And the red lion club.

And the homes of the chemists.

I don't know when I sought out the rest of their network, or how. I knew only by the news reports the next day, announcing murders (with strangely missing bodies) and blazes all over town. To this day, I don't know who I killed or what I burned.

But I knew, that night, who it was that needed to pay.

They were the ones who'd crossed us.

They were the ones who'd taken Daisy from us.

She, who'd become everything that still seemed to matter.

When I returned to Celeste, I was empty. I was barely ambulatory. She fed me on her own blood, purely for the thirst of it, then brought home two drifters to sate me. This, she did at great personal risk. The sun was still out. She'd hunted in the early morning shadows same as I had, because — and this, she told me later — she'd been sure I'd die without nourishment to revive me.

Maybe.

Because in truth, vampires can't die from thirst.

But they're not supposed to be able to die from broken hearts, either.

53
————————

MONSTER

THE OFFICE WAS QUIETER than the subaural echo of an empty tomb. Silent except for the ticking of that same clock in the corner. The one Annabel got from a drug rep. Or was it an uninventive cousin? She couldn't remember. But she couldn't see it from here, and for some reason it felt wrong to turn her wrist and look at her watch. For now. For now, she needed to sit still and listen, and keep her peace.

Maurice had been talking for hours. It must be the middle of the night. Her husband was probably worried. Oh, who was she kidding?

"Did it help?" Annabel asked.

Maurice turned his head without lifting it from the pillow. It looked like he'd forgotten she was there.

"Did you feel better, afterward?" she tried again.

"No. I felt worse."

"Celeste?"

"We never really talked about it. We were quiet for a few days after that, just milling around our apartment and keeping out of each other's way. I remember feeling like we were alone inside of a crowded city. Every place we went — every place we tried to move after it was all over — seemed too empty. We were finally being left alone in Chicago, and I couldn't take it."

"Did the vampire mafia ever come after you?"

"*What* vampire mafia?" Maurice gave a bitter laugh. "I'd wiped it from the planet. Almost all of it was in Chicago at the time, and after Logan's regime grew, local Councils filled the void the mafia might once have been able to fill."

"Logan, then?"

"Let's just say we've had our disagreements."

The way he said it, Annabel decided not to ask further.

Then Maurice turned to her and said, "So? What do you think?"

"What do I *think?*"

"I've been sitting here listening to my own story," Maurice went on, "and I have some idea what *I'd* think in your shoes, hearing it for the first time."

"You wanted to know about Daisy," Annabel said. "You wanted to explore why you turned her, as relates to the reason you turned ..." She groped for the name, but it was like it didn't exist. Nothing modern existed. Her mind was still in the twenties.

"Reginald," Maurice said.

"Yes. *Reginald.* Does the relationship between your three turnings — him, Daisy, and Celeste — still strike you as most important?"

Maurice, still reclining, shrugged. "Does it strike *you* as most important?"

Annabel was torn. As a psychiatrist, she was most interested in Maurice's self-hating tendencies and his identity crisis about the vampire he'd be until the day he died. But right now, something deep inside wanted to focus on Daisy, same as his story had focused on Daisy. There was so much she didn't understand. So much that still must be incubating inside that vampire brain of his.

"I think we should explore whatever's bothering you most."

Maurice stood from the couch. Annabel thought he'd go for more wine, but instead he went and stood with his back to her, his face to the window.

"I came here because I was bothered about Reginald," the vampire said. "He'll go on trial, and he'll die. It won't matter that he lived. All that will remain will be a scar. Up here." Maurice touched his temple. "When you lose progeny, you feel it forever. I will have done that to him. To Reginald and to myself, just like I did it to Daisy. And ... *yes*. Right now, that's what's bothering me most. I'd managed to forget most of what I just told you, yet I dredged it all up. But for what?"

"To heal," Annabel said.

He spun. She saw anger, and it startled her.

"To heal *what*? She's still dead. I could have left her alone. *I should have let her die.*"

"You don't mean that," Annabel said.

"Don't I? What did I do for her, other than give her pain? She was born drug-addicted and never shook it free. Her family didn't have to die; that happened because I didn't pay enough attention. The war wouldn't have happened if I hadn't turned her. If there'd been nobody for Isaac to drag off and party with, I'd never have gotten involved. Maybe I wouldn't even have killed those first mobsters, that night at The Bomber."

"Yes," Annabel said, holding her ground, "and who knows *what* the vampire mafia would be up to today?"

Maurice grunted.

"What about Thrill?" she asked. "Can they still make it?"

"Not without the chemists. Not without the paperwork and places I burned. Today, they'd have file backups all over the world — but this was the twenties, and the internet didn't exist. If someone had gone back to making it, I think we'd have heard of it by now."

"You said your Vampire Council was involved in Thrill bootlegging ..."

"Yes, and they got away with it. Logan is still in power."

"But how much richer would they have been, if you hadn't stopped the trade? How much *more* power would they have if you hadn't shut down the mafia?"

"You don't know what our society has become," Maurice said, "with or without Chicago muscle."

"*I know,*" Annabel countered, "that if you hadn't intervened, it would have become something worse."

He was still at the window, but now he turned. The expression on his face was skeptically hopeful, wanting to believe.

"You can't know that," he said. But she could see him thinking, agreeing with her without wanting to. In his story, he'd suggested things worse than the Council. Greater evils that even Logan was keeping at bay ... and that might have come to power, if there'd been funding and sway.

"Of course I can't," Annabel told him, "but you'd be stupid not to agree anyway."

There was a long, tense beat. She'd taken a calculated risk. His story had been full of others calling him stupid, and she hoped he'd take the lesson.

Maurice smiled. Only barely, but he smiled.

"Sit down, Maurice. Please," she said.

He looked at the clock she couldn't see and said, "No. I've taken up enough of your time."

"I don't mind."

"It's very late. You need sleep, and I need to feed."

Spontaneously, with absolutely no thought or sense, Annabel blurted, "Feed on me."

He laughed. But Annabel rose. Obeying an absurd impulse, she took his hand. It was cold.

"I'm serious. I need to know more."

"What more?"

"All of it. Everything." Her eyes went to her desk, which was full of photographs of other people's babies: cousins, nieces, nephews, celebrations even from unrelated friends. There wasn't one picture of her horrible husband, probably because she found him horrible. They'd been together for ... oh, she didn't even know how long. And yet he didn't warrant a picture? *Nothing* in her own life merited a photograph on her desk? What had she done with herself all these years? After hearing Maurice's story, her adventures seemed lacking. She was so ... *ordinary*.

She realized she was begging. Subtly, but begging nonetheless. She backed off, letting go of his hand. She was a professional, after all.

"I ..." she stammered. "It's just ... *You* need more. We've barely scratched the surface."

He took a long breath, again looking out the window. What did he see out there, with his vampire eyes? What could he hear? What could he smell on Annabel, and how fast could he strike if he chose to do so? She realized, quite suddenly, that she was helpless. She was with an animal, and only his choices were keeping her alive.

"I changed my mind," he said.

Annabel shifted in her chair. The skin of her neck prickled.

He looked at her, seemed to realize what she was thinking, and said, "About Daisy, I mean."

"What about her?"

"I suppose I feel better."

"Oh. Good. But still ..."

"Maybe there's a world where I can see her becoming a vampire as for the best, despite the outcome. It's a long shot, but maybe."

"And Celeste. You said you've been married for a thousand years."

"Yes. That one worked out."

"So that's two out of three," Annabel said.

"But Reginald ..."

"Don't judge Reginald yet," Annabel told him. "There might be something yet, to that fat vampire of yours."

He stopped. But then slowly, he nodded.

They stood at impasse. She knew what she should say, but it was perhaps too strong an opinion for a therapist, who was supposed to reflect and evaluate — who was supposed to remain neutral.

She said it anyway.

"You're not a monster, Maurice."

"You don't know what I am."

"I know enough."

They matched eyes, each waiting for the other to flinch. Maurice, despite Annabel's glamour, flinched first. This time, the smile he gave was a bit more genuine. He put a hand on her shoulder and said, "I should go."

"Until ...?"

He was already going. He turned to look back.

"Until when?" Annabel repeated. She was moving toward her desk, pulling up her appointment calendar.

"You've been very helpful, but this isn't something I can make a habit of," Maurice finally said.

"Bullshit. You literally have all the time in the world, and two millennia of issues to work through. That's forty times more neuroses than even my worst patients."

He seemed to consider.

"I won't charge you," Annabel said.

"Oh, yes you will. I have more money than I know what to do with."

"So ... *yes?* You're agreeing?"

Maurice laughed. "Friday?"

"Fridays," Annabel said, enunciating the plural.

"Fine. But it has to be after sundown."

"Seven PM, for now."

There was a long pause. Then he nodded.

"All right, Dr. Rice," he said. "We'll try it your way."

54

THPECTACULAR

THEY SAID GOODBYE. She closed the door behind him. She could tell the glamour was still on her, but it felt thin. Just enough veneer to give tonight believability — just enough lubrication to keep her from telling the world, without changing her way of thinking or changing who she was.

It was quiet again. Just the ticking of the clock.

With the vampire gone, the office felt too empty. Creepy, almost. As she moved around to collect her things, she noticed cold pockets in the room — spots Maurice had deadened with his presence. There were no lights moving beyond the windows, no sounds of activity in the office at all.

She spied the clock. It was almost two in the morning. That gave her a start. She'd guessed 11pm, maybe midnight.

Annabel took her purse from behind her desk, then located the miscellany of modern life she'd left scattered around the room: phone, lip balm, that pen she really liked but kept misplacing. She had a light jacket on and was headed for the door when a ring stopped her. Not from the phone in her purse, but the one on the desk.

She picked it up, said hello.

"Annabel? You're late."

Her horrible husband.

"I know. I'm sorry; I had an emergency client that went very long. I just noticed the time. I'm leaving now." She heard herself and realized that in her shoes, she'd never believe that for a second. Who stays at the psychiatrist's office until 2am? Clearly, she must be having an affair.

But it's not like he'd care about that. There was only one thing he *actually* cared about.

Instead of pushing back, he asked, "How did it go?"

"Same old. Neuroses and tics. How was your football game?"

"Thpectacular," he said.

"Did your team win?"

"They did. Did you?"

"Did I what?"

"*Win*," he answered.

"I'm not sure what you—?"

"Annabel," he said, his voice dropping into that soothing, soft-lipped rhythm he had — the one that always made her lower her guard and ... yes ... do whatever he asked. "We've talked about this. We've talked about it for a very long time."

"About what?"

"About Maurice." It came out as, *Maurithe*. That soft palate of his — the one he hated but swore the best surgery couldn't fix.

"How do you know about ... ?"

But she trailed off, and her husband let her. He was waiting for her to remember. Because she didn't *usually* remember. Usually, Maurice and all that she'd done tonight was beneath her conscious surface. Usually, she didn't know Maurice Toussant existed. Or any vampires, for that matter.

Her eyes lost focus. She felt herself entering her familiar, light-bodied trance. It was the same trance she entered every time he was particularly horrible and she went to leave him. And not just when he failed to lower the toilet seat or didn't respect her opinion — this happened more when he came home covered in blood. When people went missing, and he convinced her to forget them.

"He didn't know who I was. Or who you are," Annabel said. Even to her own ears, her voice sounded neutral and droll.

"What did you talk about?"

"Daisy."

"Did you guide him there? To Daithy?"

She hadn't, had she? Somewhere in the back of her mind, Annabel seemed to remember a reason why she might have guided Maurice toward discussing Daisy and how she might have been able, given what she now realized she knew. But she didn't think she'd done that. She'd felt clear-headed when Maurice had entered, not this foggy sort of miasma. It meant she sincerely hadn't known who he was at the time ... and, by extension, hadn't had a clue who Daisy might be.

"I don't think so."

"Did he talk about Thrill?"

"Yes."

"What did he say?"

"Only what you already know."

There was a pause, and in it, the part of Annabel that wasn't entirely glamoured cringed. He didn't believe her; he thought Maurice must have said *something* in all these hours that he didn't know. It meant that when she got home, he'd reach into her head with extreme prejudice, and scoop out the entire night's information.

"There was *one* thing," Annabel said. Saying it took strength, as she pushed through his glamour. But despite the long years and the prison of a marriage, she'd found she was always able — just a little — to resist him. She almost knew why: something deep inside, far past the place where knowledge of her husband's past lived, told her that she was stronger than most humans. No idea why, but the will was there. Hiding.

"What one thing?"

"He told me that during Prohibition, they used to call you—"

A note entered his voice. He said, "Enough."

But Annabel managed to say, "—'*Puffed Wheat*.'"

Then the door closed, his will reasserted itself on Annabel like a vault door closing, and her mouth shut so decisively, she almost bit off her tongue. After, she heard him on the other end of the phone, shifting and seeming to wait to see if she had any more smart shit to say.

"Did you arrange for him to come back?" he asked, now with an edge in his voice.

It took new effort to speak. His will was back upon her, too strong.

"Yes," she finally said.

She could almost hear him nod with satisfaction.

"Pay close attention, then," he said. "Because it's only a matter of time."

The End

Resurrection

Save the City

Save the Girl

Save the World

Longshot

———

THE INEVITABLE:

Robot Proletariat

The Infinite Loop

The Hard Reset

Cascade Failure

Reboot

En3my

———

DEAD CITY:

Dead City

Dead Nation

Dead Planet

Dead Zero

Empty Nest

———

THE DREAM ENGINE:

The Dream Engine

The Nightmare Factory